TWELFTH KNIGHT'S BRIDE

TWELFTH KNIGHT'S BRIDE

E. ELIZABETH WATSON

Entangled Publishing, LLC
644 Shrewsbury Commons Ave
STE 181
Shrewsbury, PA 17361
rights@entangledpublishing.com

Scandalous is an imprint of Entangled Publishing, LLC.

Edited by Erin Molta
Cover design by Mayhem Cover Creations
Cover photography by Period Images
kamchatka/Deposit Photos

Manufactured in the United States of America

First Edition November 2020

To the "Morning Writer Chicks."
Without this motivated group of talented women—and lots
of coffee—my book might not have crossed the finish line!

Chapter One

Urquhart Castle; Scottish Highlands; 24th of December, 1545

"A little farther, man," Aileana encouraged her brother's horse as she rode hard through the snowy glen.

The beastly stallion panted, leaping over drifts with fringed hooves. She leaned over his neck, which lunged and retracted with each bound while his mane blew wildly in her face, her hands close to the bit. Her bundle, wedged between her belly and the saddle pommel, threatened to jostle loose. She pressed her stomach into it to keep the stolen goods in place and glanced over her shoulder, fearful of her pursuer.

"Mayhap we've lost the cretin."

The snow was falling in thick gusts by the time she thundered across the bridge to Urquhart Castle's gatehouse, blazing beneath the portcullis. Her brother's head guardsman came out of the gatehouse to investigate.

"'Tis only me, Sir Donegal!" she called, sweating, and pulled the reins back to stop the horse short.

"Lady Aileana? Why arrive in such haste? And dressed

in trews?" Sir Donegal asked as soldiers craned their necks through the merlons atop the curtain wall to see if danger lurked in the hills beyond.

Aye, she wore pants, a tunic, a cloak, and boots. With her hair pulled back tightly and hidden in the neckline of her cloak, she likely looked like a skinny lad.

"No reason," she replied. "I thought to give the horse a good romp considering he's been cooped up due to our *fine* weather." A lie, but Aileana flashed a confident smile as she gestured to the falling snow as dusk darkened the already-gray sky looming over the fabled Loch Ness. Fine weather indeed.

She shrugged nonchalantly for good measure and draped a hand over her bundle of thieved vegetables, holding it steady while she flung her cloak over her shoulder and dismounted, though her heart pumped from the exertion. Fear at being caught trickled through her blood like spring snowmelt down a mountain and was just as icy. This food, pilfered from that bastard Laird James Moidartach MacDonald—the once-outlawed Earl of Ross—would feed Urquhart's inhabitants for one night, and a thin broth it would make at that. But her people were desperate, thanks to the Devil MacDonald's aggression toward them, and scant nourishment was better than none.

These vegetables are the least the ruthless MacDonald can do for us.

Life had been lean since the MacDonalds' last raid two years ago, which had seen her people evicted. Laird MacDonald had occupied Urquhart, and it had been thanks to the Earl of Huntly himself for demanding the laird relinquish the stronghold back to her brother, Laird Grant. But not before he and his ruffians had depleted their buttery, packed away their livestock, and devastated their seed stock for planting, meaning the last two harvests had been paltry at best, in spite of the meager grains her brother had bartered from the Frasers. And to add insult to injury, this last growing season had been unseasonably wet. They'd reaped an even worse harvest than before. Their petition for a recompense from the MacDonalds still sat before the Crown, and if it wasn't awarded soon, they would surely starve this winter.

"Are ye sure ye're being honest, Lady Aileana?" Donegal persisted as she passed off the reins to their lone stable groom, the seneschal's son.

Trepidation ate at her. She'd barely escaped MacDonald's hunting camp, for his men had made chase as she stole away to the glen at the base of *Carn Eige*, where she'd stashed her horse for her flight home. She glanced over her shoulder again. The hills that loomed over Urquhart were shrouded in fog from the snowflakes falling down onto the frozen banks of the loch—

Her stomach dropped.

A shape emerged from the fog, like a death knell, the thudding of hooves growing louder. Bright, tightly woven red plaid, blond hair—in part flowing free, in part braided—and shoulders shielded in fur, rode out of the hills atop a leathery-black destrier. Damn the man! He'd followed her trail.

"Of course I'm being honest," she croaked to Sir Donegal, who leveled a glare at her. She lifted her chin, having claimed the lie and knowing she must own it. "I, eh, must depart."

She hurried away, clutching the vegetables.

"Look lively!" a sentry called while Grant soldiers clattered to positions.

"Drop the portcullis!" shouted another, and the chains ground on the winches, the forces of Earth pulling it down to land with a rattling pound.

"Ready at arms! It's Devil MacDonald! Inform the laird! Archers! To the walls!"

Aileana jogged through the yard sodden by cart wheels

and ducked through the kitchen door. Sakes! Anger at herself nipped at her heels. She'd been so sure she could outsmart the hunting party and get home unscathed! And now she'd brought trouble to their threshold. Her brother, Seamus, didn't need to fend off the likes of their enemy after all that had passed between their clans.

The kitchens were hot with dinner's meager preparations. Flatbreads baked in the ovens from what flour grains they had been able to grow and harvest this past autumn, and leftover venison boiled in a pot to make a broth.

"Good day, Lady Aileana." The head cook curtsied, oblivious to the mounting commotion outside.

"A good day it is." Aileana dumped the bundle onto the scullery table. Dried carrots, onions, leeks, and beans tumbled across the board. "We have a wee blessing for our supper, but ye must cook it with haste—"

"Goodness!" the cook exclaimed as the other kitchen maids gathered around the bounty in awe. Aileana smiled, but a pinch of sadness sparked in her chest that these basic foods should be so exciting.

"Does God favor us this Christmastide?" the cook continued. "Ye've obviously made some fruitful bartering."

A lie she'd let them believe, for there had certainly been no bartering.

"Quick," Aileana instructed, ignoring the cook's remark. "Chop and boil it so we might eat it fast, and say no' a word that I delivered anything."

"Whatever for?" the cook replied. "Such a quantity can be divided in two and shared with tomorrow night's bread—"

"Look no' a gift horse in the mouth," Aileana urged, adding a grin in hopes it would put them at ease, but they must eat the evidence. The commotion from outside now echoed within the castle. Seamus's demands for reinforcements rang through the great hall. She swallowed, then urged, "We—

eh—could use a filling meal and, for once, feel satisfied."

The cook bobbed in another curtsy and began doling out orders, and Aileana shook the snow off her cloak onto the rushes, then dashed through the kitchen, out into the corridor, and up the winding stairs to where her bedchamber was located. She shoved through the door, barred it, and flung her cloak upon a chair, kicked off her boots, stripped the trousers so that she wore only her hose and tunic still damp from her ride, and hastened into a simple brown gown, just as plain as she was.

"Mi lady!" came a masculine call at the door, accompanied by a knock.

Donegal.

That was quick.

"Mi lady! Devil MacDonald storms our gates and demands to see ye for his own eyes! He swears a lad stole away with goods from his traveling party and rode to safety here. We've sworn the only person to pass our gates this eve is the youngest sister of Laird Grant, but he'll nay be deterred until he sees ye. Yer brother tries to placate the *nàmhaid*, but he threatens to return with more men if we do nay comply... or worse, complain to Huntly!"

She sucked in hard, then exhaled. Her brother would *know* it was her who had committed this thievery, for it wasn't as if she was innocent of such a crime.

"One moment, Donegal!"

She raced back to the door, having yet to catch her breath, and knew her cheeks were splotched with sunbursts from her exertion. Opening it, she twirled around to the man, giving him her back without greeting.

"Lace me up. Quickly," she breathed.

"God have mercy, lass," the guardsman muttered with exasperation, but thankfully he was used to her unorthodox mannerisms, for he'd been her dear friend since childhood, her first kiss, and her father's finest squire. "'Twas ye, was it nay? That bundle on yer saddle? Ye've invited trouble of the worst kind—for MacDonald will bring another raiding party if he suspects he was abused."

She snorted. "Oh, him—abused, the misunderstood violet." Bitterness tainted her tone. "He stole *everything* from us, and yet we're no' entitled to a menial amount of food? We shall die without any, Donegal."

"And yer brother made war on James MacDonald four years ago, aye."

"Because he reaved on us six years ago," she snapped.

"And yer *faither* the same to his *faither* before that."

And so on. The feud between their people had existed since the Grants had established themselves in the Highlands at the request of Huntly. Before the Grants, it had been Huntly himself who had endured raids. Before that, the Crown had fended off renegade MacDonald parties, shoring up the rampart defenses to deflect the lairds of the isles. Urquhart was a strategic stronghold and would consolidate power over the entire region should the Devil acquire it.

"The history matters none," Donegal said, jerking the laces tight, drawing her clammy tunic tightly against her body. "He'll retaliate."

"Ye're nay to say another word to my brother until I've spoken with him," she replied.

"That matters none, either. The laird kens ye must have done it but has demanded ye come to the gates so MacDonald can see for himself that ye cannae possibly be a *lad*."

The guard braced his knee against her rear and cinched the strings, causing her to lurch.

"I'll nay ask"—she gasped as the dress was put into place—"how ye became so deft with a lady's garments, my friend," she teased.

He leaned around her face as he now tied the laces, a grin

softening his jaw and brow.

"Ah, well, I've been known to make the lasses swoon. Ye being the first, eh?"

She batted his face away, and he chuckled. "Indeed I was young and misguided, aye? My *faither*'s boot to yer rear and a sennight of hard labor taught ye never to take such liberties, I recall."

The chuckle rumbling in his throat intensified. "Nay, lass, on the contrary. It taught me never to get *caught*."

"Ye're insufferable!" she jested, smirking and scurrying away to grab her shawl.

She fixed the tunic, which protruded from her dress sleeves, for she hadn't had time to don a proper chemise. With her proud Grant tartan cast about her torso, she looked the picture of plain and proper.

"Ah, but now ye've done it, mi lady, aye?"

"I fear I have," she mumbled under her breath, exhaling. "I'm sorry, Donegal. It's just…we're desperate."

"I ken that," he replied soberly. "Let down yer auburn hair, mi lady. It's one of yer beauties and the most un-*lad*-like thing about ye."

She blushed—of all the ridiculous reactions—at his compliment for he meant it purely in the spirit of friendship these days. But her hair, in truth, was her one vanity, for compared to her older sister, she'd always felt plain.

Her gown in place, she slipped her feet into a pair of ankle boots made of soft lambskin but, like all her things, were worn through. A hole had abraded the outside toe on one, and they needed resoling desperately. Still, all in the castle had made concessions, and she wouldn't complain. It wasn't her brother's fault that this sorry poverty had been thrust upon them due to the MacDonald bastard's relentless greed.

She let down her wavy curls from the utilitarian bun she'd

concealed within her cloak and tried to run a comb through the ends. No use. The prongs snagged in the hopeless tangles, and there was no time to wet it and make it manageable. Instead, she fluffed it down her back, where it tumbled to her waist, and hastened to tie it back in a plain ribbon as she accompanied Donegal downstairs, through the hall, and out into the bailey.

Servants scrambled across the slush, pushing carts to safety in a shed, and took shelter in case the enemy laird had returned for a rematch, while guardsmen lined the curtain wall to assess the threat, arrows trained upon their *guest*.

"There's my sister now," she heard Seamus say.

She stalled in her tracks, her throat constricting, and a leaden anchor sank in her stomach. Although they'd never been introduced, she knew it was the Devil MacDonald himself perched in the saddle on the opposite side of the portcullis grate.

"Ye were just out riding, were ye no', Aileana?" Seamus demanded as his wife, Elizabeth, and their sister, Peigi, flanked him demurely, watching her, ever the beautiful ladies that she had never been and would never be.

Her gaze flitted from her sister-in-law to Peigi, then to Seamus once more, so regal in his deep-blue plaid draped over his shoulder, his heavy belts, and—she noted—his claymore sheathed across his back. Dagger hilts protruded from his waist, and his *sgian dubh* was lodged strategically in his boot. He'd prepared himself to greet James MacDonald as a proud, stoic warrior and their parents' only son to survive infancy.

But as her eyes returned to the laird atop his glossy stallion, she didn't see the disgusting cretin she'd expected. She saw striking blue eyes, dark-blond hair waving wildly around his face and neck with those ever-present braids which she could see, now that she was close to him, were knotted with *wooden* beads—not bones, as he'd been rumored to don—and he was obviously disheveled from his chase. His jaw was scruffy in dark whiskers, those of a young man filling into his prime. His cheekbones were cut high; his nose, long, but firm and proud. Around his shoulders hung a heavy pelt of deerskin over his doublet coat, and a bright red tartan draped across his chest, held in place at the shoulder by a bejeweled badge denoting the clan's symbol.

His thighs, partly visible due to his kilt splaying about him, were powerful and bulged with bands of long muscle, and his boots, deerskin insulated in fleece tufting out of the tops, were fine quality—and certainly not wearing through the toes or soles like hers were.

She nearly scoffed at the thought and instinctively wiggled her little toe rubbing through her lambskin as a chill shivered through her. She should have changed into a fresh chemise.

He was magnificent, *not* the beast she'd always conjured to mind when reliving the horrible day they had last been besieged, even if his face was filled with fury now. Her stomach twisted nervously as he managed the reins of his cavorting destrier puffing steam into the air. Blast it, but she hadn't expected *handsome*. Nor had she expected his gaze to hold hers as if she'd surprised him, too.

Memories swirled to life of clenching sweet Peigi's hand and ferrying her to safety as Urquhart was attacked by men whose faces were muddied and painted in blue woad. She lifted her chin to push away the unwanted thought. Rolled back her shoulders. This MacDonald bastard, no matter how handsome, was a *nàmhaid*—an enemy—if there ever was one. She wouldn't allow him the pleasure of watching her shrink from his hard gaze. Instead, she walked up close to the portcullis as if to taunt him, folding her arms and examining his features for herself. His piercing blue stare followed her, evoking shivers across her skin.

She could feel her brother's glare upon her, too, though she ignored it. She might feel guilty about bringing trouble, but she wouldn't apologize for stealing a wee bit of food. She was a noble-born Grant. It was as much her duty as Seamus's to look after the folk who supported this home with their labors, and they could no longer afford to await word from the Crown as to whether or not their recompense would be awarded.

Seamus leaned into her ear as she felt Laird McDonald's gaze still scrutinizing her, perusing her figure with his devilish eyes. His moniker was proving to be true. Devil indeed.

"Pray tell," Seamus whispered so softly she could barely make out his words, "why I must face down this bastard and his accusations of thievery."

She remained high-chinned and gave the MacDonald a searing perusal of her own, as he was doing to her, causing his eyes to narrow curiously. He was probably conjuring some nefarious plot, for he looked as if he contemplated something.

"Sakes, brother, but I can barely stand to be so close to him. Breathing the same air as him will surely bring about a case of hives."

A nearby guardsman snorted at her jest, and she smiled sweetly at her adversary, knowing by the tightening of his brow that he had heard her. Then his gaze dipped to her lips, then back to her eyes again.

"Sister…" Seamus rubbed the bridge of his nose. "Were ye outside the gates today?"

"I was. 'Tis a lovely day for a country ride, one of the few pleasures we still have, since all other pleasures have been *stolen* from us," she replied, making no effort to hide her flippant tongue as her gaze bore into James MacDonald's.

The MacDonald harrumphed, grumbling, "Yer sister has a disagreeable tongue. Nay a wonder why she's no' married yet."

The nerve! Anger flared in her chest at his insult, even if it had been delivered by a deep, husky voice, inducing more shivers across her skin than she should be proud of. What did he expect from the Grants? Kindness and benevolence?

"Too bad ye'll never ken a whit about my tongue," she snapped in return.

James's brows shot up in surprise at her lewdness, and she smirked, crossing her arms with satisfaction and popping her hip.

"That's enough, Aileana," Seamus admonished her. "God in heaven, why must ye be so brash?"

She scoffed. "And why must we pretend to offer this man salutary kindness? He rushes to our gates, accusing us of…of *what*, this time?"

"Of a lad thieving food from their camp," her brother replied, his head turned toward her and away from Laird MacDonald as he raised a knowing eyebrow.

"Oh, a lad thieving, eh?" Aileana scoffed, then addressed MacDonald still perched in his saddle, seething. "An eye for an eye, then." A twinkle glinted in his too-handsome eyes, as if he wished to return her insults with delightfully accurate precision.

"Nay, lass. Yer clan reaved us first, remember?" James argued.

"Because who reaved us before?" She tapped her chin, feigning to ponder. "Oh, that's right. Yer *faither*."

James groaned, raising his eyes heavenward with barely leashed composure.

"But what does this have to do with us?" she asked. "Or more specifically, *me*?"

"The lad rode here. Through these very gates, nay more than ten minutes ago," MacDonald said. "And they say ye're the only one to enter this afternoon. Coincidence?"

"Ach, do I look like a lad?" she asked, though she

regretted her question the moment she asked it. His smile lifted dangerously. Good God above, she'd opened herself to an insult of the worst sort.

"Ask no' a question ye wish no' to be answered," he quipped. She balled her fists. "Produce the culprit, and we'll have nary a problem," the MacDonald said, holding her glare as he resituated his grip on his reins with a creaking of leather, clearly annoyed that this questioning was taking so long.

"Yer thief didnae come here," she replied. "I'm the only one who's been out riding. Our lads must labor overmuch to compensate for all that has been stolen from us and havenae time for countryside leisure, and if ye must ken, in sooth, I was out hunting." That much was true. She'd been pursuing hares when she'd left Urquhart and had merely happened upon the MacDonald camp. "Unsuccessfully, I might add. Which means, once more, we'll go hungry."

She folded her arms, unable to tame her tongue. She wanted to needle this bastard who had made life difficult, made her and her sister's marriage prospects sink as deep as Loch Ness, for with their poverty came the *lovely* benefit of no dowry. Hers had been stolen, complete with the beautiful pearl earrings inlaid in gold that their mother had gifted both Peigi and herself. Aileana had kept hers in her jewelry chest, which MacDonald had stolen. No one would wish to marry a lady who brought no wealth to the table, except maybe a lowly baron.

But her attempt to thwart his curiosity backfired. The anger in his brow softened as his eyes drew together to search her face, traveling over the ridges of her cheekbones and nose, her earlobes that sat empty of adornments—unlike Peigi's, for Peigi still had the earrings their mother had given *her*. She'd been wearing them that fateful day. *I suppose there is merit in decorating myself like a lady.*

His assessment traveled over her wild red-brown hair

tumbling over her shoulder from her ribbon, over her figure again, making her squirm while fluttering ravaged her belly. What was he looking at? She'd never been the bonny sister that the men enjoyed glimpsing. Peigi was comely, with soft, tantalizing cleavage; flared hips that she'd heard men mutter were good for birthing; pink cheeks; pillowy lips; and rich brown eyes like their brother, while Aileana had been blessed with plain hazel eyes and a faint speckling of freckles across her nose. And yet not once had James MacDonald turned his head toward her older sister who *always* turned a man's head.

"On second thought…perhaps it was a *lass* who stole from me," James finally concluded, a satisfied smirk darkening his face once again as he sat upright in the saddle. "Tell me, do ye wear trousers, my lady? I can see ye looking like a lad."

She gasped. As did Elizabeth and Peigi. Shocked at his rudeness, she saw the corner of his mouth tip up. He *knew* he'd gotten under her skin. So he hadn't been intrigued by her femininity, as she'd dared to think he might be—and why on God's green earth did she want the animal to be interested?

"Mind yerself, James," her brother growled, straightening his belts and filling his chest with a deep breath to broaden his already-broad torso. "There's no need to be insulting. She's lady-born and bred and will be treated so."

"My sister doesnae see her beauty like we do," Peigi spoke up. "Yer arrow, sir, was aimed to hurt."

Bless her siblings for defending her. Still, the remark stung, reminding her that even with a dowry, she'd likely remain an untouched spinster, for what man wanted a woman with freckles?

"I ken nay who yer thief was," Aileana began, her throat scratchy with emotion. "But I commend the lad for delivering justice, no matter how menial as a pile of vegetables, to a thief like ye," she replied, and though she tried to bolster her confidence again, she knew the sting of his remark tainted her words now.

"I never said the thief stole vegetables." Laird MacDonald's smirk rose into a dastardly grin.

Her mouth dropped open to launch a rebuttal, when her words froze in her throat. Seamus exhaled long and low and perched his hands on his hips, his gaze flitting sidelong at her with increasing frustration.

"Aileana?" Seamus said, his voice gruff. "He speaks honestly—*this* time. He didnae say vegetables. Only food."

Dammit! She'd ensnared herself in her own lie!

MacDonald, his handsome face, littered with scars, brightened with amusement as he leaned his forearm on the pommel like a spectator at a tourney. "Seamus Grant, have ye sunk so low as to send yer *sister* out reaving?"

Seamus's frown deepened as he turned back to James. "I would never ask such a thing of a sister!" he erupted, then took a deep breath and turned to Aileana once again. "Ye conceived of this plot yerself, did ye nay?"

Aileana gaped at Seamus, gesturing to James like her brother was blind to the truth. "Because *they* have starved us out. They have left us with naught, and the king takes his sweet time deciding to award yer complaint. We have *nothing*. Am I supposed to let my people go hungry because this greedy cretin wishes to amass *all* our lands, *all* our cattle, and own *all* of the Highlands for himself?"

"This land was my birthright," James growled. "It was stolen from the MacDonalds and parceled off to the king's favorite men."

"That was *two* centuries ago," Aileana snapped. "Why continue to battle for something ye never had?"

"And why continue to aggress against me?" the devil rumbled. "For ye act like an innocent, but yer brother took up arms with our enemies and evicted *me*, declaring *me* an outlaw when I'm my *faither*'s direct and rightful heir."

"Oh, posh! He'd never do anything of the sort!" Of what lies did he accuse her brother?

James's mouth twisted as if he desired to deliver further rebuttal, but he chewed his words and clenched his teeth. "We all await the king's decision on how to recompense ye. But it nay changes the fact that ye've stolen from me again."

"*Vegetables* for our people. Nay coffers and cattle!" Aileana said, sweeping her arm wide to encompass the stronghold.

"Mayhap I ought complain to the king myself. That Seamus Grant's sister is a thief and ought to be named an outlaw if she cannae be controlled."

Aileana's jaw dropped, but it was Peigi who found the quickest words. "Then yer cruelty kens no bounds."

James's eyes only flitted to Peigi for a moment before settling back on her, and the twinkle lighting them sent a nervous pulse kicking through her blood. He released the reins and scoured a palm over his face, looking away as if to hide his expression, as if suddenly hot. Curious.

"One moment," Seamus said to James, then gripped Aileana by her upper arm and marched her away, not stopping until they stood across the yard from the gate.

She wrenched her arm free and pushed his hand away as she fought to secure her tartan again while the midwinter wind whipped mercilessly through the bailey.

"Why, sister?" he finally demanded. "Why take such a risk as to steal from the *MacDonalds*? Of all the people, ye chose *him*? What were ye thinking? Or were ye even thinking at all?"

"Aye," she said, seething. "I was thinking that our people surely willnae make it through the winter unless the MacDonalds pay restitution soon. Our pantries are barren—"

"I'm aware," Seamus ground out through clenched teeth. "But right when the king is positioned to rule in my favor and grant us our justice is *nay* the time for ye to diminish our reputation. God above, lassie, I'm *this* close to achieving my desires the diplomatic way." He held up his finger and thumb to indicate just how little time they had left to wait. "My messenger arrived yesterday to inform me that the king has decided and sends his writ to me within the next fortnight. But James, the bastard, kens ye're guilty now, and if he makes a royal complaint of his own, the king is likely to dismiss us all as warring clans who retaliate back and forth, therefore giving us naught!"

She flinched at his anger. Seamus was typically a gentle soul, and he'd never treated her to the deep, rumbling voice he used when intimidating his foes. He pinched the bridge of his nose again, closed his eyes, and inhaled deeply. Her eyes flitted to James afar, who was poised in his saddle and, this time, wore concern on his face. Concern for her? Her brother would never raise a hand to her, but James didn't know that.

Weariness sagged her brother's shoulders, catching her off guard, causing sadness to lodge in her chest. The corners of his eyes were crinkled, his brow pleated with the burden of responsibility on his shoulders. No doubt he was also worried about his wife, Elizabeth, who was due to deliver their first child in the spring. A lean winter might cause the lady to miscarry. Such a loss would devastate her, and thus, devastate Seamus, too.

"I'm sorry to shout," he amended after a moment's thought, then dragged her into a hug. She wrapped her arms around his waist, belted in thick leather, resting her cheek against his tartan mantle. "I try to balance many needs, Aileana. We have no Yuletide celebration. No feast. The castle wears no evergreen boughs, for there simply hasnae been the will to decorate. I ken yer heart was in the right place today, but what ye did was dangerous and impulsive. I now need to settle a compensation with Laird MacDonald, as much as it sickens me to barter with him. I must appear honest in every regard, for my royal recompense will be the equivalent of three *hundred* head of livestock, and I cannae risk having it rescinded."

"Barter with him?" Aileana knew what Seamus meant, yet it still left a rancid taste in her mouth. "How can ye lower yerself to do such a thing—"

"*Wheesht,*" he said, silencing her. He stepped back and cupped her cheeks paternally, for he was years older than her. "What's done is done. Now, we must sort it out. Come."

He escorted her back to the gates, though each step she took sent trepidation through her core. How would this be sorted?

"Laird Grant," MacDonald said as they approached. "I've decided. I leave ye to yer Yuletide celebrations and will go to the king to complain." He glanced around at their drab walls, slowly chipping with disrepair. An obvious sign that the Grants hadn't rebounded. "A victim of a brash woman."

Victim. The jest made Aileana want to vomit, for the MacDonalds were rich and powerful.

"There's no need for that. Ye were obviously hard-pressed for yer vegetables," Seamus said, with sarcasm dripping from each word.

"I am. The winter is thin to us all," James said.

"Then suppose we come within to discuss what I can do to recompense ye."

"I do nay believe it," Aileana gasped under her breath. "He's coercing ye, Seamus—"

Her brother clenched her elbow to silence her.

James nodded once. His eyes caught hers again and held the stare, as he'd been doing since his arrival, as if assessing her for something...*more.* Though his expression remained unreadable. "'Tis agreeable to me."

Seamus sighed, then called up to Sir Donegal. "Raise the

portcullis, man."

"Raise it?" the head guard questioned, and a murmur swept through the servants who had gathered in the bailey.

"Indeed," Seamus replied. "Only for Laird MacDonald. If ye have other men lurking, James, tell them to stand down."

MacDonald shook his head. "They packed camp and returned to Tioram Castle. 'Tis only me."

"Raise the gates!" Donegal called. "By order of the laird!"

The winches began churning again, and slowly, the gate was lifted as servants gaped at the welcoming of the enemy wolf among the flock.

MacDonald trotted boldly into the yard as if he owned it, glaring down at her as he passed. Aileana straightened, felt her pulse quicken at the strength he exuded. He might try to intimidate with his imposing presence, but she would not be cowed, no matter how handsome his features or how hard his stare.

The groom hastened to the laird, holding his horse at the bit. Still, MacDonald's gaze remained fastened to hers. Blast it, but her fingers felt as if they trembled. Snow landed upon her skin, stinging with the initial bite of coldness before melting. Could it not chill her mounting nerves?

His horse, hooves fringed in shaggy feathering, shook his mane and tossed his head, grunting.

"He's a spirited beast, lad," James said to the young groom. "Ye got him?"

"Aye, mi laird," the boy replied, but Aileana noticed James steadying his horse anyway to ensure it would acquiesce. A tiny kindness, as was the mindless tousle to the child's head after he swung his leg over the cantle and jumped down with a firm thud.

She crinkled her brow. Softness? From this hardened warlord? And sakes, but his horse was a beauty—his coat so dark and rich, mane thick and windswept, muscles well pronounced. He must be nearly eighteen hands—

"Ye like my stallion, lass?" James wore a cocky grin, folding his arms. "I dare say ye'd have a hard time stealing *him*. His name's Devil for a reason," he taunted.

She scoffed and folded her own arms, glancing askance. "A fitting name for the Devil MacDonald's steed."

He stood to full height, towering over her, though now that he was on foot, she could see he wasn't massive with muscle so much as he was bulky with tartan and fur. Rather, he was lean, like the Norsemen from whom he'd descended. And young. Mid twenties, perhaps.

"Disarm yerself," Seamus ordered, and with a firm face, James complied, unstrapping his back sheath and depositing his claymore in her brother's hands.

She sidestepped the men, allowing them to lead, as Seamus ushered him toward the keep. Guilt sliced through her like dirk blades for putting her brother and their clan in such a position. True... She had acted impulsively. And perhaps with a pinch of spite fueling her small act of retaliation.

The doors swung open, and James shook the snow off his furs on the top step, then stepped over the threshold.

So he does have some manners bred into that bull head of his. Aileana smirked, though the way in which he assessed their hall and sparse furnishings made her wonder if he was assessing the castle for more signs of weakness to exploit.

"Join me at the board, James," Seamus began. "Supper will be served soon, and we can discuss over our victuals how I might make amends for my sister's ill-conceived plot."

"Mayhap ye can tell me why the lass is riding the countryside like a ruffian in the first place," James groused. "Oughtn't she be housebound with needlepoint or a lute to pass her time?"

He spoke with exaggerated enunciation, as if he wanted

to get a rise from her. Ach, she couldn't help giving it to him.

"My sister is—"

"No' only would I nay be caught dead sitting on my arse whilst my people suffer," she interrupted, "but we havenae the leisure or the money to buy such resources for needlepoint and music thanks to y—"

"*Aileana* has always been our wildling," Peigi interjected with a sidelong glance, the soft edge of love coating her words. "Our dear mother tried to mold her into a lady, but she's always been headstrong, and since our *eviction* two years ago"—Peigi's implication was the closest thing her ladylike sister would make to an accusation, and James's eyes cut back and forth between them as if bracing for an onslaught—"my sister has done everything she can, as have we all, to help uplift our people. She's a skilled healer and prefers romping along the shores of Loch Ness or tending our parents' graves in the cemetery or helping the peasants with their tasks. *But* a real asset, she is, for she's never afeard of rolling up her dress sleeves to get work done. And she's always been motivated by kindness and love."

Aileana drew her brows together and gazed at MacDonald. "I suppose being like a lad has its benefits, eh? I make a good work mule, is what she's saying."

"'Tis nay, sister!" Peigi protested.

"*Enough*, Aileana," Seamus said, with little conviction to his voice, as he dragged his hand through his hair.

The kitchen maids began delivering meager platters of flatbread and roughly hollowed wooden trenchers of watery broth and bits of floating vegetables. A cowbell was rung in the bailey, and off-duty servants and guardsmen hurried through the front doors, bringing a draft of cold air and sprinkling snow across the threshold as they cast wary glances at their supper guest. *Pathetic*, Aileana thought, feeling her throat thicken with emotion. Their meal was already so meager, and now they had to share it with the Devil MacDonald. He'd see firsthand how little they had to celebrate this Christmastide.

Aileana breezed around James, who examined the hall as if assessing the worth of it all, before sitting. Perhaps lamenting that he had missed his chance to own it when her brother had returned with the Earl of Huntly's soldiers to evict the MacDonald squatters. His eyes cut to Seamus while he twisted the stem of his goblet, as if weighing options, and she squirmed with curiosity to know what he was thinking. His eyes lifted to hers as if sensing her stare. Aye, her guard rose. Without a doubt, he was scheming something.

The meal began solemnly, and Aileana tried to stare at her bowl instead. Watching their guest sent butterflies through her stomach with each searing gaze and did nothing to keep her nerves calm.

"And so, James," Seamus addressed him, "let us discuss how to make my sister's thievery right with ye."

Just like that, her eyes lifted to the enemy's again. She shivered. Watched him tear off a bite of flatbread, watched his jaw muscles bulge with each chew. His gaze held hers so tightly, she couldn't look away. Another shiver washed over her, for he seemed ready to voice whatever he'd been thinking—

"I need a wife," James said as if this somehow answered her brother's question. Peigi gasped. Aileana's stomach roiled. Silence fell like an iron gate upon the hall as utensils clattered down. "One of yer sisters will do."

Trepidation washed over Aileana like floodwaters. She knew which sister he wanted.

Chapter Two

Ye're a whoreson, James, for playing at such an intrigue. But this infernal lass, with the glossy voice of an angel belying her barbed words—and the Highland clans called *him* a devil—had given him an opportunity he desperately needed that he never thought he'd get. He desired his inheritance. And thanks to restrictions thrust upon him, more like a *curse*, the only way to claim four hundred pounds was to take a Grant wife and conquer Grant lands by his twenty-fifth birthday—which happened to fall upon Twelfth Night. *Best never let her ken that I'm desperate for a wife, or she'll be sure to rib me mercilessly.*

The people of the western isles and Highlands feared him as a warlord dominating the MacDonalds of Clanranald, who'd claimed the Earldom of Ross. They needn't know that while his castle coffers were rich, his personal ones were not, thanks to his stepmother—

Enough about that.

The silence in the wake of his demand was deafening. Grant wouldn't marry a sister to him. Still, he chewed the unleavened bread, swallowed, tore off another bite, and chewed, remaining impassive even though the spark that had ignited in Lady Aileana's eyes intrigued him further. He'd heard that Clan Grant bred fetching women, but this one... He'd been unable to look away from Aileana's untamed beauty since she'd squared off with him, her chin high, her auburn waves bonny on the breeze.

What fool had allowed her to think herself plain? Aye, she was fresh-faced, unpainted by makeup, but she looked like Scotland would look as a person. Wild. Unyielding. Proud. Beautiful around every curve, every edge, as the crags and straths appeared in the glowing sunset.

"Too bad ye'll never ken a whit about my tongue..." Christ above, didn't Lady Aileana know a remark like that would do nothing but pique a man's curiosity and heat his blood for a challenge? Add brazen to her list of qualities. That comment had repeated in his mind like a bell tolling. He couldn't shake it away. What gently bred woman spoke like that, challenging him to pick up his sword of words and parry with her?

Yet wouldnae that be the ultimate conquest? To determine more than a whit about her tongue for myself?

No. He'd never been one to play at intrigues with women. In fact, being raised a bastard had instilled fear in him. How could he ever be flagrant with his male urges and make bairns out of wedlock on a woman, shattering her reputation and shrouding his seed in a lifetime of shame, to be raised in the shadow of criticisms, whispers, and gossip, as he'd been raised?

"Mine ears must have misheard ye, *friend*," Laird Grant said, seething.

Ha! Friend indeed. More like a knife in me back the first moment I turn around.

Aileana snorted, too. Damned lass. "Aye, a friend who leaves wreckage in his wake."

"Ye want to act like a victim, lady?" James challenged, taking the bait, and did he hope for her rebuttal? "Yer *brother* rode on Tioram Castle and helped the Frasers evict me to instate their own choice of chief, a cousin of mine so distant, and with so thin a claim to the lairdship he was easy enough to quell, thank God—"

"I willnae dare believe yer accusations that Seamus is guilty of the cruelties ye've bestowed on others. And it nay changes the fact that ye reaved against us, stealing our cattle, our stores of grain—"

"Aileana, for bloody's sake—"

"Aye, as was deserved." James cut off Seamus's attempt to interrupt the argument. "Because yer brother rode on us, too, stealing *ours*," he retorted.

"And 'twas yer *faither* who maimed mine," she seethed, sitting forward in her seat as if she wished to claw her way across the damned table into his lap to scratch at him. He wouldn't mind her in his lap. "He—"

"Enough, both of ye!" thundered Seamus, shooting to his feet.

Aileana jumped at her brother's outburst, and again, the strange protectiveness that had afflicted him when he'd watched Seamus scold Aileana outdoors flared in his stomach. *Why? Because of Marjorie...* Nay, Aileana could clearly hold her own. He was daft to fear for this hellion, who would just as soon see a dirk lodged in his heart at first chance.

Grant jerked his belts straight and eased back into his seat.

"Yer ears have nay misheard me," James finally replied. "I need a woman. Ye have two sisters, Seamus, neither of whom ye can afford."

Horror dropped Peigi's mouth wide, as it did to the silent Lady Elizabeth. Aileana gaped at him.

Ye, James mouthed at her so boldly, it was a wonder he

wasn't a randy stag who regularly bedded wenches.

Her eyes widened farther. *Why does needling the lass please me so?* Aye, his curiosity was piqued. He watched sunbursts erupt on her creamy cheeks, sprinkled with endearing freckles... *"Fairies' wee kisses,"* Marjorie had always told him when he was a lad and his own face had been plagued with freckles—now faded. He swallowed at the stab of pain thoughts of his oldest half sister always induced, willing the memory away. Why hadn't anyone made Aileana believe the truth? That they made her beautiful? His blood stirred at the mere thought of pecking kisses upon each one. A man *would* think them kissable, *until she opens her mouth and tells him off.* He harrumphed to himself.

"I'll consider the debt owed me paid. It would ease yer purse strings to have one less mouth to feed."

Seamus harrumphed now, too. "Try again, man. Why the hell would I give a beloved sister to such a *bastard*?"

James swallowed the anger that flared at the insult and sat still.

"Surely ye would be cruel to her out of spite," Grant added.

Hell, he'd never been cruel to a woman in his life. He thought of Marjorie again, one of the two older sisters who'd doted on him, despite their mother's hatred of him. She'd been married off to that brute... In sooth, Marjorie's lot had made him think closely about his. Would he be able to remain tempered? Careful? Rational? With a woman of his own? Or did all men turn into unfaithful husbands like his father or violent beasts like Marjorie's?

"The absolute horror," whispered Peigi to Aileana, whose hazel-green eyes were still wide.

His brow knitted. Shock and surprise were understandable. But horror? He knew these people disliked him, but was he really so repulsive, too? Still, he felt an ounce of satisfaction. *So it* is *possible to render this hellion Aileana speechless.* The satisfaction induced a fleeting smile he tried miserably to suppress as he filled his mouth with another bite of bread.

"And besides, what does needing a wife have to do with anything?" Seamus Grant growled, rising slowly from his seat. "My sister stole vegetables. Coin is a sufficient compensation. She ought no' pay with her life."

"That's a fatal way of putting it," James replied. "No one aims to send her to the gallows. I seek an accord, 'tis all. Yer clan wronged mine. I need a wife. Ye have two unmarried sisters with no dowries, no doubt." He eyed Lady Aileana again. "And I'd never harm a woman—"

"Because ye stole them from us!" she exclaimed, slamming her goblet down like a man at a tavern and jumping to her feet. "And as to yer claim that ye'd never harm a woman, true, yer reputation for benevolence and compassion are known throughout the land," she said with a dramatic sweep of the hand, as if entertaining a court.

She was trying to piss him off, and succeeding. He mustn't give her the satisfaction of winning. "I speak truth, woman," he drawled, his mouth tugging up so that he knew a divot creased his cheek. "Nary a complaint I've heard from the maids yet."

"So smug," Aileana muttered under her breath. "And they are no doubt women with poor taste if they lie with the likes of ye—"

"Sister, I demand ye stop." Seamus's reminder for silence, however, still didn't seem to affect Aileana, for she lifted her chin, then lifted her goblet and took a measured sip, her hazel eyes never leaving his, as if daring him for a rebuttal.

James's blood burned for the challenge. Aileana had better be the bargain bride Seamus chose for him.

"I stole no dowries," he scoffed, leaning back.

"Aye, man, ye did," Seamus rumbled, defending her. "Ye stole Aileana's jewels, and ye stole the purses set aside for their marriages."

Jewelry. James took in the plainness of Aileana's appearance. No jewels about her neck, nor bobbles hanging from her ears. Mayhap she wore none because she no longer had any. And at Peigi's ears, he now noticed a pair of pearls inlaid in gold suspiciously like the ones his men had presented to him after their reave of Urquhart two years ago... *Shite.*

What had he just asked of these women? For the sake of fulfilling obligations for his inheritance, when he'd stolen theirs? And Aileana might be desperate and altruistic enough to accept his demand, to help her people, even if her bold tongue's retribution would likely lash him at every opportunity for the rest of his days.

Aileana's lips finally parted to argue, but Seamus held his hand to her for silence.

"I would speak, brother," she argued anyway.

How did she do that? Speak such commands with softness in her voice? It was misleading, and it had the power to transfix a man right before she struck her target true.

"He's coercing ye. He's nay going to run to the Earl of Huntly over vegetables, nor is he going to run to the king. I say we call his threat what it is—a bluff—and send him on his way. I can keep helping the crofters and tending our sick, and if ye continue to hunt and barter, we'll find a way to make it through and pray our recompense is awarded. Peigi's piecework brings in some coin, too, during the convent's seasonal faires. Bollocks to this tyrant."

A twinge of guilt assailed James for insulting her outside, for right now, her face pinched with distress like it had then, as if her strength were an ugliness that made her repulsive, made her more suited to help haul hay, wearing a lad's trews instead of a lady's kirtle. And if she'd been the thief who'd successfully raided him, she was an expert horsewoman, who would no doubt love to gallop the hills with him—

Do nay be an eejit, man. The woman would spit in yer porridge with gladness.

"Ye can call it what ye like, lass, but my request is genuine, and I'll turn a blind eye to the theft."

"Nay, and that's final," Seamus growled. "My sisters are nay free for bartering."

James leaned back in his chair, haughty as a monarch, and slung his arm over the back. At one point in time, his ancestors had truly been monarchs of this land. "I understand that the king might indeed rule in yer favor and order me to pay ye a handsome sum. Three hundred head of cattle and bundles of commodities? But if I bring a grievance before the court, I dare say yer sister's thievery might put yer sterling reputation in jeopardy."

"I offer ye hospitality and an honest wish to make amends, and ye would blackmail me into giving ye a sister? As if she were naught but a cow for bargaining?" Seamus's voice rumbled, and now he unsheathed his dirk from his belt.

"Nay," James said, shoving to his feet, too, and withdrawing his dirk.

Soldiers clattered forth.

"Drop yer weapon, MacDonald," the man named Donegal said. "Ye forget yer place right now."

James, his chest rising and falling, fuming, sheathed his dirk. He instead withdrew his riding gloves and shoved aside his chair.

"Ye all act wounded, as if yer clan has done no wrong to me. As if my anger is unwarranted. As if my raid on ye wasnae to resupply everything that *yer* clan stole from *us* when ye evicted *me*. Except I didnae go crying to the king like a bairn throwing a tantrum. I handled it and moved on. Fine. I care naught at all if she stole a pile of vegetables, or a bundle of coin. I go to complain and play dirty the way ye do."

He stalked down the dais.

"I want my sword," he called over his shoulder.

"He's nay bluffing, sister," he heard the Lady Peigi whisper through the silence.

He was nearly to the door beneath the censuring gazes of Urquhart's inhabitants when Seamus called, "Stop!"

He stopped, pivoted over his shoulder, and grabbed the latch, for the guard at the door seemed disinclined to assist him.

"Please. Return to the board. Let us barter with words instead of weapons."

Aye, Seamus Grant the peacemaker, the one to *first* draw his blade. James snorted.

He took his time deciding a course of action, then lumbered back to the dais. Aileana's gaze was fixed on him. He assessed her, watched her sip more wine, watched the moisture make her lower lip glisten, watched her tongue run along the flesh to clean the remnants of drink. That tongue. He wanted to know much more than a whit about it. He wanted to silence it with his.

He, too, scooped up his drink to take another sip, still standing. "She'd be taken care of in a rich house, would want for nothing, and would have a position of rank. *And* yer debt to me would be paid."

Seamus scoffed, but it was obvious by the thoughtful furrow capturing his brow that he was beginning to consider the merits of the offer. Seamus sighed. "I'll need to discuss the matter with my sisters—"

"Ye cannae be serious!" Aileana exclaimed. "Did ye nay hear a word that I said? The *nàmhaid* is coercing ye!"

Her wild hair was fraying in wisps about her face, and her pert nose wrinkled. She'd be a handful as a wife, for certain. Peigi would make a more agreeable woman, and she was clearly a cultivated beauty who would do her duty. But James's eyes remained trained on Aileana.

"I'd never make either of ye marry a man who ye didnae wish to wed," Seamus said, trying to placate Aileana, though Peigi, to her credit, looked just as mortified.

"Come, sisters, let's leave the Devil to his meal for a moment—"

Ah. "Devil." They use the ugly moniker, dubbed me by my enemies, right in front of me.

"I'd like to speak with ye privately. Wife? Will ye see to the laird's companionship whilst I'm away?"

Grant's eyes flitted to the man, Sir Donegal, at his back, more the intended companion than his wife, James assumed. He shifted in his seat to keep an eye on the guardsman's blades.

Lady Elizabeth frowned but nodded once in acquiescence, and Seamus led his sisters down the servant hallway that led to the kitchens. James sipped from his goblet, glancing at the pregnant lady who took measured bites and did nothing to engage him, rather, sat stiffly like a statue. He scooped up a spoon of the watery broth, letting it dribble pathetically back into the bowl. Was this honestly all that the Grants had to offer a guest? True, they liked him about as much as they liked cattle dung cached to their boots, but customs of hospitality were never shirked, and the best meal a laird could provide was always offered.

Which meant these people had naught. Except for a couple chunks of carrots and spring onions that looked suspiciously like the ones stolen from his camp, the flavorless liquid was barely salted with a sparse sprinkling of venison. A glimmer of the desperation Aileana felt infiltrated his mind, as did memories of the raid that had seen *him* evicted, *his* cattle stolen, *his* goods depleted before he could fight his way back within and chase away the usurper that Seamus Grant had helped to instate.

Damnation, but if it wasn't the MacLeods of Skye bombarding him from the water, it was this bloody clan attacking by land.

He ought to feel more pissed than he did. He certainly shouldn't feel guilty for turning back on the Grants what they'd turned on him. Christ, he needed to let this sympathy go to hell where it belonged. A laird had no use for it regarding his enemies. Being firm, bold, direct, and unapologetic were the qualities that held up a man's continued repute.

"How could ye, Seamus?" Aileana whined from within the bowels of the corridor, before her voice fell muffled again.

A whine? This woman wouldn't whine unless she felt desperate. He strained to listen, since Lady Elizabeth was disinclined to speak and sat trembling like a leaf in his company. Seamus's voice rose, too. Clearly, they were in disagreement.

"And sweet Peigi? What on earth has she done to deserve such a sentence?"

"If our brother asks it of me, then I must do it out of duty," Lady Peigi replied, though James noted the forlornness in her voice. "We've erred, and yer skills would be missed here—"

"As has he! He eats the very food we cannae afford to spare, after he put us in this position of poverty," Aileana argued.

"Yer brashness isnae helping, sister. And I dare say, if I agreed to marry *ye* to him, ye'd start an all-out war before the sennight's end. Peigi is the better choice."

Disappointment caused a tumble in James's stomach. Grant was going to give him Peigi?

"Ye cannae mean this," Aileana now said, though her whisper was so impassioned, her voice bounced off the stone. "Seamus, what ye propose is cruel, especially when it was *my* fault. James lies. A man like him would be just as cruel to a woman when she errs as he is to an adversary. Peigi would never survive."

A swell of irritation bloomed in James's chest. He'd taunted Aileana about women, but he'd spoken the truth. MacDonald women were kept well, and sweet Marjorie, who had not been so loved by her husband…had been avenged. He couldn't abide a man who lorded over the fairer sex, for in truth, it was only weakness in the man's heart that compelled him to do so.

"Sister, I ken no' what else to do, and—sister? Aileana, come back—"

Aileana blazed out from the corridor to James's side so quickly, he jolted with surprise and instinctively reached for his dagger.

"I'll do it," she breathed.

"I accept." He nodded.

A strange wave of relief overtook him. Aileana's bonny eyes were resigned, and rimmed with…redness. Hell, was the lass going to cry? This was a business deal. But the fear he saw on her face made more guilt nip at his conscience. Force the enemy woman to marry him so he could claim his inheritance? Except… Ah, he was daft. Why had he not thought about this before?

I can either marry an enemy Grant by this Twelfth Night or unite these lands to gain it. Would this marriage sufficiently satisfy both conditions for his inheritance in one swoop? He'd always thought the MacDonalds must conquer Grant land, but now that he thought about it, nothing in the documents said a whit about ruling Urquhart—only uniting it with MacDonald lands. This could work. And was far less violent than a raid.

It felt strangely right.

Seamus emerged behind Aileana and then Peigi, whose

cheeks were damp with tears.

Seamus squared Aileana in front of him while the hall stared raptly at the dais. "Aileana, this is folly, and as yer laird, I forbid it. Renounce what ye've just offered—"

"Nay, ye cannae sentence Peigi to a life with this brute when it was my fault. Since ye're bent on gaining yer recompense from the Crown, as ye should be, I'll..." She took a deep breath and extricated herself from Seamus's hold, summoning that stubbornness James realized he expected from her, and rolled back her shoulders. "I'll take the punishment," she said, much gentler this time.

Gasps and murmurs rattled the hall, breaking the silence like a split of lightning.

Punishment? James smarted. He hadn't intended it to be a punishment...or had he? If anything, it was justice. This marriage was a bargain, but it wasn't intended to be a life sentence of misery.

"Are ye certain?" Seamus asked, also more gently, taking her by both shoulders again, refusing to be cast off. "Sister, this isnae what I wished for ye."

She shrugged. "Be honest. I burden ye, and with nothing for a dowry—"

"Nothing *yet*," Seamus emphasized. "But when the king's ruling comes back to me and I'm awarded, I'd have much for a dowry, and yer prospects would change. The Fraser laird's nephew is seeking a woman and leads a powerful stronghold. He'd be pleased to consider ye."

"Aye, and he's already had two wives who've preceded him in death. Is he as old as *faither*? Or nearly as old?" she replied with dry sarcasm. Seamus sighed. "At least James is a far cry better look—"

She snapped shut her mouth, but James heard the direction of her remark, and a silly bout of excitement lurched in his chest at the knowledge that she found him handsome.

Seamus rubbed the bridge of his nose, heaving a hand to his hip. "Do ye ever think before ye speak?"

Aileana looked down at her hands, subdued by her brother's censure. "*Mither* was right. I'm hopeless as a lady."

The dejection in her voice made James uncomfortable. Hopeless? Nay, she was bonny, strong, skilled, and she loved her people enough to steal—and not just from anyone. From *him*.

Drifting in thought, James twisted the stem of his cup. In truth, Seamus was right. She'd only stolen some vegetables, nay his coin or valuables. He was doing this just as much to lord his command over the Grants as he was to gain his inheritance.

"How old are ye, lass?" James asked.

Aileana frowned at him. "I have nine and ten years."

His thoughts deepened. Nineteen was certainly older than many a maiden upon their marriage.

"If Aileana continues to be stubborn about this, then I'll agree to betroth her to ye," Seamus began. "We can send for a priest, for we havenae a regular holy man, and this will give us time to post the banns—"

"Nay, we'll handfast. She comes with me now," James replied.

More gasping. More shocked utterances.

"Ye would deny a lady of rank, no matter how penniless, her kirk wedding?" Seamus demanded, this time, rage ringing unchecked in his remark.

"I dare say ye cannae afford the priest's fee or the cost of hosting guests," James replied.

He glanced from Peigi's grief-stricken face to her hands clenching Aileana to her red-rimmed eyes. Aileana gripped her stomach, pulling away. Was she about to swoon? Fall ill?

He ought to back out of this now. But stubbornness or greed for his money—or perhaps...desire to learn more about this enigma of a woman—refused to topple his stance. A warrior would be weak to make demands and then wave them off as whimsy.

"It's all right, brother," Aileana croaked. "Let us please just…get this over with."

"But ye *must* have a stake in this bargain, too," Seamus replied, then turned on James again. "I must demand that if Aileana do this, that she be given a degree of latitude or else there's no deal and I'll await my chance to defend her against yer formal complaint."

"What are yer terms?" James quirked his brow.

"If ye handfast her, I demand that she be given until Twelfth Night to decide if she'd like to remain as the Lady of Tioram Castle, or if she's too miserable as yer trophy of humiliation and wishes to return home, that the handfast be severed. Promise me this, as an official term for everyone in this hall to bear witness to, or else we have no accord."

Grant sliced the air to emphasize his point.

James swallowed. The leaden weight that dropped in his gut caught him off guard. Be damned, but he needed this marriage to be permanent. He should have opted for a kirk wedding and scrounged up a priest. For if she left him on Twelfth Night—as she undoubtedly would—he would miss his chance at the money. What was the point, then? And yet, if Seamus called him on his threat to lodge his complaint with the Crown, Twelfth Night would come and go before his grievance was even heard, making a quest for compensation moot. He huffed and eyed Aileana. He'd felt the stirring of lust for her each time they'd parried with words, and he knew he'd have no issue feeling passion for such a woman. But would she reciprocate in time? Could he achieve the ultimate conquest and convince her to stay?

Damn, but this was the only chance he had now. His plan had ricocheted back on him. He took a deep breath. He'd always loved a challenge. He had a mountain of one now.

"All right. I agree to yer terms, Grant. I'll return Lady Aileana, the handfast revoked, with yer full rights as her laird to marry her to another as it pleases Clan Grant, by Twelfth Night"—his eyes cut to hers—"*if* she so chooses."

"What of yer recompense for my thievery if I leave?" she asked, that haughty lift of her chin a tough expression on an increasingly fragile face; that voice, so barbed with words and yet so smoothly spoken. A defense, he realized. Aye. She wasn't really so tough, and this handfast frightened her.

He nodded once. "I'll consider it repaid, lass."

His statement hung in the ensuing silence, until Peigi's sniffling became too much for her to contain. She threw her arms around Aileana, who stood stone still like a tree trunk. "But my dearest sister! He'll strip yer innocence!"

James frowned. Did they think he'd force Aileana to his bed? He wasn't like his horrid brother-in-law, who now resided in the fiery pits of hell, where he belonged. He'd never stripped a woman of anything she didn't *want* to be stripped of. And besides, a handfast was as legitimate as a wedding registered in a kirk. There was no shame in lying with one another if they'd handfasted with an agreed set of terms.

Seamus placed a hand on Peigi's back but glared at him. "Do ye aim to punish me by putting one of my sisters in yer bed only to give her back when yer amusement abates?"

Peigi gasped at the lewdness of Seamus's statement.

"I'm a compassionate man," James replied.

"Sure. Ye attacked our walls when I and my strongest contingent were away and now play nice with neighborly alliances. Compassionate. And the Loch Ness Monster comes ashore to dance jigs at the faire. I smell a deeper motive for demanding a woman in exchange for a potful of vegetables, and I do nay doubt ye'd find pleasure in returning my sister at Christmastide's end with her reputation in tatters."

James took a deep breath, anger mounting at being so likened to Marjorie's husband, and snarled, "*Ye* suggested terms, nay me. I merely agreed to them. I'd prefer any marriage I enter to be for life."

"Ye do nay strike me as the type to have care for a lady's honor," Seamus taunted.

"Then ye ken nothing about me," James muttered, so low and soft, he saw a flicker of surprise cross Grant's face, as if he believed him.

Hope seemed to light Aileana's face, too, but shrewd disbelief captured Seamus's brow now.

"I ken what ye really want, James MacDonald: my lands. And this nay doubt is part of a scheme."

James didn't deny it. No one else knew about his inheritance, trapped in the care of Fearn Abbey thanks to his stepmother's conditions that he earn it, first—a task she'd thought would be impossible, which was why she'd stipulated it. He shrugged.

"I can come home on Twelfth Night, brother, for there's no circumstance under which I'd choose to remain," Aileana said softly, taking her brother's arm. "Laird MacDonald is simply like a hunter toying with his quarry, but I'll be no victim. Fear no' for me. I'm strong. I can withstand this and will return home. This, I vow. Even if I have to claw my way back."

Peigi sobbed even harder now, clinging to her and drawing a kerchief to her nose. "But he'll bed ye, and then ye'll have shed yer maidenhood for naught."

A blush captured Aileana's cheeks—to have something so intimate discussed so openly—and she cast her hazel gaze askance. James inhaled long and slow. This pity was growing strength in his gut. He'd stolen all from these people in the name of conquest. True, they'd stolen from him, too. And back and forth the rivalry had seemed to always swing. But these people were suffering and might not last the winter, and now that he was catching a glimmer of the Grants at the supper board instead of at the point of a sword, he thought, *Does this fighting need to persist?* At some point, someone would need to cut their losses. Could he be the one to finally lay down his sword and wave a white flag of truce? In his older years, James's sire had seemed to tire of fighting, and he had set aside his armor and sword. He'd been anxious to see his daughter marry an enemy man, in hopes it would bring peace between their clans.

Mayhap peace would have better results than warfare. Mayhap the terms of his inheritance had been put in place at his stepmother's insistence, but his father had never crafted them to be about conquering at all.

He pushed to standing.

"I'll add a further term, then, to put Lady Peigi's heart at ease." Peigi looked up at him with splotchy cheeks and a sniffle, though Aileana, still standing stone still, stared stoically at his chest as if he were a reaper come for her. "No consummation unless she chooses to remain."

"How can I trust yer word?" Seamus growled.

Sakes, but this might be the only time he acquiesced to touching Seamus Grant without it being to drive a blade into the man's ribs. He thrust out his hand to shake wrists. Seamus frowned but finally accepted the offering.

Aileana swallowed so hard, he heard the gulp, and she pushed back her wild wisps of hair that seemed determined to irritate her eyes. James watched the trail of her slender finger across her cheek, over her ears, a sweet gesture from an otherwise confounding creature. He withdrew his *sgian achlais* from beneath his shoulder where it was sheathed. Seamus tensed and whipped loose his blade at his hip once more.

"Ye invite trouble?" Seamus said. "Ye might overpower

us with sheer numbers, but I'll remind ye that right now, ye're the one *alone*."

His gaze never wavering from Grant's, James fished up the hem of his mantle tucked through his belts and sliced away a strip of red MacDonald tartan, then sheathed his blade once more.

"Give me yer hand, lass," he said to Aileana.

Her eyes dipped to her feet. Was it possible for this feisty woman to feel sheepish? Or was she merely reluctant? Still, unceremonious or nay, it was best to get on with the custom and ensure she'd promise herself to him for the next fortnight, even if the coercion now left distaste in his mouth. A maiden and lady deserved a celebration, with finery and a delicately beaded gown, with feasting and bards and dancing. Nay this.

I can still release her of this trap. Yet he couldn't bring himself to say those words.

Aileana finally looked him squarely in the eye before lifting the end of her tartan shawl and withdrawing her own dagger from her bodice, slicing off her own strip of plaid. She held out her hand with the cut of Grant fabric, her chin raised high. She'd made her point. She wasn't owned by MacDonald colors, and she wasn't owned by *him*.

He took the offered tartan and handed both cuts to Seamus, who ran his thumbs over the enemy plaid thoughtfully.

"If I hear of abuses toward my wee sister," Seamus finally said, his eyes dark with intent and a low rumble to the back of his throat, "I'll nay give one shite about a royal recompense. I'll kill ye. Ye can count on it."

"She's safe," James replied, and swallowed hard at the grief he felt for sweet Marjorie, who had *not* been safe.

Solemnity overcame him. It might only be a handfast, but he'd never been married. And he hadn't come here with a marriage proposal on his mind. But now that he pondered it, it felt...sacred. In this exact moment, a stranger was giving herself to him, even if it was just for a fortnight, trusting that he would take care and uphold his honor when he'd never been honorable to Clan Grant, nor them to him. There were neither altars nor blood of Christ to sip nor words of wisdom for a newly wedded couple. In this moment, as he picked up Aileana's trembling fingers, he felt another wedge of compassion infiltrate his heart.

He set his brow. "I give ye my word."

In spite of the lack of fanfare and celebration, the impact of the moment rocked him. How brave of Aileana to commit herself to the unknown. What an arse he was for demanding it. His people were going to be stunned.

Chapter Three

Aileana's hand was burning. James's fingers were thick, rough, and his palm was more like the paw of a giant, all encompassing. His calloused skin snagged hers, and the warmth of his touch surprised her, both easing her trepidation a degree and agitating the butterflies breezing around her belly into a gale.

Seamus held the cut of MacDonald fabric, his face gray, as if unsure whether to treat the scrap with respect or spit on it and toss it in the hearth. He cleared his throat. The muscles bulged beneath his ears as he pumped his jaw, causing a new surge of anger to wash over her. Even though her brother made peace to protect his recompense, the revelation that she *was*, in truth, no better than a cow for bartering gouged like a blade.

"Hold out yer clasped hands," Seamus said, clearing gruffness from his throat while Peigi's eyes overflowed with tears and she clenched Lady Elizabeth's hands.

MacDonald lifted their shared grip, and Seamus draped both plaids around the knot of their fingers, wrapping them around and around, tying the ends.

"Upon Twelfth Night, Aileana Grant may choose if she will remain as yer wife or return home, *unharmed*, and if the latter, this handfast will be void," he added for good measure. "Let it be so known!"

It took a moment for the hall of people to lift their goblets in a salute that sounded more like a toast of condolences than jubilance.

MacDonald lifted their clasp to show the hall proof of their unity, stretching Aileana's arm over her head, and in truth, only raising his hand by degrees. Confusion and sickness swirled in competition in her gut, causing the meager food she'd consumed that day to threaten rebellion, but she swallowed hard at the urge.

And then James squeezed her fingers. It was slight, but reassuring. Her eyes flitted upward at the unexpected gesture, his own cast sidelong down at her as if to see if she would notice, and their gazes connected. Though his brow remained stern, his blue eyes twinkled and his expression... softened.

The handfast complete, her new husband—sakes, what a title to think—lowered their arms, and for a moment, neither of them moved. Numbness coated her skin, and she was certain she'd lost her ability to speak. Would he insist upon a kiss to seal their agreement? Her cheeks flamed with heat, burning, and she cupped her hand over one as if to contain the blushing. Would she dare to allow him his kiss? She doubted it would be as repulsive as she wanted it to be. She examined his lips—soft, in spite of his strong mouth and jaw. It wouldn't be repulsive at all. His eyes dipped to hers, too, staring at her mouth so intently, it was as if he was also contemplating what a kiss would feel like.

Instead, James untangled their fingers and shoved the knotted tartan into his sporran.

"I'll wait in the bailey whilst ye pack...*wife*," he muttered, and turned to leave.

Aileana's eyes widened. James had struggled to push the title over his lips. Was he, too, just as affected by the moment and the newness of the title? Seamus postured next to her, and Aileana gripped a chair like a lifeline. She had to leave this minute? Would James be gentle if he insisted on breaking their agreement or... Goodness! Took her to bed?

She doubled over, her mind foggy, and swayed on her feet.

"Sister," Peigi fretted, helping lower her into a chair, then glaring at James's retreating back and righting her posture, she beseeched him, "Ye would drag my sister away *right now*?"

James turned and looked over his shoulder, stopping, his brow crinkling with concern at Aileana slumped in a chair. She glanced up from her seat as the dizziness thankfully passed.

"There's no time to spare, Lady Peigi," he replied. "Already it grows dark, and I must return to Tioram soon, or my men will worry and send a search."

Seamus furrowed his brow with barely contained rage at being so cornered. He stepped in front of her as if to protect her while the staff looked onward, and Aileana peered around him to watch her new husband. Peigi threw her head in Aileana's lap as if she were being sent to the gallows.

"Sakes, dearest sister! Why did ye do it? Why?"

"Would ye rather it be ye?" Aileana ground out, her knuckles turning white around the chair arms as Peigi fell to sobbing again, gripping her so hard that her nails bit through Aileana's clothing. But she wouldn't fling herself against her sister. This was her yoke to wear, no matter how heavy, and she rose to stand on wobbly legs, determined to remain composed.

"Go and pack what ye will, woman," James said gently.

"I shall be quick and pack light," Aileana replied. "For I do nay intend to remain at yer castle for long."

She left the hall alone, her shoulders back, her head high, and her heart sick with regret and...confusion. So far, James Moidartach MacDonald hadn't been nearly the beast she'd thought. And the way he gazed at her, so intently, sent shivers of traitorous curiosity over her skin. It was as if he liked what he saw. She ought to be frightened. But his surprising gentleness had eased her distress. Would an alliance with the MacDonalds, even if she was the tribute to be exchanged, be so bad? Or would it maybe, *blessedly*, bring this warring clan to heel?

• • •

It was nearly dark by the time James stowed his claymore on his saddle and hoisted Aileana up pillion behind him. Her arms slid instinctively around him, sending a shiver across his skin at the intimacy of the contact, to be so held by her, even if it was purely to keep herself aloft. They set out through the gates, rocking together with Devil's lumbering, making use of what midwinter light was left.

They traversed the countryside in silence, save the creaking of leather, shrouded in wintry white. The snowdrifts made their surroundings bright enough to decipher, in spite of the cloudy night settling upon them. But Aileana was shivering against him, and her grip about his waist, tight, felt as if her arms had frozen. A warm fire and a night beneath his heavy fur might do her well.

"Up there. We'll stop to make camp," he finally said, breaking the quietude.

Aileana said not a word as he steered his horse through the glen where a cluster of boulders had long ago tumbled down the surrounding hills. They would make a good shelter.

Her stomach rumbled so loudly, she resituated herself. She was hungry, and come to think of it, he didn't recall seeing her eat a bite at supper when her fate had been sealed. When had her last meal been before that?

He pushed Devil onward until they reached the boulders next to a frozen burn meandering down the glen. He dismounted and reached up to help Aileana down, but she swung her leg over and slid down Devil's rump on her own, glanced at him silently, and then bypassed him without a word. He inhaled deeply, exhaled. He deserved her anger.

Instead, he removed his packs and unfurled a bedroll, hauling them within the boulders, and dropped to his knees to scoop out the snow to make an embankment around them when he felt Aileana come up beside him. She knelt next to him and began scooping out snow. He took in her slender arms shoveling the snow, the torque of her waist as she did exactly as Peigi had said—helped with the labor to get the job done. Okay. Perhaps he could make this the first step toward a truce betwixt them.

She glanced up at his staring, crinkling her brow questioningly.

He severed his gaze and returned to work. "Thank ye for helping."

"It's what I do best," she retorted.

He ignored the displeasure in her voice and continued working.

"We'll make an embankment around the entry," he said. "Such will insulate us whilst we sleep."

She nodded her understanding, and the two of them finished the task silently. Too silently. He wanted her spitfire tongue to lash him so he could lash back and feel the sparks flying between them again.

"Aileana," he finally said, resting back on his haunches. "I propose a truce. At least, for now."

"A white flag? From ye? I didnae ken ye owned one," she said as her body jolted with each thrust of snow. "But I suppose ye've gotten all ye want, including my dignity. 'Tis easy to sue for peace when ye walk away the winner."

The softness he'd begun to feel grew brittle, and his lips thinned. All right, so her spitfire tongue was lashing again, just as he'd wanted, which was daft of him because arguing with her would surely become damned exhausting. "And apparently ye forgot yer white flag at Urquhart," he grumbled.

She smiled sweetly at him, a smile that didn't meet her eyes. "We have none. They were stolen, along with all our other goods…" She tapped her chin. "By *ye*, I believe."

He took a slow, long breath and restarted, for she seemed to have this strange ability to bring out his brash side. "This union is a chance to reunite olden MacDonald lands. I seek to gain my inherit—" He cut himself short. *Be damned and hold yer tongue*, his conscience chastised him. If he spilled about his inheritance, she really would leave him—just to spite him. "And I've won nothing."

"Won *nothing*? Is yer memory so poorly that ye can nay remember—"

"Remain here," he ordered, interrupting her stream of venom. "I go to collect kindling."

He shoved to his feet and stalked off, needing space to think. He trudged to the edge of the glen where the tree line started upon the hillside, and rummaged through the snow to pile sticks in his arms. She hated him—and yet she thought him handsome. He'd seen her rake her eyes curiously over his form, his shoulders, and his braids, her hazel gaze wide. And how could he help but stare at her beauty? But physical attraction alone would not a marriage make. If she continued to harbor anger for him, their union would remain poisoned with bad opinions and resentment. Perhaps he ought to return her and agree to a voided union now—his reputation as a warlord be damned—to spare her a fortnight of misery, which was pointless anyway, for whether he returned her now or on Twelfth Night, dear old Stepmother had still cozened him out of his inheritance. Besides, would his people be accepting of a Grant woman?

"Just what my step*mither* wanted: For me to fail. For the lairdship and all its benefits to pass to anyone but me."

His mind made up to take her home, he turned back toward camp. But as he crunched near their shelter with his arms full, it was empty. He peered within the rocks.

"Lady Aileana?"

He dropped the sticks with a clatter and walked around the boulders. No one.

"Dammit," he cursed, turning in all directions. Had she fled?

No, his horse was still there, and she no doubt had common sense enough not to run off in the middle of a freezing night. Unless she knew shortcuts to reach home that he didn't.

"Aileana?" he boomed, though the surrounding snow dampened the echo.

Silence answered him. Nerves pulsed in his gut.

"Aileana!" he rumbled, though again, the echo was thwarted.

Sakes, was she lost? Injured? Stolen away? Of all the nights to leave a lass unattended, this one ought to have been the safest. What if something horrible had befallen her? Seamus Grant would make good on this threat to kill him; James had no doubt. Their clan rivalry would rage onward, this time with no hope of abating.

"Good Christ," he cursed under his breath. "Aileana! Answer me!"

He squatted down to inspect her tracks, then hastened after them, losing them at the bank of the frozen burn, a skinny trickle gurgling down the middle.

"Aileana!"

In the distance, he saw a shape. Was it an animal? It moved like a dark presence against the snowy backdrop, and he drew his dirk, when the shape began to take form. A long, flowing mass of fabric became obvious, as did the wavering of long hair, the shape of a woman.

Exhaling hard, he paused, then wiped the sweat that had beaded his brow. He sheathed his blade and jogged to her.

"Where were ye?" he demanded, right as he looked down into her arms to see the load of kindling she also carried.

"Helping," she muttered, then moved to step around him.

He blocked her path, taking her arms. She stiffened.

"I told ye to stay at the camp."

"I was freezing, sitting there, when the exertion of moving about would warm my muscles. That, and two people can gather as much kindling twice as fast as one."

"Ye disobeyed me."

"I suggest ye become used to it, for I answer to no man save my brother, who is laird."

And she hardly listened to him, James thought wryly.

"I had good reason for ye to stay put. Ye could've gotten lost, frozen to death, and yer brother would've had my head—"

"I ken these hills far better than ye do, for we're nay even off *Grant* land yet."

Emphasizing Grant. True, for all the claims to birthrights, he didn't know this region the way her clan did.

"Ye do nay listen well," he growled, leaning down into her face.

She met his nose with her own, thrust up to meet his menacing glare. Their lips practically touched. He could feel her breath warm upon him, could see tiny details in her face in spite of the nighttime, and his scowl unfurled as he leaned in closer to smell her scent and decide if he liked it. Fok, but he did. *So close to knowing more about her tongue.* As her husband, he had a right to know this tongue if he wished. In the dark, her eyes were more like gray crystals with the lack of sunshine to ignite their color. They sparkled with mischief and perhaps a small amount of satisfaction that she was a nettle in his saddle.

"And I suggest ye get used to *that*, too," she replied. "I'll nay be bullied or abused by any man, least of all a *nàmhaid*."

Hurt lashed him, and the bruises he remembered on sweet Marjorie's face haunted him once more. If Aileana meant to strike pain on him, she had. In spite of his pulse racing to know her more intimately, he stepped away, clearing the gruffness from his throat that thoughts of Marjorie always induced. Tears a man like him would never be allowed to shed. Marjorie had loved him as her full brother, in spite of her mother's hatred of him. And he'd been unable to protect her.

Aileana's eyes widened with surprise at his retreat when she'd clearly expected him to double down. Her lips parted, but he turned away before she could speak, his thoughts afluster, and left her to stand alone.

Be damned. Be damned to high heaven. He rubbed the bridge of his nose. He'd intended to make *her* want to stay, but he'd never anticipated *wanting* her to stay. And he wasn't sure he could handle the constant reminders of Marjorie she was certain to evoke.

He huffed into his hands to warm them, rubbing them together, hearing the soft swishing of her skirts behind him. Good, she followed. He squatted to arrange his pile of kindling—wee tinder on the bottom, larger sticks and twigs on top. Aileana came up behind him, causing tingling to skitter across his skin that she would be so close again. She stepped over the snowy embankment they'd formed around the shelter and set down her armload of wood, then maneuvered around him to collect her small pack and withdraw a thin sheet of wool from it to wrap around her shoulders.

James's eyes followed her as she settled down opposite the fire ring from him—

Damn! The stick in hand slipped from his grip in his distraction and bit his skin. A sliver.

He unsheathed his *sgian achlais* from his underarm sheath and pushed it out with the flat of his blade, but his gaze landed back on Aileana across from him. Did she hope to keep her distance? She was shivering like a pennant on a blustery day. They'd do well to nestle together to generate more body heat, but after her biting words, the notion of sleeping together was sure to sit poorly with her. He withdrew his fire flints to spark against the metal plate and induce a fire.

"In my packs, I've bread, cheese, and jerked beef," he said. "Help yerself."

"Is the beef from one of our stolen cows?"

His jaw ticked at her sarcastic reply, and his lips thinned. If she thought to do nothing but needle him until Twelfth Night, he'd make sure her play was turned about fairly.

"Indeed, and it was delicious," he grumbled, looking up at her to await her retort.

Her mouth opened, aghast at his rudeness, but no sound came out, and she closed it. She finally managed a reply. "Well then. I believe I'd rather starve."

"Suit yerself." He shrugged, then continued to strike his flint.

A spark took hold, a tiny flame catching on dried leaves that spread to the twigs. James leaned low to the ground and blew gently, encouraging the flame to catch. As the fire began to curl the twigs and spread, he pushed to his feet and retrieved his packs, unstrapping one and withdrawing his foodstuffs. Aileana, now lying down, shivered beneath her cloak and blanket, gazing at the flame as if deep in thought.

He walked around the fire to sit beside her, noticed her glance up at him, noticed sweat beading her forehead. His brow furrowed. To be shivering *and* sweating could only mean the lass was falling ill. *No good.* Now more than ever, he needed to get her beneath his furs or else a fever might set in.

He tore off a bite of jerked meat between his teeth and dropped to his rear, leaning against a boulder. Her stomach growled so loudly now, he couldn't withhold his chuckle. Yet wariness remained. He couldn't allow her to become sick.

"Ye ken the expression, 'biting off one's nose to spite one's face'?" he said.

She shot her hazel glare at him and sat up, too, sparkling warmly in the firelight and her hair glossy with dark-red hues as the light wavered against her. A bonny sight.

"Ye're hungry. And nay just hungry, but it's been some time since ye've eaten well."

He held out his food, this time under her nose so she could smell the saltiness of the meat and cheeses, and he saw a tug-of-war commence in her mind. He gestured with it once more, and she finally acquiesced, taking a piece of meat from him and bringing it to her mouth to nibble.

A smile pulled up his mouth.

She glanced at him, a smirk forming on her face in reply. "I only eat because I'm famished, nay because I accept any sort of truce."

He lifted his eyes heavenward, shaking his head. "My sister Brighde says there's no one as stubborn as me, but I now believe her to be wrong. Ye exceed me."

He dropped his last bite in his mouth and grabbed his fur, piled next to them, and dragged his saddle pack close. Shifting himself beside her, her eyes widened.

"What are ye doing?"

"Readying to sleep," he replied. "Ye may no' be tired, but I'm weary from spending my day chasing down a *lad*."

"And ye think to sleep with me?"

He felt the need to smile again.

"Aye. Nay only right here, but beneath the covers with ye, too."

She gaped at him as he stretched out flat and draped his tartan and fur over their legs. Plagued by another rare moment of speechlessness, her mouth remained open, and her lush hair fell like a tapestry around them.

He flashed a grin, amused by her sudden surprise. "What?" he asked innocently, her body so close he could once more smell her.

"Ye intend to strip me of my honor right here, at the point of force, only to toss me back in a fortnight—"

"I wish to remain warm. Nay slake my lust on ye, lass," he growled, shoving himself up, too. His smile dropped, and his eyes narrowed. Anger over Marjorie's lot, always simmering beneath the surface, bubbled over now. "If ye ken one thing about me, let it be this: my sister Marjorie died because of a brutish husband. My *faither* married her to a *nàmhaid* MacLeod in hopes it would create peace, but it only put her, a wee mouse, betwixt the jaws of a lion," he spat. "He humiliated her, raised his heavy hand to her more times than could be counted, and sent her home in such dishonor, my *faither* and I thirsted for blood revenge. I was nay even fully grown, but when she passed away, we sought it.

"I've *never* forced a woman to my bed, and I would *never* force ye, either. I trust that if I were to cause ye harm, yer brother would come for my blood, as I avenged *my* sister."

"A mouse and lion…" she whispered to herself, as if his comparison meant something more. She sat stone still and then looked down at her hands as the popping of the fire intensified the silence between them. "I didnae ken that about yer sister. I didnae ken ye had sisters before tonight. Ye must have loved her very much."

The gentleness in Aileana's voice took him aback. No barbed words? No kicking the "*nàmhaid*" when he was down?

"Why did he send her back?" she asked, twisting a loose thread on her sleeve.

Blast it, he'd never talked about it, and he struggled to find the words.

"She lived there for more than a year," he finally managed. "But the man couldnae get a babe on her, least of all a son, and blamed her for it. When illness began to take her eyesight, he—" Shite. His voice cracked, and he raked his fingers through his hair, snagging on his braids, then propped his arm upon his knee. Composure regained, he cleared his throat, and gazing into the flame, continued, "He disgraced her dignity in such a way, I wanted to..."

He couldn't finish, and silence, once more, stretched between them.

"What did he do?" she whispered, and this time, a gentle hand came to settle upon his.

Ah, he'd thought Aileana's willingness to help set up camp might be the beginnings of a truce, but *this* was their actual truce. She was in the position Marjorie had been in, and he'd just given her a piece of his soul by telling her about it. *This* was the common ground upon which they could build a temporary peace.

"He sent her home upon a blind ass. She never healed from the humiliation. Never spoke again, for the month it took her to waste away and pass on."

"James, I'm sorry," Aileana breathed.

He cleared his throat again and took the fingers she'd laid upon his in hand, looking down to examine them. They were icy. And yet the gesture was warm. "Brighde and Marjorie are, in sooth, my half sisters. I was bastard born upon my *faither's* favored leman. But my *faither* saw fit to recognize me and raise me with his daughters, though at times, I wished he hadn't, for my step*mither* never accepted me."

He stopped. He needn't spiral down the high road of emotional scars inflicted by a woman who'd sabotaged him and needled him at every turn, all because of who he was through no fault of his own.

"My sister, Lady Brighde, lives with me still. I'll nay bless a marriage for her until I ken the man who seeks her hand is honorable."

Aileana looked into the fire beside him, pulling her knees up and wrapping an arm around them. "And yet I've been married off, on almost a whim, to someone my family only kens as an enemy."

James said nothing. It was true. He knew he would never lay a hand on Aileana to hurt her, but Seamus couldn't have been certain of that.

A fingertip caressed the back of his hand. "I'm sorry that the Lady Marjorie suffered...and that ye suffered, too."

James lifted his eyes to hers as she gazed back to him, and he cleared his throat, setting his brow. "'Tis the way of things. Brighde will be pleased to meet ye, and mayhap, find a sister in someone new. At least for a fortnight. Losing Marjorie was hard upon her, too, for they were close."

Aileana took a deep breath, still holding his other hand—a small acquiescence on her part. Pleasure at the gentle act warmed him, and his thumb took to caressing her skin, too.

"Mayhap ye best wait for the shock of a Grant wife to dull first before ye decide if she'll be pleased," she said, the corner of her mouth lifting in jest.

James chuckled, grateful for a reason to smile. "Aye, to

be sure I'll confound my people, for I've never kept a wom—"

Again, his eyes snagged hers at such a personal confession. A laird who had never kept a leman was an oddity. But his father and stepmother had taught him all too well the consequences of sowing bastards. He'd not do it to a bairn of his own.

He cleared his throat. "But Brighde will welcome ye with open arms. She's kind like that. Always cheerful in spite of the rough lot dealt her. And considering what happened to Marjorie when she was married off to a *nàmhaid*, I suspect Brighde will be more understanding of yer position."

Aileana smiled. "Peigi is like that. Normally, she's always smiling, even when there's so much bearing down on us."

The fire crackled in the ensuing silence as their hands remained touching. The point of contact made his skin buzz, and he was reluctant to let go of this fragile connection.

"But now the real question is," he continued, "are ye willing to freeze the night away because of yer pride? Or are ye willing to lie with me so we both might keep warm?"

She contemplated him, severing their hands' embrace. A shiver racked her frame, and she looked longingly at the fur he'd piled up their legs, resigning to a decision and flashing a wan smile.

"I'll lie with ye, *nàmhaid*. Ye are, after all, my husband."

Chapter Four

This is the wise thing to do.

More sweat beaded Aileana's brow—a bad omen, for with a still-damp tunic cold against her skin in this freezing night, she ran the risk of fever. Yet try as she might to convince herself that sleeping together for added warmth was best, she still couldn't settle her nerves.

Slowly, she settled down on her side, turning to face the fire as her cheeks raged red with nerves, embarrassment, and perhaps more than a little excitement to be so held by this man. In the span of only a moment, James had become a human to whom she could relate—as he'd shared the wound that losing his sister had left on his soul—even if she still felt anger at him.

She swallowed hard. What sort of pain had he and his surviving sister endured, watching Lady Marjorie's demise and death? She wouldn't be able to bear it if something like that happened to Peigi. And yet that explanation was all she'd needed to feel safe in his presence. A man who had watched such a horror unravel with his own sister wouldn't perpetrate the same thing upon another, would he? And he had been right as he'd negotiated with her brother that evening: their clans had clashed back and forth many a time. Her brother, and her father before him, weren't innocent, and neither was James or his father.

At some point, this violence needed to stop. What if she and James could be the start of that change? Nay. He'd forced her to marry. Even in the face of his sister's memory, he'd still held her brother by the proverbial bollocks to gain a woman—

His hand gently swept her hair over her shoulder, the coolness of the night air mingling with the heat on her exposed nape, inducing a shiver. Gooseflesh tingled her skin as his roughened fingers dragged across her flesh. His arm then slid beneath her neck to cradle it upon his bicep as he stretched his long limbs and contorted himself to fit against her. The blanket, then the fur, slid up them both to cocoon them together.

Her heart kicked up a notch at the gesture—*imagine, gentleness coming from this upstart warlord.* And knowing he thought her plain only made her heart pinch. *Which is daft. I shouldnae want him to like me.*

His chest came flush with her back, his, his...sakes, his masculine parts nestling against her rear, his legs now purposefully tangling with her skirts. He rustled for a moment to settle into a comfortable position, and her body burned where he shifted against her. And then his other hand fished for the hem of her cloak, migrated beneath it, and his arm settled heavily around her stomach, toned, long muscle, cinching her tightly to him.

Goodness, she trembled now, and not from shivering. To be touched so brazenly when a man had never wrapped her waist in his embrace before. And still, as if unconsciously, his thumb began to rub back and forth across her stomach, calming her jitters.

"I meant what I promised yer family," came his voice, husky and deep against her neck and inducing another shiver as she imagined him whispering in her ear, perhaps nipping at it.

But after a moment of rubbing his head against the pack to dent a comfortable position, he exhaled, breezing against her nape, relaxed, and moments later, seemed to fall into the easy breathing of sleep.

Just like that? He could fall asleep tangled with her so, when not long before they had been enemies? Fascinating, for her heart was skipping frantically, and her chest rose and fell with ragged, ill-measured breaths, so much so she was certain she wouldn't sleep a wink. Had he been speaking the truth when he said he'd never kept a woman? Was she the first that he would publicly announce? Even if this marriage was only an illusion? Either that or he was lying and indeed was no novice wrapping himself around a woman abed any night that he wished. She lifted her eyes heavenward and exhaled harshly. She wanted the latter sentiment to be the truth so she could continue to hate the handsome cretin, and yet he'd made her doubt all her beliefs about him.

How long she lay stone still, listening to the wood pop and watching the fire turn slowly to coals, it was impossible to say. But at some point, her shivering subsided beneath his possessive grip, and her eyelids grew heavy. His breaths came in deep, steady puffs upon the back of her hair. Slowly, she relented to the comfort of his embrace, drifting, as visions of his feral hair and sparkling eyes from astride his stallion, as he stared at her through Urquhart's portcullis, danced in her mind.

• • •

25th of December

James smelled the herbal scent of Lady Aileana's hair all damn night. So soft, so silky against his cheek and nose. And this newfound gentleness in her beckoned him to move closer. To be wanted by her. He opened his eyes, giving up on sleep, and took in the dark sky of early morn…and felt the warmth of her breasts pressed against his stomach, her cheek upon his pectoral, her palm slung upon his navel beneath the covers as if to torment him, for his manhood was well aware that her slender fingers lay so close to his belts. His skin buzzed as he tried to tether his wayward thoughts, squinting out at the predawn light casting grayness upon the snowy world. From this barbed woman, her touch, so gentle, was a gift.

She shifted ever so slightly, her fingers brushing upon his belts, and he froze, swallowing a groan, closing his eyes. But hell, if his thoughts didn't gallop away, imagining things he would never do with her. Motionless and daring not to move, lest he disturb this sliver of contentment, when yesterday this woman had attempted to shred his patience, he tightened his arm around her, holding her more snuggly upon his chest.

Yet the throbbing of blood pulsing through his loins couldn't be helped, lying so intimately with her. Fok, but he couldn't remain any longer, cocooned together, while her wild hair filled his senses with desire, tickling his stubble. How had he lived his life at Tioram, a mere day's ride from Urquhart, and never met Aileana Grant? Not even at a gathering or council between clans?

A breeze disrupted the surface flurries and sprayed them inward, causing them both to shift, and she softly sighed, a high, groggy moan drawing from her throat. He pondered her: such a spiked tongue when awake, such an angelic doe when asleep. Hell, it was just an innocent sound, and yet sensual, wanting.

He released his hold upon her, easing himself away and from beneath the covers to stand. The stark chill of winter stung his arms through his doublet and his bare legs. Oh, to tarry on this journey home with Aileana, joining in a kiss, a dalliance of lips and tongues... Would she be just as acerbic abed as she was when she was verbally sparring with him? Or would she blossom into a seductress?

Eejit. I build fantasies where there are none. Lady Aileana wants nothing to do with me. Even if she softened to me last night. She softened because of Marjorie's plight, nay mine. Nay that I actually did much to win her affection yesterday, coercing her into a jest of a marriage...

Aileana's eyes fluttered open as he gazed down at her, and he settled the fur around her, tucking her back in. "Sleep, lass."

Her eyes drifted shut and she rolled over. "I thank thee, Jamie..." she mumbled so softly, it was clear she wasn't awake, to have spoken so kindly to him.

Jamie. His breath caught. Only Marjorie had called him that, a sweet pet name that had been enough to feel loved.

He stalked out of the shelter to tend to his morning ablutions and catch his breath. Did such an unconscious utterance on her part mean she might feel affection for him? Or at least a desire to forge trust? *Daft man. Ye need her to remain in this union so ye can claim yer money.* But it was going to become hard to manipulate someone who didn't want to stay into staying, if he started having feelings for her.

He found the nearest dip in the hillside to flip aside his kilt and take care of his morning needs, then wandered until light brightened the eastern horizon, losing himself in thought. He'd meant to offer her a return home last night, but her disappearing act, and ensuing argument, had thrown him off course. As he returned to camp, he glanced at her form. She lay still. She'd been nervous and as rigid as a curtain wall in his arms, and she must have stayed awake half the night, to sleep so now.

Devil flipped his ears backward at his approach. Coming up beside the beast, he stroked his powerful neck.

"Good morn, man," he whispered, and he reached into his sporran for a wrapping of dried apples he kept stashed there, palming one to the horse's mouth.

Devil lipped it up, and he rubbed the stallion's muzzle. Turning toward the countryside, he plopped a bite in his mouth, idly offering another to his horse, who nudged his sporran for more, when a rustling noise drew his attention, as if something was routing through leaves buried beneath the snow. A critter. He quieted, until the pointed black tip of a nose attached to red fur and a bushy tail peered out from behind some rocks.

They regarded each other, the fox's tail flicking curiously. James smiled and squatted. The wee beast would harm them none, and probably hoped for a nibble of food. Digging out a strip of jerked meat from his sporran, he broke off a piece and held it forth while the fox's nose sniffed the air.

"Come hither," he rumbled softly, clicking his tongue for encouragement. "I'll hurt ye none."

The fox darted back and forth, edging its way forward, tantalized enough by the prospect of meat to dare a closer encounter.

"That's the way, beastie." He wiggled the meat as he rested on his heels and lured the fox closer.

Furtively, it strained forward and snipped the treat out of James's fingers, scurrying back to its den. James shook his head with amusement, slipped another piece of apple into his mouth, and chewed. But as he glanced back at Aileana, he saw her propped on her elbows, watching him.

His smile fell and he pushed up. How long had the lass been spying? He cleared his throat and returned within.

"Did ye sleep well?" he asked, and a sliver of concern gripped him. Her face was pale. He leaned down and touched the backs of his fingers to her forehead.

She gazed up at him, crinkling her brow at the unexpected contact, perhaps thinking about something she wasn't sharing. "Ye're fond of animals."

He straightened and shrugged noncommittally. "In sooth, I like them more than most people."

She laughed softly. "Aye, indeed I often think the same thing."

Their eyes connected. "Aileana." *Why'd ye call me Jamie?* He didn't ask the burning question on his mind since he'd woken, and he cleared his throat. "Would ye like me to return ye home this morn? I worry that ye might be taking ill."

Her eyes widened and she wrapped her cloak around her frame more tightly, pushing to stand, too. Her rich hair, slung over her shoulder, was tangled in such an unladylike fashion, he wished he'd been the one who'd cast it into such fetching disarray.

"Ye would do that?" she asked. "And what of my thievery?"

He huffed. "I was angered, aye. Our people have flung unkindness upon each other for so long, 'tis hard nay to feel affronted. But, eh..." He raked his hand though his hair. "I ken ye'd be unhappy. That I forced yer hand."

She looked askance. "I'm nay averse to spending a fortnight at Tioram before I go home," she finally replied. "I suppose, if ye and I can forge a trust, then mayhap we can return to our people and spread goodwill. I'm nay privy to the disagreements that pitted our *faithers* against each other. But should such madness continue?"

His heart skipped a beat at the same time it plummeted. A fortnight at Tioram would give him time to become better acquainted with this woman, who had been quick to despise him, even if she'd still be leaving eventually.

He nodded once, then turned away from her, scooping up his packs to heave them onto his shoulder. Whatever their decision, they needed to get moving and get indoors, in front of a crackling hearth.

"Let's break camp and eat, then," he said, and strode over to Devil to load his effects.

The peaceful morning spell was broken. Or perhaps, they finally had a spell cast on them.

. . .

The morning was clear and crisp, the storm having passed. Sunlight blazed off the snow, sparkling white crystals, the air around them blessedly still, making the cold bearable. At long last, as they came out of an upland, Tioram Castle loomed into view beneath them, a proud tower perched atop a wee peninsula lording over the confluence of the River Shiel and Loch Moidart. No doubt the stretch of land and rocky uplift became an isle when the tide was high. Distant, white-capped peaks upon the Isle of Skye loomed like sentries in the distance, guarding the great expanse of ocean beyond the Hebrides. Surrounded in snowy banks that glistened like fluttering fairy wings in the sunshine, the earth seemed deceivingly pure.

"Goodness..."

James glanced over his shoulder at Aileana's sigh. She leaned around his torso to see. A wide-eyed expression had captured her visage, as if she were awed or overwhelmed by the beauty.

"I've only heard tales of this place from my brother. It truly is magnificent."

James nodded once to her in acknowledgment of the compliment. He'd always been proud of his castle. Bastard born or not, he'd been afforded comforts as his father's proclaimed heir, and these walls held the whispers of his childhood.

"Urquhart used to be so magnificent, too, before the reave," she continued.

Was she censuring him? Knee-jerk irritation gripped him before he could temper his tongue.

"Tioram, too, was a shell of itself after yer brother and the Frasers unseated me, chasing me out and burning our stores before I could finally afford to refurbish the damage," he retorted.

She sucked in a lungful at his admonishment. "And at whose expense did ye rebuild? Ours. Ye simply terrorized all the innocent people at Urquhart to steal what ye needed. I see ye use yer white flag of truce as a nice doormat for yer mucky boots."

"Ye imply that Urquhart's problems are *my* fault instead of yer brother's for involving himself in the Frasers' schemes. 'Tis no' I who sullied the white flag, lass."

Aileana pulled away. He glanced back at her withdrawal. Be damned! Their history seemed forever beneath the surface, ready to leak anger before one could think better of it. But the sunshine bright on her face in spite of its paleness, her nose and cheeks pink from the cold, snagged his irritation, as did her hazel eyes glittering with unspoken thoughts.

She looked down. "I suppose these rivalries betwixt us willna die an easy death if we continue to parry as *nàmhaids*," she muttered.

He fished behind him for her hand and pulled it back around him as they curved down the path, revealing more of the hillside overlooking the water as descended. "Aye." They'd made a tentative truce, and he'd do well to foster the goodwill and bite his tongue next time she needled him.

He nudged Devil into a trot as he felt her shivering against him, for the path to the gates had been well trodden.

She cleared her throat, her hand at first frozen, then as she relaxed, her other arm came around him, too.

"What's that?" she asked. "Over yonder. Is that yer chapel?"

James glanced across the hillside to the cemetery buried in snow among a dormant tangle of brambles, near the trees that lined the loch. The wee chapel stood above the graves, a small, single stone chamber with a carved cross atop the ridge over the door and decorated with Pictish knots from olden days. Pillows of white rested upon the roof and drifted against the door. He hadn't gone inside that chapel or walked among the headstones since the day Marjorie had died. Even when his sire was finally laid to rest, he'd remained apart from Brighde, unable to come too close.

"Aye. And cemetery. Five generations of MacDonalds are buried there. And on the end is an empty space for me before the next row will be started."

"Just one space?"

James shrugged. "I never thought I'd marry. No sense in setting aside a plot for a wife when I assumed I'd die a bachelor."

"Why did ye assume you'd no' marry?"

He digested the question. He'd assumed he'd never gain a *Grant woman's* hand, to be more specific, and since claiming his inheritance had been the only thing consuming him—a quest he was certain he would never conquer—he hadn't seen any value in the institution of marriage. Aileana had serendipitously put herself in a bad position for her and a good position for him when she'd chosen to thieve from him.

"It looks overgrown," she muttered sadly, as if to herself.

"I do nay visit it often, nor do I spare staff to come tend it," he bit out.

"Why no'?"

"*Why*?" he countered.

As if she could sense his unwillingness to say more, she let the subject die. A blessing that she did, for each time he looked at the cemetery, overlooking the joining of the sparkling western waters upon which Tioram sat, with a heavenly view for which to spend eternity, he remembered the cold, rainy day he and his father had lowered Marjorie into her grave, bound in white cloth with a thistle laid upon her breast, feeling such helplessness... That helplessness threatened to wrap its talons around his heart and squeeze once more, as it always did when he dwelled too long on Marjorie's sad lot.

Hunger plaguing Aileana's stomach rumbled against his back, and as they neared the castle, he felt her stiffen, further distracting him from the sting pricking his eyes at the memory of Brighde sobbing, his stepmother's contemptuous glares of hurt at his father for contracting their older daughter to a fated marriage that had left her wasted.

Aileana's grip tightened as if she held herself aloft, and her breathing seemed to grow uneven. "They're going to hate me," she murmured.

And here he was, bringing an enemy bride into his fold to face the displeasure of his people, as no doubt Marjorie had been forced to do. He dragged back on the reins upon hearing the waver in her voice and glanced at her, eyes narrowing to examine her distress. She was sweating again, a sheen of illness having moistened her brow. Had her shivering finally turned feverous? No good?

"They'll be wary, aye," he said. "Ye're Laird Grant's sister. And there's bad blood there."

Best not to deny the truth. His people wouldn't understand at first. But mayhap, if she showed them her kinder, understanding side as she'd shown him last night, they would eventually warm to her, for a marriage to an enemy was where her lot ceased being similar to Marjorie's. Had Seamus Grant made this handfast permanent, Aileana's future would have looked much different, with a man who would never strike her, humiliate her, or degrade her, no matter the champion's effort she thrust into arguing, needling, and debating him.

"I should have accepted yer offer to return me," she whispered.

Vulnerable. Just as he'd thought. Her hardened facade was merely a veneer upon a fragile soul.

"Ye havenae a choice, now. Come," he encouraged. "Ye'll do fine."

Chapter Five

Guardsmen patrolling Tioram Castle's parapets winched up the portcullis, like the opening jaw of a hungry lion. James trotted Devil onto the promontory leading across the peninsula, passing rows of balingers and smaller *currachs* tipped on their sides with snow pillows atop their hulls. A wan smile tugged at Aileana's mouth as she imagined James at the helm of a watercraft, dragging the sheets against the wind and dominating the cresting waves. So long of leg and blond like his Norse ancestors, he would probably look magnificent.

Lively with folk, noise arose from within Tioram's portcullis as servants went about their jobs, making Aileana's fate real.

"Jesu..." she whispered, sucking in air as if it were drink and she, thirsty.

In truth, she was. Her mouth was chalky, her body racked with shivers, her skin clammy.

James's broad hand squeezed her trembling ones. Goodness! The gesture was brief. But much like it had been during their handfast, it was reassuring now, and she rested her cheek between his shoulder blades to steady what she feared was becoming a feverous mind.

"I train warriors who fight at my bidding," he said. "But my people will harm ye none. Fret no'."

The knot in her gut eased an increment.

"The laird has returned!" called a sentry atop the curtain wall, and a general clattering of people preparing for their laird's arrival ensued.

The knot tightened again. James raised a hand in greeting to them.

"Good afternoon, my laird!" shouted another as they rode under the archway. "We wondered when ye'd arrive back! Sir Angus is preparing a search party. Did ye catch the thief?"

"Who's the lass?" asked another.

"I did indeed catch the thief!" James replied, his voice booming. "And the woman is Lady Aileana Grant!"

God in heaven, he was going to oust her to his people! After the moments of gentleness that had passed betwixt them?

Curious faces turned to stare as they entered the bailey, now consumed within the belly of this stronghold, as maidservants gathered dutifully on the steps. Soldiers leaned warily over the walls to catch a glance of her. Her face burned with heat. Surely they were all making opinions of her. Surely they hated her, or judged her plainness for themselves.

"Ye bring the enemy?" called down a ranking soldier who wore a sparkling brooch. Was he James's first-in-command?

"Lady Aileana isnae our enemy, Angus man," he replied in defense of her.

"The Grants are our friends now, is that it?" the man named Angus replied to a rumbling of chuckles. "The scar on me arm begs to differ!"

He must rank high to talk back so freely. Aileana clenched James, her mind swaying now. She blinked to clear the headiness and lifted her chin, ever defiant. *What was I thinking, agreeing to come here?*

"What be the lady's business?" came a feminine voice in a much kinder tone.

A woman with soft blonde hair swept back in beaded netting and a braid of hair looped over her head like a crown stood regally at the steps, a MacDonald tartan wrapped around her back and clutched in the crooks of her elbows. Her eyes were a pretty blue, and her looks favored James's. Was this his sister, Brighde? And then Aileana's gaze migrated to the dangling bobbles at the woman's ears. Pearls embedded in gold in such a distinctive design, it would be hard to mimic. *My mother's earrings bequeathed to me...* that had been stolen. Aileana had coveted those precious gifts. James had gifted them to this woman!

"She comes with no business," James replied, coming to a halt and addressing the gathering. "She's my wife."

Gasps resonated. Wide eyes loomed around them, and someone, somewhere, dropped their burden with a clattering of metal. Sweat trickled down Aileana's temples, nerves chewed mercilessly at her stomach. And the fever she feared had taken root threatened to get the better of her. She focused on the one thing that wasn't starting to spin: the other lady's earrings. To know this man who she was beginning to feel fondness for had stolen them was one thing, but to see the spoils of his raid flaunted before her now stung. Her distress, held at bay by a thread, overpowered her.

"My earrings," she murmured, and she blinked desperately to clear her foggy mind but tipped off the horse, grappling fruitlessly to hold onto James's waist as her vision swirled, as she fell, fell...and lurched hard.

. . .

26th of December

Pounding. Aileana winced. Her head was pounding. She was so tired. But as her head lolled on the pillow...

A pillow!

It was soft and lush. The linen covering it was finely woven and smooth against her cheek. It smelled of lavender, a faint waft meeting her nose each time she moved. Ah, heaven, such a scent. It had been so long since the Grants could afford so fine a fragrance as lavender. And she was warm.

A heavy blanket was draped upon her, cocooning her to the firmly stuffed mattress. She basked in the sensation until curiosity got the better of her, and she dared to blink awake. Where was she, and what had happened? The chamber encompassing her was dim but, my, so fine. Bed curtains of deep-red velvet were drawn back to reveal a hearty fire crackling in the hearth, the smell of the peat both pungent and comforting. When was the last time they'd had such a fire at Urquhart? The Grants only burned one when they needed it. Otherwise, their drafty hearths remained cold.

She pushed onto her elbow and brought her fingers to her forehead to feel the source of the pounding. Surely she'd bruised herself. How? Slowly, as the memories of her arrival to Tioram Castle filtered back through her groggy mind, she recalled the sensation: feverish, shivering, vision going black, body drifting...

She bolted upright. Pain throbbed through her head. "Goodness, I fainted dead away, off his horse."

She waited for the sensation to ease and pushed back the covers to stand.

"Ohh," she groaned, and she dropped back to her rear, bracing her forehead again.

As the swirling sensation settled, she glanced around her chamber at the tapestries hung over the window shutters, wooden furnishings polished to shining with embroidered pillows upon the chairs at the table. Anger at Urquhart being so deprived of these things swarmed her thoughts like angry wasps, and she moved to the hearth to kneel before the heat. The floorboards were coarse under her bare feet, save the soft rugs before the hearth.

Bare feet.

She looked down. She was bare footed and in a chemise! She hadn't been wearing one before, only her tunic beneath her gown.

Clenching the neck hole to her throat as her sleeves billowed to her elbows, she huddled at the fire and looked about for a robe. The trunk beside the dressing table seemed the likeliest place for a robe to be stored, though it sat draped in a silken cloth, with baskets of bobbles and a mint box atop it. Who had undressed her? Dear God, had James done so himself?

The door opened. She whirled around to look over her shoulder, her chemise still clutched at her throat, and, *speak of the devil, the Devil MacDonald.* James pushed through the door. He froze, his hand in midthrust. His eyes widened an increment, traveled down her body, and lingered upon her for longer than was gentlemanly before traveling over her hands clutched beneath her chin.

"My dress," she croaked, snapping his attention back to her face.

Propelled to action, he closed the door and cleared his throat.

"Ye were burning up. Ye fainted. Yer attendants assisted ye, and thankfully, yer fever broke whilst ye slept, or else I fear it might have become something worse. Then Seamus would have had my head upon his pike."

The distress in her stomach unclenched at his admission. He strode within and plucked a garment from a chair to hold up like proof of wrongdoing at Court—his jaw freshly shaven, clamped tightly—and thinned his lips.

"Why were ye traveling in a wet tunic? As a woman whose family claims ye to be a skilled healer, I'd think ye would have more wisdom. Were ye trying to catch yer death?"

She grinned sweetly. "Aye, anything to see the MacDonald's head upon my brother's pike."

He huffed an unexpected chuckle at her jest and lifted his eyes heavenward.

"It's no' as if I planned to be whisked away upon a handfast, James," she added more seriously. "I wore what I had on."

He dropped the tunic and shook his head but seemed to let his rebuttal go. "I thought ye were still asleep. Are ye well?" he asked.

She shrugged, a wash of forlornness blooming in her chest. She was alone. Without Peigi and without Seamus. *Who sold his sister to the wolves.*

"My forehead hurts, but I shall endure. Did I hit it?"

As if she'd given him purpose, he came to her, a slow progression, his gaze seized upon hers. Each step increased his height, until he loomed above her. She craned her neck back to look up at him and tried to stand, but he squatted down, his hand resting on her shoulder and urging her back down to her knees. His palms spanned her cheeks, and his thumbs parted the hair draped across her forehead. Once more, he lay the backs of his fingers against her brow as if to check for fever. Her skin tingled. For such a merciless warrior, his touch was, once again, surprisingly delicate, as was his demeanor.

"Aye, a wee bruise ye've got. I barely caught ye, but ye still landed hard." His thumb caressed her cheeks, his gaze dropping to her lips with such intensity, it made butterflies flit through her belly again. His eyes dipped down her chemise as if an unconscious reflex, but they quickly bounced away. "I'll, eh, fetch yer maids."

He dropped his hands and stood, rummaging within his sporran. The draft through the shutters, though dampened by the tapestry, still filled the chamber with a chill, for the heat of the fire only radiated so far, and she dropped her hands from her throat to rub her arms.

"Aileana..."

Whatever he'd wished to say, he trailed off, such firmness overtaking his brow she wasn't sure if he was angry or not. Her guard spiked high, prepared to defend herself.

But he bent for her hand, pulled it outward, and dropped a trinket into her palm. Reflexively, she clenched her fist, like a child trying to resist, and watched his back retreat to the door.

"Yuletide ceremony will abound today, considering yesterday was the first day of Christmastide." he said gruffly, his voice strained and his broad shoulders tense as he gripped the latch. "If ye feel well enough, I wish ye to join me for an excursion, and to sit at my side this eve, to celebrate with us. It might ease my people's confusion over ye."

She opened her fist and looked down. Her breath caught.

"My earrings..." She inhaled deeply as trembling consumed her.

Still, he remained, his back to her and his hand on the door, as if unable to pull it back. Aileana dashed to him, embracing him so swiftly she could scarcely believe she'd done it. But to hold those precious relics again, when she'd been so certain they were lost forever, filled her with emotion. He tensed, his muscles twitching, and then he pivoted to face her, and his arms came around her, clenching her in return, holding her head to his chest and dipping his nose to her hair.

It felt so blessedly good—his arms, strong; his smell of riding leathers; his soap; his unique male scent.

"They were a gift from my late *mither*," she continued. "She had two pairs crafted. One for me. One for my sister." Silence stretched between them, pregnant with uncertainly, though his grip tightened. "Mine were stolen the day yer men raided us. It was all I had left of her. And the day I sat before her grave and confessed to her that they were lost...'twas silly that doing such felt so monumental, but my *mither* was always a good listener, and it felt as if I'd finally lost everything."

He seemed game to listen, his chest rising and falling in measured, steadfast breaths, so she continued as the sad memories locked in her heart fought to wedge a crack so they might leak out.

"Peigi always told me to wear my earrings and look the part of a lady, but I was too afraid to lose one. I was certain they'd be safer tucked in my trunks. My sister has always been the envy of many a woman. She's had many suitors, but my brother lacks the promise of a dowry, which eventually sends the suitors away in search of richer prospects... These were part of our dowries, and without them, I have no prospects at all."

He didn't seem inclined to let go, but she pulled away, and he dropped his embrace, clearing his throat.

"I could be a pros—" He cut himself off but not before Aileana suspected the direction of his remark.

She didn't consider James to be a realistic prospect...did she? And why did he want a permanent marriage? Surely he wasn't so pious and moralistic.

His gaze, aimed over her head to stare at nothing on the opposite wall, didn't drop to meet hers, and upon the lips he chewed, he seemed to stifle further rebuttal. She examined him in the firelight while the shadows played upon his tunic, the lacing loosened to reveal the muscle beneath, his features bronzed in the soft, dancing light upon his smooth face.

"My thanks for returning them."

An inkling of guilt contorted his brow, and she might do well to continue fostering this peace between them instead of spitting at him like an adder. Perhaps not only could they form a truce over Christmastide, but she could work out some benefits for her clan, too. A twinkle lit his eyes, and his mouth curved up. Not a smile, but seeming amusement, and he dug beneath the cuff at his wrist. He dragged free a white cloth and shook it out, handing it to her.

She furrowed her brow. "A kerchief?" Like a favor an eligible lady would give to her favored knight at a tourney? A curious smile captured her lips. "Are ye bestowing yer maidenly favors upon me, James MacDonald?"

A husky laugh rumbled unexpectedly up his throat. "'Tis my white flag of truce, lass." He made a concerted effort to inspect it for blemishes. "Eh, as ye can see, I've nay wiped my boots upon it."

The jest induced a giggle. A giggle! *What am I, an enamored lass?* And yet his meaning was clear. He was committed to giving this friendship an honest try and not devolving into parries about whose fault what was. And something about his determination warmed her.

He dragged back the door with a grin and strode out. "My wife is awake," he said to someone, followed by something inaudible, then, "See her dressed and ready for today's outing."

A moment later, two maidservants entered the chamber, followed by a small serving girl, bobbing in their curtsies, their arms bundled in masses of fabrics and baskets of supplies.

"We are to be yer personal maids. The laird requests ye be dressed for the morning's celebrations," the first maid said, though she regarded Aileana warily. "A traveling party goes without the walls to find the perfect Yule log and haul it back to begin burning tomorrow eve."

Morning? Disoriented, she moved to a tapestry, peeling it back and peeking through the crack in the shutters. Stark, early light leaked through. Soldiers gathered for training in the yard. Moments later, James emerged from beneath her window, slipping into a training jerkin and gauntlets and snagging the hilt of a practice sword his man, Angus, tossed to him.

"Did I sleep the whole night?" she asked as James's orders rang out into the bailey and his men took formations to begin sparring.

"Aye, mi lady," the woman said, her tone curt. "Ye passed out. The laird had ye put to bed and sat by yer side until yer fever broke."

James had done what?

"Ye'll join him for the countryside jaunt if ye feel to rights," said the other, just as warily.

She spied MacDonald tartan draped over the maid's arm. A garment for her to wear? Presumptuous on their parts to assume she'd be willing to don such colors. Unless…James hadn't told them about their marriage's lack of permanence. Why? Did he intend to dishonor his agreement to return her home by Twelfth Night? And lay complete claim to her?

A daft, impulsive reaction. She looked down at the earrings in one hand, the kerchief in her other, running her thumb across it, then out the window at him as he drilled his men, deflected his partner's blows, and shouted pointers. His muscled legs and torqued body, hugged by the jerkin, really was a thing of beauty. Nay, he'd been sweet just now, forging further goodwill and returning her most-valued possession. Could she keep taking a *nàmhaid* at his word?

The maids flitted about the chamber while the serving girl, no more than six or seven, closed the door and sat down beside it. They tucked in her bed linens, fluffed her pillows, and laid out their bundle of fabrics. Dark sapphire blue, rich hunting green, soft mauve. And that damning red plaid.

Such beautiful, rich gowns. Her heart squeezed to think of Clan Grant having gone without for so long, while Clan MacDonald seemed to have so much.

"The seamstress will visit this afternoon to take yer measurements," the first maid spoke again as she smoothed the wrinkles from the garments. "The laird has ordered a new wardrobe made, but until that can be done, these gowns might suit. The Lady Brighde has kindly offered them."

That suspicion niggled again. A new wardrobe would be costly and time consuming. Why would James invest such an expense in a temporary handfast?

"We're to see ye break yer fast, per his lairdship's request."

Not a single smile warmed their faces. Instead, they kept their eyes averted, avoiding coming too close to her.

"Come sit, mi lady," the first maid said, an air of irritation to her voice as she placed a tray of savory smells upon the fireside table, pulling out her chair. "Maudie, bring that basket of hair adornments here."

The little girl hurried from the door with a basket on her hand, bobbing in a quick curtsy.

"Ribbons for yer hair, mi lady," the girl said, eyes wide and brown, red hair curling out from beneath her linen bonnet tied beneath her chin. "The blue will be most comely on ye."

Aileana took in her expectant face and bent lower to smile, though even the child shied back from her. Were they worried she'd bite? She straightened, her smile falling.

"Have I offended?" Aileana asked, glancing at the maid who intended to style her hair, and sat.

The other servant, still tidying the chamber, stopped and glanced at her.

"The laird tells us ye're sister to Laird Seamus Grant, mi

lady." The maid tugged Aileana's hair straight.

"I am. I'm his youngest sister," Aileana replied.

The maid swallowed stiffly, and as Aileana faced the tray before her, the maid took to running a comb through her hair, yanking upon her tangles with little gentleness. "Yer brother's men killed my husband four years ago when he and the Frasers sacked Tioram and sent his lairdship fleeing."

Aileana gasped. Winded. As if she'd taken a pummel to her gut. Her clan had done what? She'd always thought her brother's campaign to help the Fraser's instate a new laird had been due to a legitimate claim to the Earldom of Ross. Mayhap all of what James had said was true. And it had affected these innocent people's lives.

"I…I'm sorry," she whispered. "I didnae ken."

The maid scoffed.

"Anag," snapped the other, flashing the woman at her hair a warning look and silencing her.

Aileana winced at the rough combing, but sat quietly, her appetite once again thwarted. She could eat once the maids left. She'd harbored such anger at James these past two years. Anger at how he'd wronged them. But blast it, the truth of who'd started the feud was murky, hidden deeply in a past lost to time. Her conviction solidified as she looked down at the kerchief once more. This bad blood would never be leeched away until both sides decided to cut their losses and move on. And that was hard for maids such as this one, who'd lost their loved ones because of it.

Her hair finally complete, the maid began to pack her bits and bobs into the basket again and swept it onto her arm, but Aileana snagged her hand.

"Anag, is it?" she asked as the maid looked down at her with surprise.

She nodded curtly.

"I truly am sorry. The menfolk make war, but the women

oft suffer the damages."

Anag's face softened, and her gaze dropped to her feet.

"Is that how ye ended up married to our laird, mi lady?" Anag asked.

Aileana swallowed, standing and turning away from them. "I was given in a trade."

Had James told them about her thievery? Sakes, the embarrassment…

"Our hunting party returned the day before, cursing about a lad who'd thieved from their camp," the maid said. "His lairdship announced at board last night that he'd caught the lad, a Grant, and that to make reparations, yer brother promised ye to him."

Aileana's heart clenched. So James had kept her thievery secret?

"My people are desperate. From Laird MacD—from my *husband's* conquest of Urquhart. We havenae much food or provisions. But it was wrong, the thieving, and yer laird demanded a wife as compensation. It was either me or my sweet sister. We only knew yer laird as a warlord against us, and my sister was so frightened…"

Should she tell them this arrangement was only temporary? For some strange reason she couldn't push the truth over her lips. She had no illusions about remaining here. Did she?

The maid dipped in curtsy to her. "Ye needn't fear Laird MacDonald. He's a good man who sees to his people's well-being. And whilst he might be able to strike down a Grant soldier, he'd never strike a lady. Indeed, we wondered if he'd ever marry, for he'll be five and twenty aye soon, and ought to have sown several children by now, but until ye arrived here, he'd refused."

Aileana squeezed her hand as thoughts of Lady Marjorie and the pain that had consumed James's visage when he'd confided his sister's fate in her came to mind. No, she was safe in his charge—of that, she was becoming certain. And yet still, his demands for marriage and desire for wedded permanence in the face of his refusal to marry until now sent a prickle of confusion over her skin of which she couldn't make sense.

The other maid guided her to her dressing table with a kirtle and bodice upon her arm, summoning wee Maudie again to pour the ewer of water upon it into the bowl. The maid saturated a cloth, wringing it, and handed it to her to wash. Goodness, it smelled of roses. Such elegant water. Peigi would have loved this luxury.

Next, the maid helped her step into her stockings, tying them over the knees with ribbons, and draped the creamy kirtle over her head, dragging it down to her waist to secure the fastenings. Her bodice was next, and lastly, the rich sapphire gown and sleeves, which hung in billows of loose trumpeted fabric that bunched in her elbows. She caressed the heavy velvet, awed and wistful. Here she was, wrapped in such finery, while her people scraped by, one breath away from starvation.

"Yer style is finished," said Anag. "What thinks ye?"

She held out a looking glass. Aileana's wistfulness abated as she inspected her reflection and slowly lifted her hand to finger the hairstyle.

For a split second, it seemed Peigi's reflection stared back at her.

"My." She sighed. "Ye've done a fine job...I ken it's unruly."

"Nay mi lady," wee Maudie now said, dropping her head to her feet. "Yer hair is so beautiful. I should hope mine darkens like yers when I'm grown. For right now, it's such an unsightly ginger."

"Yers is quite bonny, child," Aileana countered, lifting

her chin. "And let no' a soul tell ye otherwise. My thanks for yer assistance this morn. It has made me feel welcome."

The girl beamed at the compliment and curtsied.

Aileana glanced back at her reflection in the mirror. A true glass mirror! Not bronze. Her hair had never been so fashionable, even when Clan Grant had had the resources, and she touched the net at the back of her neck, beaded with seed pearls, edged in rich sapphire velvet. Her mother and Peigi would be proud to see her looking like this now.

Then her gaze settled on her face. Her smile fell. Her freckles had always been such a blemish, even if her mother had tried to downplay them by uplifting her other attributes. *"Too much time in the sun, my dear... Ye'll freckle if ye insist upon riding so much..."*

"The dark blue is fine with yer auburn coloring." The maid curtsied once more. "Surely his lairdship will be pleased."

"What normally pleases him?" she asked, before biting her tongue. *Why care about what looks or fashions please James?*

"We ken nay," the maid replied. "The laird has never made known a leman or a betrothed. Ye're the first woman that he's announced."

Had he spoken the truth beside their campfire, that he'd kept no women before? Surely there had been at least *one* to slink from his chambers in the wee hours of morning, her chemise barely clinging to her arms. A man of his prestige and fine appearance would have his selection of women any night he chose.

The maid continued, "But he chose ye, mi lady, so we ken *ye're* to his liking."

Blush burned up Aileana's neck and stained her cheeks. James hadn't chosen her—she'd sacrificed herself to save Peigi. *Aye, he did want me. He mouthed to me in Urquhart's hall.* She'd thought at the time it was because he'd wanted to punish her, not because he'd been attracted to her. Perhaps he'd been motivated on both accounts.

"How could any man no' turn his head when ye walk into a chamber, enemy or nay? 'Tis obvious why the laird wanted ye over yer sister, even if ye're thin. A good month at Tioram will put some softness back on yer bones."

She froze. A month? Then they truly didn't know she'd be gone in a fortnight—the moment Epiphany was upon them on Twelfth Night? And yet emotions swirled like an eddy, confusion and guilt chief among them. Guilt, that she was about to partake of a meal so hearty as this, when poor Peigi and Elizabeth had nothing, and further confusion at the thought of never returning home.

Why has James nay told them about Twelfth Night?

His pride? Mayhap hope that she would choose to stay? Why would she want to when her cold reception with Anag, whose husband had been slain by Grant men, was surely not the only frosty reception she would receive today? Besides, she'd been clear about her intent to go home. She'd promised her family and her people that she would.

And yet I refused his offer to return home when I had the chance.

She quelled her conscience. It mattered not that James was turning out to be much more complicated. The maids departed, and Maudie, feeling more at ease around her now that the maids weren't so wary, waved discreetly as she slipped through the door.

Aileana smiled, returning the wave with a wiggle of her fingers, then turned to her tray as they secured the door shut behind them. A hearty stew awaited her beneath the lid, savory smells of salt and saffron wafting to her nostrils. Her mouth watered and her appetite, patchy as of late, surged quickly with desire to taste the rich meal. She took up the accompanying knife and swirled a piece of venison around the trencher, plump and oily. It wasn't the watery broth and pathetic floating bits that they'd treated James to at Urquhart. Nor was the bread beside it flat and bland. It was a soft, thick cut, with an artfully whipped blossom of butter. She touched it. And still warm! And there was cheese... She hadn't had cheese in so long, for to have cheese one needed cows. And dried apples. Apples!

She placed the morsel on her knife between her teeth, indulging in the venison's hearty taste, the urge to stuff it down her throat overpowering. Bite after bite, she devoured the stew, then the pieces of apples, having forgotten what it felt like to be so sated. *Slow down, Aileana,* her conscience admonished her. *'Twill do no good to overload an empty stomach and make yerself ill—*

Guilt jarred her again so suddenly, she froze.

Her family ate watery broth, not soft breads and cheeses, and Elizabeth, of all people, was carrying a child and needed sustenance far more than anyone else. What they would do for a meal like this... She set the knife aside and slid the trencher away as emotion pricked her eyes. Unable to go on eating, she lifted the white kerchief to her eyes and dabbed them. Standing, she walked to the hearth. Why must she find pleasure here? Why was it no longer so simple as hating an enemy but, perchance, empathizing with them, too? For it was becoming clear, her people might be suffering, but one look at Anag and it was obvious that this clan had suffered as well. Clan Grant wasn't as innocent as she'd always thought them to be.

And perhaps that was the hardest revelation to swallow.

Chapter Six

"Is it true, my laird, that the lady was given to ye as restitution?" James's cousin and first-in-command, Angus, asked discreetly as they led the traveling party.

James glanced at his cousin's guarded expression while Devil plodded beneath him. The morning was fresh, and the sunlight winked upon the snow, so much so that it nearly burned the eyes. His soldiers and the wives accompanying their men on this hunt for the Yule log made merry, startling a flock of ptarmigans from their roost into flight with a beating of black-tipped wings as they passed around a flask of drink and broke out spontaneously into song.

"I saw a sweet, a seemly sight; A blissful burd, a blossom bright…"

"Why would Clan Grant give ye a noble sister?" Angus continued. "They hate us. Surely Laird Grant would prefer war over such."

In spite of his shocking marriage announcement the day before, his people remained cheerful for the advent of festive activities, for his bakers were making stacks of bean cakes as they spoke to usher in the season tonight with the traditional game of seeking the bean in the bread, and soon the ladies would begin binding ashen twigs with evergreen twines to place as blessings in the Christmastide fire each night until Twelfth Night, when his twenty-fourth year would run out.

"I was surprised, too, that Grant acquiesced to my demand," James replied.

He squinted back at Lady Aileana, riding at the end of the procession and thankfully well again. His chest clenched. Christ's bones, he could barely stop looking at her. A bonny sight if he'd ever seen one. His maids had transformed her. She'd gone from nearly feral, with her hair unmanaged, to a cultivated lady, with the simple employment of a couple maids and a wardrobe. The starkness of the snow and brilliance of her sapphire gown set her auburn locks—held back in a net—on fire in the morning sunlight, and her skin, so porcelain, was like cream with sunbursts of pink upon her cheeks from the chill. Her lips were a kissable shade of rouge, and upon her ears hung a pair of amber bobbles. Not her pearls. Interesting.

Angus chuckled. "Still. Grant woman or nay, she's a bonny prize to be won in a bartering. Is she mute? She's too quiet for a woman."

Nay. Quite a tongue she has when she wants to lash someone with it. James chuckled to himself.

"Though I dare say our womenfolk are repaying her the cold shoulder the Grants so deserve," Angus continued.

They are what? James cast a look over his shoulder once more. She rode alone, ignored by the other women, who clustered together on their horses.

"I suppose a quiet wife is better than an unruly one," Angus added. "Mayhap having subdued a Grant in such a way as ye have will keep them from meddling in skirmishes in which they have no business involving themselves."

James swallowed the sour dislike that Angus's remark put on his tongue. Aileana wasn't soft-spoken. He'd come to expect her forthright tongue lashings and, strangely, felt deprived of them since their arrival in Tioram the day before. Here, among his people and his wealth, he sensed her nervousness, and much of her confidence was now stripped. If his women were treating her unkindly, it was no wonder that she rode by herself.

"That's it, is it nay? Ye think to bed the Grants into submission since nothing else has worked?" Angus asked. "A surprising tactic, laird, considering ye're careful about yer womenfolk. But aye, brilliant. Something a MacLeod would do."

Be damned! James hated mention of the MacLeods and thoughts of Marjorie in their grips. Being compared to one? Revolting.

"We all see what ye've done, which is why we tolerate her presence—"

"That's enough," James grumbled. He'd foisted a petty punishment upon the Grants and risked Aileana's health, no matter how unknowingly, with a much bigger reason at heart: his inheritance, which none of his clan knew about, apart from his sisters, and one of them had taken the secret to the grave. He hadn't been trying to conquer the Grants by warming his bed with one... Had he? And if warming his bed was the intention, it was a chilly bed to be sure.

"I didnae force her to wife so that ye could all gloat about conquering the Grants. Our fight has never been with *her*, and I would expect better of my people. If ye'd give her a chance, ye'd see she has much to offer."

Angus cleared his throat, surprised by the admonishment. "Ye cannae expect our people to open their arms to her so easily as ye apparently did. Her brother raided upon us. Evicted *ye*, and declared ye an outlaw. Some of our fine men died that day, leaving behind widows and orphans."

"And we've raided on them, killing theirs," James rumbled. "But Aileana raided on no one." A lie, but he wouldn't lump desperate snatches for food together with larger transgressions like attacking castles for reasons of power. "She pays a price now for decades of troubles. I bid ye, and everyone, treat her kindly."

He certainly wouldn't allow his man, cousin or not, to jest at Aileana's expense.

"Apologies, cousin. I mean no disrespect," Angus said after clearing his throat. "We've clearly misjudged yer feelings for the lass. Tell me, will ye plan a kirk wedding for her?"

He shook his head. Aileana might have rejected his offer to be taken home right away—a pleasant surprise that made him wonder at a deeper motivation on her part. But she'd given him no indication that she wished their union to become permanent, either.

"She does nay want one."

"What lady wishes naught for a kirk wedding?" said one of his knights to another.

James twisted over his shoulder, wishing to quit their gossip.

"My lady!" he called.

His men and their wives fell silent, glancing over at Aileana, as if having forgotten she was riding with them. And as he suspected, many a frown captured their faces at mention of her. Be damned, but he needed his people to accept her. Aileana might be slowly warming to him, but it was only with their friendship did he hope to lay a foundation that could lead to permanence and convince her to stay.

Aileana looked up at him, surprised, as if unsure that he spoke to her. He gestured to her. "Ride aside me, wife!"

He steered his mount out of the procession and heard her palfrey's hooves escalate to a trot. She pulled up beside him, relieving him from further interrogations, for Angus took the cue.

"I'll check our flanks, laird, and ensure no one straggles."

James nodded to him, thankful for his departure, and blessedly his people fell back into song. He glanced at Aileana's profile, her bare neck and collarbones delightfully enticing as they peeked through the clasp of her cloak; her posture, straight and cultivated like a winter queen atop her mount. The maids had done her appearance justice by selecting the beautiful gown and amber bobbles, which nearly matched her hair.

And yet he wanted her parrying. If he admitted it, he enjoyed crossing swords with her. What had his womenfolk done to silence her?

"Have the maids treated ye well?" he asked.

She nodded, offering a soft smile and gazing to the hills beyond, toward which they headed.

"Then why so silent? Has something happened?"

She frowned but shook her head. "Nay. I simply find myself pondering the state of things betwixt our clans."

What did that cryptic reply mean? "Care to explain?"

Aileana sighed. "As I suspected, nay body much wants me here, for if looks could slay, I'd be dead, but having spoken to my maids, I suppose I can understand why. I used to think of the history betwixt our people in a one-sided fashion. I could only see the wrong ye'd done us. I believed nay the wrong my clan had done to yers."

He quirked the corner of his mouth, deciding not to press the matter. *Could it be that we are finding more common ground?*

"Would it make any difference to ye now to ken that the mare ye ride is light of foot and won me a race in the Inverness games four seasons ago?" he diverted.

She glanced at him. "She *is* quite spry for her age. What

does that have to do with clan rivalries?"

His semi-smile broadened, and he leaned down to her, lowering his voice as he wrapped his hands around his reins in preparation. "Absolutely nothing. I'm saying my horse could use a good jaunt, and since yer palfrey bears the record she does, how would ye like a wee competition? Up to the wood's edge where it's dense of trees and sparse of people?"

Her eyes brightened, and a smile of her own danced upon her lips as she looked ahead of them to get bearings on the mark. Just as he suspected. The lass, bold of tongue, was also competitive.

"I do believe I'm being challenged to a race by the enemy. More rivalry is what we need, then?"

"Only a gentle bird frightened of losing would refuse," he taunted, sitting upright again and staring down his nose at her like a haughty prince.

"Then I suppose the only way to silence ye is to put ye in yer place." She giggled.

A giggle. His eyes dipped to her lips.

"What's the boon for winning?" she asked.

"The chance to gloat that their clan is better, aye?"

She lifted her eyes heavenward. "Childish of ye, Jamie."

And damn, but the moniker again made his heart skip like an eejit. She gathered her reins alongside her mount's neck, patting the pretty beast. He grinned.

"Ye bring out the best in me, lass." Turning to his nearby guardsman, he ordered, "Bother us nay. We're off for a gallivant and will await the party from the forest's edge."

The knight nodded his nasal helm in compliance.

"Since ye challenge me, *laddie*," she bated further, though he wondered if she, too, was anxious to break away from the party. "Ready...go!" she breathed, tapping her horse into motion, and launched ahead of him.

His grin never faltering, he shook his head and tapped

Devil into a charge, overtaking her.

"I see ye're a cheat, *nàmhaid*, jumping the start!" he taunted.

"As are ye!" she called back as her cloak billowed like shimmering banners behind her, and sakes, but a gorgeous, full grin had split her lips, the likes of which a man would want to litter with pecks as he acquainted himself to every secret within her kiss.

"How so?"

"Ye challenge me, and yet it's ye who rides a prime stallion who isnae even exerting himself yet! Ye're certain to win, and I needed the head start to even the stakes!"

He laughed, a husky, hearty sound. "I'd expect something so underhanded from a Grant!"

Her mouth dropped in feigned shock, though she laughed. "As I would from a MacDonald!"

"Careful, woman, ye're one of my kind now!"

"Never!"

She urged her horse onward, overtaking him by a neck, which he leveled out easily, surging ahead.

"Cheat!" she called, inciting more laughter, and he glanced back to see plumes of powder rising in their wake as she made a champion's effort to capture the lead.

Devil puffed onto the air, stretching his muscles after a day of lazing in the stable, and he indulged the horse, achieving the tree line several lengths ahead of her and jumping nimbly off his stallion before the beast had completely halted.

He dashed to a nearby tree while Devil panted, propping his shoulder against it, giving Aileana his back as she fast approached, and slouched, folding his arms and crossing a leg. Was he daft? Why was he playing at such sport with her—or anyone—when he, a grown man, had always been so serious? He'd had to be, as his father's only son, and disdained by his stepmother at every opportunity. And yet it felt good to flirt.

He harrumphed at that.

He peeked over his shoulder to see what Aileana was up to. She would need help down in her heavy layers of finery.

He yawned, stretched. "Ach, lass, I've been waiting for ye to catch me for so long, I must have dozed off—"

A hand ripped down the neck of his doublet, and an icy pillow of snow shocked his skin.

"Christ's bones!" he cursed, jumping and whirling around as Aileana fell into a fit of laughter.

He shook out his doublet, feeling the snow melt down his back and soak into his tunic, and his shock slowly turned to mirth. Even in layers of beautiful but useless fabric, she was as nimble as he was, sneaking up on an enemy.

Giving her his full front, he smirked. "Would ye like to ken why they call me the Devil MacDonald?"

She righted herself, though her smile remained, as did a quiet giggle behind her pinched lips as he continued.

"Because of this!"

He swiped a branch of its snow and lobbed the powder back at her.

"Oh!" she jumped, the snow leaving a starburst upon her stomach.

He tipped his head back and guffawed a deep, rumbling laugh—

A wad of snow hit him square in the jaw.

"Ach, *nàmhaid*, ye'll pay for besting yer laird," he baited, and soon the two ducked and dodged each other, flinging up snow. Her hair was falling loose from her netting, and she didn't seem to notice or care, as her face remained light with laughter, and his heart opened an inch farther to her. Snow landed upon her cheek. She smarted, backing up a step, then swooned playfully.

"'Tis a good thing I have yer flag of truce with which to wipe my brow." She sighed, and withdrew his white kerchief from her sleeve to dab her face.

"Oh, ye insult the enemy by sullying his flag?"

She nodded, grinning, and scooped up another fistful to lob at him. He dodged it, withstanding a barrage of snowballs and guarding his face with his arm as he encroached upon her.

"Nay..." she breathed at his approach, and took flight, tossing poorly aimed fistfuls at him. "Do nay capture me!"

He snagged her about the waist, spinning her around as a squeal escaped her throat, and they stumbled off balance. He caught her as she fell against a tree, barely catching himself before he crushed her to it.

"Do ye surrender, *nàmhaid*?" he breathed.

"Never, *nàmhaid*!" she declared, as if a valiant warrior going down a hero while he held her to the tree.

Their laughter subsided. He could feel her chest heaving for air against his abdomen, could smell the rosewater used to freshen her skin, could feel her body heat, steamy from their exertion and damp clothes. He took in her hazel eyes, glowing in the stark midmorning light, took in each fairy kiss upon her nose and the bonny wisps of escaped tendrils that hung loose around her face. Her lips parted, and his eyes dipped to them. Her smile fell, and her hands...sakes, he could feel her palms braced against his belly, palming him through his doublet. His mind ran wild with sudden thoughts of those hands, what they might feel like snaked beneath his coats and tunic, skin to skin, fingers inducing quivers of delight, burning patterns across his flesh...

Her breathing grew erratic, and uncertainty sprang to her face. Desire throbbed unchecked through his blood. His hands dropped his grip upon her shoulders and migrated to her fingers, peeling them away and enfolding them, lifting them over her head and pinning them to the tree. Their bodies flush, her wedged beneath him, he stared at her lips as desire to taste them nearly overpowered him.

Could he steal a kiss? Could she not give him a sign as to whether or not she wanted one? For he wouldn't kiss her otherwise.

Singing in the distance was faint but brought with it reality, and reminders that the Yule party would eventually join them. Yet he remained against her. She had yet to indicate she'd prefer him to relinquish her—a prize in itself, to have her acquiescence. But the singing grew louder, and as he glanced toward it, he could see Angus and the others approaching with a clear view. Had they watched the entire snowball spectacle? Jesu, they probably thought their laird had gone daft.

Aileana, too, seemed to come to, and she dropped her head. "Mary mother..." she prayed beneath her breath, wriggling her hands from his grip. He released them. "Ye're nay like what I expected."

She didn't sound as if she'd intended to speak the sentiment aloud. His brow lifted, and he glanced askance to examine the dips and rises of the landscape.

"What did ye expect?"

"I wanted—nay, needed—ye to be the same beast ye were when ye attacked Urquhart, with yer face covered in woad and mud, who cut down our sentries and breeched our curtain wall, so that I could remain shielded to ye. I didnae expect someone who feeds foxes and finds pleasure frolicking in the snow."

He frowned and eased back an increment so that she wasn't so flattened beneath him. Cleared his throat. Was she saying that she liked him? But the remark poured cool water upon his lust, quelling the throbbing. They'd shared amusements and playful ribbing, but there was much that still lay between them. Wrongs he'd committed against her and her people, wrongs *they'd* committed against him and his.

Would such an obstacle ever be overcome?

"My thanks for the jaunt," he said, clearing his throat again. "I sensed ye'd like to be free of my folks' scrutiny, and in sooth, I wearied from my cousin's questions about ye."

She nodded with understanding. "I do nay think yer kin and kind will be overly sad when I depart come Epiphany," she jested, though like most jests, he could sense an undercurrent of truth.

And didn't the constant reminders of their union's fragility nip him with unease. He pushed it aside. He still had more than a sennight left with her to build upon this truce and, perhaps, claim his money.

"Mayhap ye should be yerself to them," he suggested. "Ye'll grow on them, as ye're growing upon me."

As she opened her mouth to refute his suggestion, the plodding of horses approached and the singing tapered off. A whistle at his expense ensued, and Aileana's face reddened with embarrassment.

"Aye, he does indeed subdue the Grants abed," sniggered a soldier softly.

Aileana, scalded, yanked away from him, turning from them to hide the distress that had sprung to her face.

"Aileana," he began, reaching for her hand, but she ripped it away from him.

Instead, James scowled at his people for the thoughtless remark, though they were preoccupied with their merry singing and once more passed their flasks about. Instead, he swiveled away to fetch the horses as they rummaged alongside an overturned tree buried in a snow drift, the magic of the morning ruined. Shame washed over him as he collected the reins and brought Aileana's palfrey back to her—at the taste of the acerbic disapproval from his people, at her recoiling from his touch as he tried to help her mount, when moments ago he'd had her willing body against his. He'd wronged this woman, who he was starting to—he swallowed—feel something for. He'd forced one of Grant's sisters to endure this hostility all because of his inheritance, no thanks to his stepmother. He should have known this would happen.

Mounting up, his thoughts strayed as he guided Devil into the woods, once more leading the procession. After he'd had time to wrangle down his anger and frustration, he'd make his displeasure known to his people.

Chapter Seven

Aileana trembled still, in spite of the warm fire at her back, earning another censorious frown from the seamstress bent down before her. But she couldn't shake the morning's Yule log hunt. She couldn't quell the confusing swirl agitating her: shameful cravings to be kissed that spiraled through her at memories of James's body pressed to hers while desire burned hot in his eyes, hurt burning like a cauterizing iron when she'd realized it wasn't passion fueling his seduction but merely the opportunity to squash her brother under his thumb, and *all* his people were in on the knowledge. *Nàmhaid* indeed. She'd known she was a bargaining chip from the onset of their handfast, but she'd been a fool to consider that his attraction might be genuine.

The smell of bean cakes filtered through the crevice beneath her door with warm, delicious scents, bringing with it bygone memories of festive breads at Urquhart and traditions filled with excitement to see whose bread contained the wee bean, for the lucky finder would get to make a wish. As if the insult of the morning wasn't enough. She'd never once gotten the bean, though Peigi had been lucky twice, and both times, her sister had wished for a valiant suitor and prosperous marriage—a destiny stripped from her the moment MacDonald men had stolen their dowry coin.

Aileana swayed from the hours on her feet and gripped the edge of the table to hold steady while her traitorous stomach growled.

"Hold still, mi lady."

The seamstress sighed, an exasperated sound she managed to keep tethered low. Was the woman annoyed? Of course she was. Aileana had known from the moment she'd been punished by Anag's anger, followed by the rude remark spoken under the soldier's breath this morn, that those wouldn't be the only signs of displeasure from the MacDonald people she would have to endure. James's white flag—a lie— certainly wasn't the banner under which his people marched, either. For all the rich finery and prosperity at Tioram, the castle still managed to be chillier than Urquhart's chipping walls and barren hearths.

Aileana cleared her throat and gazed at the wall.

"The bread smells delicious. I commend Tioram's skilled bakers. Making so many loaves in a day is to be admired." Once more, Aileana tried to begin a conversation to ease the woman's reservations and, in truth, distract herself from her anger while she considered what to do about James, though nothing had worked yet.

"And do ye, a ranking lady, ken much about bread baking?"

The question, uttered plainly enough, still carried with it a thread of sarcasm.

"Indeed, I've helped Urquhart's bakers numerous times." As if Urquhart could afford for her to sit on her ladylike rear and be waited on hand and foot. She knew well the ache in her wrists, arms, and shoulders from hours kneading and the feel of sweat trickling down her temples from the hot ovens. "There's always work to be done and nay enough folk to do it."

Again, silence met her ears. Her eyes flitted down again to the crouched woman, who pinched a pin in her lips. James had suggested she be herself, yet it was clear she wasn't winning any points of favor for it. And even though his reasons for wanting a permanent marriage were apparent now, how on earth had he expected this to work? Did he honestly think his people would welcome any children she bore with open arms? Or would they see James's heirs or heiresses as half enemy?

Sakes, why think on children with such a man? To think on children meant to think on how children were begotten—

Butterflies once more erupted into a swirl within her belly, confusing her, whispering reminders of how her fickle body had reacted with shivers of delight when James had pinned her to that tree and the look of unabashed desire contorting his face. She might know his true colors now, but her body still seemed to delight in thoughts of his playfulness—a secret side she'd never thought the Devil MacDonald could harbor. No wonder women had children—many of them, sometimes. If the excitement James's flirtations that morning had induced within her were any indication, eventually the burgeoning attraction that flared for him would get the better of her. And where would that leave her? Just as Peigi had feared: deflowered and divorced. She *had* to return home before that could happen, and get her clan out from beneath his domineering thumb.

"I'm content to wear the borrowed gowns my maids supplied me with instead, good woman," Aileana said. "Rather than use up yer lovely fabrics."

The seamstress plucked the pin from her lips.

"Our laird ordered these clothes made, mi lady." The

seamstress placed the pin in the fold of the beautiful burgundy wool—the overskirt to a matching burgundy kirtle made of samite and patterned in subtle, darker damask—then plucked another pin from her cushion and gripped it in her teeth as she bunched a pleat together along Aileana's hip and gave it a stiff tug to pull into alignment. The utter richness of the fabric was enough to steal a lady's breath. Peigi would be in awe. "I'll nay defy him," she said through clenched teeth.

"Mistress." Aileana stepped back, knowing it would annoy the woman even more that she wasn't just swaying but deliberately interfering now. "I ken there is bad blood betwixt our people, and I'm sorry that—"

"I believe I'm finished, mi lady." The woman stood and began packing her pins and shears, unwilling to meet Aileana's gaze, and in the distance, a bell clanked. "There is the supper call. Food is served."

"Did my brother's raid kill one of yer loved ones, too?"

So blunt was the question, but the directness caught the seamstress off guard, and Aileana had to know. The woman froze. Her eyes flashed to Aileana's. Pain poured from the silent stare. Finally, the women shook her head and once more began packing up her basket.

"Nay, I was a lucky one. My husband passed on of natural causes several years ago. But the raid saw my entire shop gutted. All the fine fabrics and threads, the imported passements from the Continent I used to use to trim Lady Brighde's gowns. All of it, up in flames when they torched it."

Aileana absorbed the woman's grievance as echoes of screams rang in her mind from that terrible day at Urquhart. Then she began unpinning the waist of the overskirt. She'd known this same heartache. James's men had done the same thing to each and every office and outbuilding at Urquhart, and part of her wished to take the woman's hands in her own and share in her grief.

"And now I must use the lovely supplies his lairdship paid a pretty penny for to clothe one of the very people who so wronged us…"

The desire to take up the woman's hands vanished. Hurt once more burned a path down Aileana's spine, and she hurried out of the loose sleeves, slipping them off onto the table, then allowing the skirt to drop in a bunch around her feet. Her brother might be guilty of transgressions, but she was not, and yet she was bearing the brunt of Seamus's punishments.

She hastened for her robe to cover her chemise, leaving the seamstress at her back. *She'd* never been part of the Grant raiding party. *She'd* never harmed a living soul. How she so wished to shed the woman's presence now. After a bout of silence, the woman cleared her throat.

"I'm sorry, mi lady," she muttered.

"I refuse yer gift of clothing," Aileana croaked, allowing bitterness to taint her words, and pulled the robe tightly to her neck, shivering. She paced to the window shutters to crack one open and stare out at the afternoon light hanging low over the horizon and sparkling off the waters. "I'm certain the pieces you've cut today can be adjusted to fit Lady Brighde."

The luster of the beautiful fabrics had been tarnished. Wearing any specially made garments would forever be blemished by the hurt she felt and the anger within these folk who she'd known wouldn't give her a chance. Yet why should she wish for their acceptance when she was only going to leave them?

"But it's the laird's wish, mi lady," the woman replied softly.

Aileana shook her head, still not turning around. "But it's nay mine. He's nay the one who has to wear them and be disdained for it. The expense is nay worth the trouble, considering I can always send for my trunks from Urquhart should I desire them."

More silence. *Please leave.* Blessedly, as if the seamstress had heard her thoughts, the door finally opened, then closed. She exhaled hard and dropped her hands clutched at her throat. The robe sagged open. What to do? She glanced at her borrowed sapphire gown lying smoothed upon her bed, ready to once more be donned. And groaned.

"I'll need the help of my maids to tie each lace, fasten each opening…"

There was no way to do it on her own—and in her hurt, she'd failed to ask the seamstress to summon her maids back. She scurried to the door, drew it back, careful to hide her undressed form behind it and peering around it.

"Anag, would ye mind helping me…"

No one was there. Anag had helped her undress. She'd known Aileana wouldn't be able to assemble everything again for supper. Had they left her on purpose?

"No matter." She lifted her chin, refusing to allow further hurt to spike her.

At Urquhart, she would simply don her brown woolen dress and wrap her tartan around her shoulders. That's what she'd do now… *But James will wonder immediately why I'm wearing my old, ugly dress again.* Worse, her maids *would* know why she was so poorly outfitted. Gossip, a blasted plague in any self-respecting castle, would surely cast her in a poor light.

Nerves, once more, surged through her blood. Couldn't she just remain hidden in her chambers, like a coward, or escape home sooner than planned and shed their presence? Shake James's false seductions off like a dirty shoe fit only for the rubbish heap? Aye, that was it. Leave.

"Ye're nay a coward, Aileana Grant."

No, she wasn't. But she also wasn't daft, and she'd bide

her time for the first moment available to depart. She lifted her chin and strode to her trunk to find something else to wear, prying up the heavy oaken lid and resting it against the wall. On top sat the green ensemble, a deep velvet over-gown meant to fall open at her waist for the associated kirtle. She lifted the over-gown. It laced beneath the arms, up each side from her hips. She would never be able to tie them properly, and the sleeves themselves needed several eyelets tightened at the wrists. And her hair, besides, was wrapped in netting adorned with *sapphire* embellishments, nay green.

After dropping it, she held out the mauve fabric instead, a soft silk gown with a furry sable lining and hooks up the back that she'd never be able to fasten. Then let it drop. It was no use. Folded in the bottom was her brown dress. She'd have to wear it. She scooped it up and shed her robe upon her chair by the hearth, slipping the thin woolen garment over her head to tug tightly at her waist. The laces still hanging loose at her back, she plucked each pin from her hair with growing urgency and dropped them in a pile upon her dressing table, until the coif and net slackened. She flung it beside the hairpins and shook out her hair so that it tumbled down her back, then dragged her meager bag of possessions out of the trunk and took them to the bed, dumping them out to sort so she'd be ready to flee at first opportunity—

Knocking thumped. Had her maids taken pity on her? Already her ears were ringing with what rumors had been started about her tarrying when by now the hall was likely well into their meals.

"Who calls?"

"James. The hall is feasting, and yet my wife has yet to show her face."

His deep voice greeted her. Anger lashed through her, at the same time that her heartbeat kicked up traitorously at the thought of seeing him again. Blasted heart, defying her sensible mind. Looking down, she frowned at her unlaced bodice in her impoverished dress. Could this moment become more embarrassing?

Nay tempt the fates to take ye up on the challenge, Aileana, for embarrassment seems to be yer lot recently.

On a sigh, she strained to fumble with her laces, ignoring him. The latch lifted, and the door pushed open without invitation. Her eyes flitted to the ajar door, glaring at his presumptuous entry. Handsome and clean-shaven, in a newly cleaned red-and-green great kilt pinned ceremonially at his shoulder and billowing down his legs, his loose locks and braids had been pulled back at his nape so that the cut of his jaw was more pronounced. He looked fit for Yuletide ceremony, and here she was in rags. Her stomach did a flip as his twinkling blue eyes roved over her state of dress, as he then spied her traveling bag upon her bed.

"Aye, he does indeed subdue the Grants abed."

Her heart clenched angrily at the bitter reminder of his people's disdain, and she turned away, her brow tight and furrowed in an attempt to bite her tongue.

"Sakes, the crestfallen expression contorting yer face is almost believable," she muttered.

And yet heat splotched her cheeks as misplaced guilt cut through her, knowing he was putting the clues together that she was readying to depart.

"What's this? Why are ye packing?" he demanded, not responding to her remark.

Her mouth opened to argue as she cast a glance backward at the sight of his unabashed hurt.

"I was simply looking for extra hairpins."

His gaze darted to her dressing table and the heap of pins upon it. He leveled a disbelieving glare at her.

"Ye're shite at lying." He frowned, striding over to her window to secure the shutter closed against the chill. "Ye're packing. Why?"

"Why?" she gasped, then swiveled to face him. "I should have gone home the moment ye offered to take me. Why should I remain now that I ken the true folly in thinking we could forge a thread of peace? When yer people look at me, they see *only* my brother. They see an *enemy*, and considering this farce will only last a fortnight, I see no reason to attempt to win their favor when they wish nay to give it. Name *one person* who wishes me to remain."

"Me."

He spoke the single word with such ardor, he nearly sounded desperate, sincerity alight in his blue gaze. *False* sincerity. Yet still, her eyes watered with no control to stop them, and she fought desperately with her dress to tie the strings.

"Aye, to put me in yer bed so my brother will forever be kept at bay." His face grew stormy, but she continued, "To keep my brother under yer thumb so that if ye should ever wrong him again, he'll have no recourse for fear of hurting me in an attack. From the beginning, I knew, deep down, this was merely an attempt to overpower us, but I'd hoped that mayhap, just mayhap, *especially* after ye confided in me about Lady Marjorie, that ye felt differently, and I was a fool to think yer attempts at flirting were because ye might fancy me—"

His hands gripped her arms, and his brow, tight, drew together over his eyes into an angry scowl. "Stop."

She shook her head. "I'm a foolish lass, even to consider a MacDonald who forced—"

"Aileana. *Stop.*"

Her fingers slowed. Then stopped. And she blinked her eyes to stave off the mist, her gaze bouncing around but not landing upon him.

"My man was out of line this morn. My folk were nay at

Urquhart when we made this agreement, and they ken no' my true reason."

"Then what is your true reason?"

His jaw tightened as words seemed to tangle on his tongue and then die before passing his lips. The muscles beneath his ears bulged as he gnashed whatever his reason was into submission, and his hand migrated up to her cheek to palm it. He swallowed, and his tender touch induced a tingling of gooseflesh over her skin. "We agreed ye'd stay until Epiphany." His brow softened. "At least give me that." His thumb began gently caressing her cheek, and her belly twisted with frustration and warmth. "The Aileana I ken isnae a coward who runs and hides when there's work to be done," he said more softly.

"Did ye forget the way in which we met?" she muttered.

He expelled a relieved breath. A smile tugged unexpectedly at his lips, dimpling one cheek. Blast it, but she, too, felt her mouth mirror his. She'd certainly run fast and hard to evade him back to Urquhart. His eyes dipped to the tiny concession of truce quirking up her lips, and his thumb swept softly over the pad of flesh as his fingers still gripped her cheeks, splaying into her hair, his eyes watching his thumb's caress.

"Aye, lass. And a fine game of cat and mouse ye played." He chuckled. "But I still tracked down the confounding *lad* who stole my foodstuff. And when I look upon ye, here, at Tioram, I cannae help but think that mayhap I was meant to discover *him*."

She swallowed. Her fingers drifted to her stomach, to the swirl of butterflies that once more fluttered in her belly at the desire and relief upon his face and the confusion that once more twisted her heart—to desire the enemy's affection, to desire to be home among her people, where she was wanted. And the worry she felt for her people while she indulged in the frigid yet generous hospitality here.

His hand dropped, and he moved to the bed, picking up the hem of the blue velvet and severing his tingling connection. "Do the gowns Brighde loaned ye nay suit?"

"They're beautiful. But the seamstress just finished her measurements, and the blue gown requires assembly, and considering I was alone, I was in a quandary as to what to do so decided to put on my old gown."

"Why did yer maids nay assist?"

A scowl turned down his lips, and he strode back to her. He took up her face in his hands once more, cupping her cheeks gently in his roughed palms.

"Anag and the others are well into their meals. Have they ignored ye?"

Aileana clamped her mouth. She would never tattle. How on earth could she expect women to wait on her hand and foot?

"I'm sure they had many tasks to do, and I nay fault them," she replied.

Sunbursts of energy erupted on her skin beneath each point of his contact. It wasn't the touch of a *nàmhaid*. And such gestures were beginning to feel comfortable. As if he was used to holding her so.

But his jaw, clenched tightly, whitened his lips, and so suddenly Aileana knew he suspected what had happened.

"I shall fetch them immediately—"

"Please, do nay."

"I assigned them to ye," he insisted.

"Ye cannae possibly understand, Jamie. If ye fetch them, it will seem as if I complained. And they'll only dislike me more. Ye cannae force them to *like* someone. How am I supposed to win any points of favor with them if ye demand they serve at my beck and call?" Her eyes held his, then she began lacing up her back again, determined to finish dressing, and turned to face the crackling hearth. "I do nay fault them for their anger."

"I do. It's misplaced upon ye," he retorted, his voice soft and low, and his hands coming to rest upon her shoulders.

"Is it, though? I thieved from ye. They might no' ken that, but I'm still guilty."

"Because ye were desperate," he argued.

She looked back up at him, her eyes widening; her lips parting once more, then closing as an ill-timed smile curved her lips. "Have we truly reversed positions? I justifying why I ought to be in trouble, ye justifying why I should nay be?"

He grinned with resignation, then shook his head. "Confounding, is it nay? Here. I'll help ye dress for supper," he said, flicking her laces playfully.

She froze. The fire popped and hissed, drawing her attention to the intrusive silence.

"I can manage *this* dress myself, thank ye," she croaked.

"Nay, take that rag off so ye can don the blue one again. The one that makes yer hair look like it glows red and brightens yer fairy kisses."

"'Fairy kisses'? Ye mean my *freckles*?"

He grimaced at her flummoxed tone.

"Aye, yer freckles. They're fetching."

He wished her freckles to stand out *more* than they already did?

"Jamie—"

His hands touched hers at the base of her back, trying to sort her laces out, settling upon her trembling fingers, and pulled them down to her sides. Her pulse fluttered at her throat, rattling her good sense, for all afternoon she'd resolved herself to give him a piece of her mind, and now here she was, melting like butter upon warm bread.

"Ye're my wife. At least until Epiphany. You'll dress the part."

He stepped back. His hands fell away. She peeked over her shoulder and watched James stride over to her bed to retrieve the kirtle and velvet overgown. Still trembling, Aileana inched her gown up her body, revealing her chemise beneath, catching James's reflection in a bronze plaque upon the wall and knowing his eyes were upon her back, caressing every ounce of her chemise that she uncovered with roving curiosity. Did she want him to see her? After moments ago, being resolved to flee from him? She saw him inhale deeply, his chest rising, then heard him exhale. He turned away, finally.

Each piece of the gown was then draped over her. Her whole body shook with heat and nerves at his proximity as his fingers skimmed her curling tresses over her shoulder and out of the way to tumble over her breasts while he deftly worked the laces on the garment. His hands tugged her skirts together to fasten them. His breath caressed the back of her exposed neck as his scent and heat filled her senses with desire to know what he was thinking and why he knew so well how to assemble a gown. And who knew a fire could crackle so loudly!

"Nary a complaint ye've heard from the lasses, eh?" she teased.

His reflection in the bronze plaque grinned smugly, then he leaned into her ear. "Did I get under yer skin, lass? Because I dare say, the moment I met ye glaring at me through Urquhart's portcullis, ye crawled right under mine, and I'm pleased to finally return the torment."

She rolled her eyes. "Ye have to work harder to torment me, man."

"Is that a challenge?" He chuckled before continuing, "Ah, but we've a truce betwixt us, woman, and I've no wish to think on past *exploits* when I've already got a fine challenge at my fingertips now," he murmured, his breath warm upon her lobe. She shivered. "No need to start another skirmish when I've already thrown down my flag of truce."

She took a ragged breath as he slid a sleeve up her arm and tied it at her shoulder, then did the same with the other. Fickle heart, indeed. He was working his seduction upon her again, and her whole body was craving more.

"Why do ye nay wear yer pearls?" he rumbled softly, as a finger rose to touch the amber bobbles she'd donned that morn, pushing on her ear.

The heat simmering within her chilled like feverous skin doused with ice. She stepped away from him, shaking her head, as thoughts of her and Peigi's pillaged dowries churned up that old hurt she couldn't seem to forgive.

"And appear in front of everyone, wearing the jewelry confiscated from yer sister to give to yer bargain bride?"

"They were yers," he replied, ignoring her tasteless comment, as if he knew her needling remarks were a blatant attempt to push him away.

"The castle folk do nay ken that—my hair! I already took it down."

She grabbed at the loose curls to hurry them into some semblance of a style, but James took her fingers in his and settled them at her stomach. He lifted the ends of her curls to rub them between his thumb and finger.

"Leave it. It looks spirited like this, hanging free. It's bonny."

Heat stained her cheeks at his soft compliment.

"Besides," he added, a cheeky grin contorting his lips upward in determination to regain their flirting from moments ago, "'twill look as if I thoroughly disheveled ye."

"Ach!" she exclaimed at his unexpected debauchery and smacked his arm, eyes widening, though he only chuckled, dodging her playfully.

"There's that feisty lass." His eyes, twinkling, gentled,

though his smile lingered. "I much prefer the upstart to the meek lady who runs and hides."

She shook her head and hurried to retrieve her Grant mantle, draping it over her shoulders, and finally turned her gaze upon him. His eyes roved over her blue enemy tartan, as if a million thoughts competed for dominance in his mind, yet he was unable to focus upon one. Finally, he offered his arm, eyes still twinkling.

"Come, *nàmhaid*. Supper is well underway by now, and the people expect their bean cakes, whether a Grant dines among us or no... Give them time, Aileana."

Aileana slipped her fingers around his elbow, and they walked through her door. Facing the MacDonald folks seemed more manageable when she had James's strong arm to hold. "Time...the one thing we have too little of."

· · ·

Aileana's remark hung in James's mind, and a furrow creased his forehead. *Time.* The end to their handfast didn't have to be so final. They could have all the time they needed to turn his people's hearts toward her, if she would only give it, but still, his people needed to give an inch, too. Why would she give their marriage an honest try if everywhere she turned, she was shunned? He knew his people were loyal and good folk to him. He'd hoped they would be willing to give Aileana a chance, based on their respect for him, at the very least.

The din of the hall echoed loudly into the gallery as he escorted Aileana to supper. The rich smells of succulent meats and the savory bean cakes wafted to his nose, and clanking, laughter, and benches scooting bounced off the walls in their typical cacophony—a sound that normally gave him pleasure, to know his people were well fortified with food and warmth. Not tonight. Not after today. Not after he'd watched his

people quietly spurn Aileana, from the morning Yule log
hunt to this evening, finding her in her chambers, unable to
avoid embarrassment. Never had he felt such disappointment
in the MacDonalds of Clanranald, as he did right now.

But bad blood was apparently too thick and deep to
simply wash away like suds off hands. His people had suffered
because of Seamus Grant and his Fraser conspirators. Wives
had lost husbands. Property had been destroyed. He might
have delivered the same retribution to the Grants, but the
score clearly wasn't considered even, by either clan. He'd
put Aileana in a grave position, bringing her here for the
sake of his inheritance and not considering these deeper
ramifications.

He stepped into the hall as Aileana's hand stiffened in
his elbow crook, yet he led her onward without faltering.
A hush muted the din at the sight of her on his arm in
her contemptible tartan, and for the first time, he felt her
embarrassment. Considered how their piercing gazes infused
her with discomfort. Instead, he wrapped his other hand over
hers, cupping her gripping fingers, and glanced askance at
her, noticing her look up at him.

He smiled. She took a deep breath.

She righted her gaze as the chattering intensified once
more, but James glanced over her head and caught the eye
of the maid Anag upon a bench along the wall with the
other maids, clustered together and chattering happily. Anag
looked up at them, double taking his dark expression. Her
grin fell. Frustration bloomed in his chest, his gaze boring
into hers as her eyes widened and redness crept up her neck
to her cheeks at her laird's displeasure, until she had enough
shame to look down at her lap.

"There ye are, Lady Aileana," Brighde chirped merrily
as they arrived upon the dais. "I was beginning to worry that
ye still felt unwell, though I needn't have done so, for James

worried enough for the both of us."

Bless his sister. She'd been a kind face to Aileana since her arrival, and after he'd confessed to her about the earrings, he'd felt such shame because Brighde had not only insisted he return them but admonished him, too, as only an older sister could. Seeing Aileana seated beside his sister, James took his seat on Aileana's other side, at the helm and forked a pile of meats and vegetables upon her empty trencher, as if heaping food at her would somehow make up for the awful feeling churning in his gut about what had happened.

"Are ye excited?" Brighde bubbled to Aileana.

"Excited?" Aileana asked.

"The bean cakes," his sister replied.

"Oh, aye, the bread smells delicious," Aileana replied, pasting a smile upon her face.

Wee Maudie, Anag's young sister, slipped by beneath them, flashing Aileana a bright smile. As if the frost of his people's disdain melted, a warm smile tipped Aileana's lips up, and she gave the child a tiny wave. The girl beamed at the treat of her lady's attention and scampered away. That single gesture warmed the tight lines of Aileana's face.

"Such a sweet lassie…" she murmured under her breath.

"I've never gotten the bean, except for once as a little girl," his sister continued, and slowly, Aileana seemed to relax.

Yet James's eyes continued to rove over the hall while Brighde prattled on and Aileana blessedly began to warm to conversation, taking in his people, how they looked upon Aileana, catching their gazes from time to time but letting them go so that he didn't spiral into glaring. He leaned back and slung an arm over the back of his chair, imbibing slow draughts off his tankard and occasional bites of fish from his eating dagger. Aileana was right. He couldn't bark at them to respect someone they only knew of as an enemy, for his displeasure might make them obey, but it would only make them disdain him in their hearts, too, and he'd always had a strong relationship with his clan—

"James? Brother, are ye hearing me?"

Brighde's voice cut through the haze of his pensiveness. Sakes, had she been speaking to him? He leaned forward to look around Aileana to his sister.

"Aye?"

"Lost in thought, are ye?"

"Ye could say that."

His sister offered him a suspicious smile, as if she knew he'd been thinking about Aileana.

"The kitchens wish to bring out the bean cakes. Are ye going to announce them? It's the first festivity of the season."

God's blood, how his mind was wandering. The head cook stood before him, awaiting his permission, and he hadn't even noticed her arrival. He pushed to standing, straightened his belts, and glanced at his guardsmen, the serving women, the maids. And forced a pleasant look onto his face.

"We've much to celebrate this year!" he boomed. "Prosperity, hard work, and a people who are loyal to each other above all others." A truth he was realizing more deeply than he'd ever thought before. "I shan't preamble much, for that is saved for tomorrow night."

He tried to grin, and his people groaned with good humor, as if enduring a speech from him was akin to their ears bleeding. But the mood was still tense. Beneath the expectant brightness upon the surrounding faces, there lingered curious muttering under their breaths, some glances at him, as if they could tell he was uneasy.

"And so, enjoy the bread. And whosoever finds the bean must make their wish known for all to hear. Bear in mind, it must be a wish I can fulfill—*Angus*."

He leveled a knowing glare at his cousin, who laughed at

the memory of the previous year, when he'd found the bean and made preposterous wishes for amusement's sake.

"No wishing for piles of gold this time, laird? Or the MacLeod's head upon a platter?" Angus shouted, cupping his hand around his mouth, and chuckles rippled through the hall.

James waved him off and sat, slinging his arm back over his chairback and sprawling lazily while picking up his tankard once more. The bread, stacked on trays, was delivered to tables, and excited folk grabbed the small loaves, tearing them open, looking for the bean. Brighde, too, claimed a loaf from the tray laid before them. James eyed Aileana, who had yet to take her helping.

"Well, go on, lady," Brighde encouraged her. "Aren't ye going to take one?"

Aileana smiled but shook her head. "I think no.' I'm growing full as we speak from the fish."

"Posh, ye mustn't do that. What if yer loaf is the one with the bean?"

"I do nay think yer people would be pleased if *I* found the bean," Aileana replied. James frowned again as he eavesdropped on their conversation. "It's probably best if I forgo the tradition this year—"

"Here. Ye have this one."

Brighde placed her loaf on Aileana's trencher as if she hadn't heard one word from Aileana's lips and snagged the other from the tray, leaving none for James, though James never had one. The treat was for his people, not him. Aileana's chest rose and fell on a deep breath, an imperceptible sign of frustration, but unwilling to disappoint Brighde, she flashed his sister a smile.

"My thanks, Lady Brighde."

Aileana tore off a small piece of the loaf and ate the morsel, hesitating, before tearing another piece, then another.

Sweat had broken out on her brow, glistening beads collecting at her temples. She swallowed hard enough for him to see the shift in her throat, though there was no need for her to worry so. The likelihood of her finding the bean among so many loaves was such a small one—

Nay...

The tiny bean fell out of the bread onto Aileana's trencher. She stared at it, freezing. James glanced at her face, impassivity capturing her brow, so impassive, it was obvious she was trying to be. Her gaze met his. He eyed her trencher, then *her* once more, then nodded almost imperceptibly and sipped his tankard as if nothing was amiss. He'd keep her secret. The day had already been a strain on her.

She furtively tried to hide it, nudging it toward her fish to push it underneath, when Brighde, after tearing her bread into crumbs and frowning playfully, glanced over Aileana's arm to peer at her bread.

"Ye found it!" she squealed, clasping her hands together. The hall hushed as faces looked around.

"Who found it?" muttered voices.

"Sakes, what are the odds," Aileana whispered through barely moving lips, then inhaled shakily.

Blast it, Brighde! James took Aileana's hand in his. Aileana's terrified eyes widened upon him. James nodded, took a gulp, swallowed, and wiped his tunic cuff across his mouth. "It appears ye have, lady, though ye needn't—"

"Oh, delightful." Brighde stood, announcing, "The bean has been found! The laird's new bride is the lucky finder!"

Aileana froze as utterances echoed, then silence fell. Brighde sat back down, clasping Aileana's arm. All eyes turned toward her, some frowns, some jaws slackened in disbelief. Her back straightened, and her chin lifted in that strong, unyielding manner. James set down his tankard and leaned forward to bring her hand to his lips and press a reassuring kiss upon her knuckles.

Sakes, had he just done that? Kissed her hand so naturally?

"I wasnae going to say a word, lass," he muttered, though her fingers felt like ice against his mouth.

She smiled, strained.

"Ye must make a wish, of course," his sister bubbled on.

"Brighde," he began. "I nay think—"

"What will it be?" his sister continued, waving him off as the silence stretched.

Aileana cleared her throat, smiling.

"Lady Brighde, why no' ye take the bean and take my wish. I ken how ye wanted so much to find it." Aileana held out the bean to Brighde.

"I certainly *willnae*," Brighde replied, affronted. "The wish only works for the one who found the bean. That's the magic of it."

"But this was yer loaf before ye shared it with me. Surely it's yer wish."

Brighde shook her head and folded her arms, smiling like an imp. "I gave it up fairly, which means it was intended for *ye* by the fates. Besides, coming here must have been hard for ye, under the circumstances," his sister said, softening. "It's surely a pleasure to have found it. Is it nay?"

Aileana cleared her throat and forced her smile back into place.

Frowning further, James leaned close to Aileana, but she pushed to standing before he could say another word, scooting back her chair with a slow scrape that echoed off the plastered stone. Rapt with interest, quiet mutters ensued, hanging on the silence for the new woman to speak, and James's ears didn't lie. Knowing remarks that the bean must have been intentionally given to her tainted the mood.

She cleared her throat again. Pulled her Grant tartan

tighter around her shoulders. Looked down at James, then at Brighde, then out at everyone.

"I ken my coming here must have been a surprise."

A few muffled snorts sounded, and that anger James had felt at his people today burgeoned anew. He scraped back his chair, shoving to his feet to confront the problem head-on; his jaw tightened, his teeth clenched so firmly, they would ache come the morrow.

"Nay, James. It's all right," Aileana muttered, grasping his forearm to stay him.

"It's nay all right," he growled, then turned to the great hall to administer the scolding he'd been mulling over all day. "Where is yer hospitality?"

The mutters ceased, and all eyes widened upon him. Did he look as irritated as he felt?

"Please," she said softly, and squeezed him.

He gazed down at her, feeling himself soften. This is what Seamus must have felt like when his youngest sister challenged him at every turn: wishing he could silence her, yet the soft tones of her voice and passion lighting her bonny eyes stayed a man who cared about her and willed him to listen to what she had to say. Duly quelled, he nodded stoutly and eased back to his rear, though he remained on edge.

"It was a surprise to me, too, for I didnae expect to be bartered in a marriage deal the day yer laird rode to our gates. He has his reasons for demanding marriage. Mayhap it truly is to try and bring my brother to his heel."

Again, James felt the need to rise, this time to defend himself, but defend himself from what? His reasons had been just as selfish, even if it was what he *had* to do to get the money. Yet Aileana didn't give him a chance to speak as she continued.

"I remember no such day, in either my lifetime or in the lore that has gone down in history betwixt our people, when the Grants and the MacDonalds have ever bestowed a single kindness upon the other. The true reasons for our rivalry, I do nay even ken. Do ye?"

The hall remained silent. The hearth flames danced and crackled, and one of his hunting hounds paced across the floor, rummaging for food scraps.

"I understand why ye dislike me. In sooth, I thought much ill of yer laird...until I met him." Her eyes once more fluttered down to him but didn't remain upon him. "To me, a MacDonald was always a beastly, frightening warrior, with a face painted in woad and mud, raising their swords high, battle cries spilling from their lips, destroying our home. Burning all we had worked so hard to plant and reap, stealing our livelihood, making widows out of our maids, and leaving my sister and me terrified, in hiding, and with naught. But that's nay who ye really are. Is it? Since coming here, I've seen jolly folk, anxious to sing and celebrate. Children healthy and excited for Christmastide. I've heard stories about yer suffering that ring true in mine own ears, of losing *everything* due to my brother's raid upon ye. And I've come to understand that the anger and passion that lies betwixt us is shared mutually *by* us."

James peeled his gaze away from the command Aileana gripped upon the hall, and he once more perused his peoples' faces. Who knew she might be an inspiring speaker? As if spellbound, they listened to her every word.

"I've never gotten the bean before tonight." She held up the bean for the hall to see. "And I ken my finding it seems unfair to many of ye because of my surname. And so, for my wish, and since the Lady Brighde willnae take it as I requested—"

She cast a fond smile down at his sister now, and Brighde reciprocated, taking Aileana's hand in hers and squeezing it. A wistful smile feathered across James's lips, realizing that on this front, he'd been right. Brighde missed having a sister, and although no one could replace Marjorie, it was because of Marjorie's lot in an enemy clan's household that Brighde could be as sympathetic as she was. Aileana might one day fill that void Marjorie's absence had left. If only she would choose to stay.

"I make a wish for all of ye, instead." An impish smile tipped up her lips, lighting her face and causing her hazel eyes, made bright and rich green by the glowing hearth and torchlight, to glow like jewels. Sakes, what stunt was she about to pull? "'Tis my wish that *ye* each get a wish."

Some murmurs and a few chuckles filtered through the silence now. Aileana smiled at them.

"We *all* get a wish?" The murmurs rippled across the hall. "What would ye wish for?"

"And what if I refuse?" James jested now, feeling the pinch in his chest relent an increment, unable to resist his own smile as the chattering grew louder. He stood once more. "Ye heard Angus. Last year he begged for a pile of gold. They'll break my coffers, woman."

Aileana shrugged, though her smile turned coy upon him. "Ye cannae refuse now, for it's been so declared. And it's a good thing ye're wealthy."

The playfulness soured on his tongue. Nay. He wasn't wealthy. The whole reason he'd tried to force this marriage had been for his inheritance. Hadn't it? *Aye. And nay. Ye took one look at this hellion. Ye listened to her spiked barbs, and ye wanted to parry with her. Ye wanted to ken everything about a wee Grant woman who'd dare to steal from a MacDonald. Careful, man, that she doesnae crawl beneath yer skin and steal into yer heart, as well.*

Chapter Eight

27th of December

The hall was lively as a bard sang and musicians played in anticipation of the Yule log lighting. Aileana couldn't remember a time when such merrymaking had graced the halls of Urquhart. She watched maids dance with soldiers, smiles on their faces. Guarded smiles cast her way from time to time, too. What should she make of that? Guardsmen chanted along to the bard's song with tankards held high, and children dashed about, weaving through the others and sneaking nibbles off platters. She smiled at their antics.

"The dancing is merry," Lady Brighde said beside her as they bound their ashen twigs for the Yule fire. "Do ye think ye'll try dancing tonight? I was sad to see ye skip the fanfare last night."

Lord no. The commons floor would probably clear of all the people wanting to evade proximity to a Grant. She swallowed. Still, ever since arriving, Brighde had made an effort to be welcoming and charitable, just as James had promised she would, and Aileana would foster the chance to be sisterly.

"I admit, I'm tired this eve, but will enjoy watching the festivities. And ye?" she replied. "Do ye plan to dance?"

Brighde grinned. "The night away, aye. This is my favorite season. I enjoy this comradery and warmth and cannae imagine a winter without it."

Aileana summoned a smile, in spite of the sadness Brighde's remark evoked. If only her people, too, could find pleasure in the season, for it was an experience so far in her past, it felt foreign now. She had no right to find pleasure relaxing within this enemy hall, basking in having enough, which admittedly felt...*wonderful.*

"It might interest ye to learn that my brother is actually quite light of foot when he dances and surely wouldna' mind a good reel with his new bride, in case ye change yer mind." Brighde winked at Aileana now. "I see the way he watches ye. He's unable to peel his gaze away. I've never seen him so taken with a woman before."

Heat ravaged Aileana's cheeks to be the center of so much attention. She cupped her hand upon one.

"How are yer twigs, lady?" Brighde changed the subject.

Aileana tucked the flexible ends of the evergreen around the sticks—a never-ending process, it seemed. For each day they made more, and each eve, the womenfolk burned them with a blessing tied to them, the sparks induced by the popping evergreen fabled to be the magic of the blessing coming true. She stacked it in the basket between them.

"I suspect I've made at least a dozen," she replied.

"And yet ye give them away, and nay once have ye made yer own blessing."

God no. After last night, Aileana had learned her lesson well. These folk would certainly grab torches and pitchforks if she declared a blessing in front of everyone. And yet the faces had been gentler today. She'd been treated to a kind smile or two, a curtsy here and there.

A cluster of young girls arrived before her now, giggling, red-cheeked with embarrassment. No one spoke, as if too nervous to address her. Aileana grinned at them.

"Have ye come for more blessings?" She eyed them playfully.

The children, brimming with expectance, eyed one another, then nodded.

Aileana chuckled. "Here, then." She scooped up the bundle of ashen twigs and passed them out in turn. "Make a fine blessing with each one."

"My thanks, mi lady," they muttered, then giggled and scurried away.

Still chuckling, Aileana shook her head. "I remember all too well being a giddy wee lassie."

Brighde laughed in her good-natured way, as if none of the world's ills could dash her constant happiness. How she found such happiness after the tragic loss of her sister, Aileana wished she knew. "They're curious about ye. Everyone is. Even Angus is warming to the idea of ye living here... Sorry. I prattle too much sometimes. It's just, I havenae had a sister to gossip with in so long."

She spied wee Maudie—ever obedient—carrying bundles of table linens from the kitchen wardrobes. Maudie glanced her way, and Aileana smiled at the child, who smiled back, a toothless grin. Platters of rich foods were being laid out, and laughter erupted from the hearth, where several men sat or stood in congregation, regaling each other with tales of conquests, both on the battlefield and in the bedchamber.

She shook her head, amused. "Are menfolk so much the same everywhere? For I've watched Urquhart's soldiers do the same as they do time and again."

Brighde laughed. "Ach, menfolk love to hear themselves

talk. An illness that afflicts them all. Tell me, what are the festivities at Urquhart Castle?"

Aileana cleared her throat as memories of Urquhart's barren walls and miserable folk assailed her, dampening her smile. How was Peigi doing? How was Sir Donegal? Her brother? Was Lady Elizabeth still healthy? Bitterness still lingered at the thought of her brother, so willing to send one of them away, even if she understood his predicament.

"Of late, we havenae celebrated much," she replied.

"Why no'?" gasped Brighde. "This is by far the best part of the entire year! Midwinter is so cold, but the celebrations of Twelfthtide and all the food and drink make it such a merry time..." Her face fell. "Or is yer brother one of those religious adherents who purport that all celebrations are akin to debauchery?"

Aileana took a deep breath. Did Brighde not understand the extent of their clans' rivalries? Was she not aware of the truth that had transpired two years ago, when James had overtaken their walls, and the lingering effect it had had? Just as she'd not been aware of Seamus's transgressions?

She shook her head. "As of late, we've had less than previous winters due to raiding. But celebrations used to be such festive times."

A commotion near the kitchens rose above the cheer. She glanced toward it.

"Help!" cried a maid. It was Anag. "Come help! It's me sister, Maudie!"

Aileana thrust aside the twigs in her lap. What had happened? Maudie had been fine moments ago.

The guardsmen clattered from their posts, and the hall swarmed toward the corridor.

"She chokes! She cannae breathe!"

Anag's frantic cry continued, and Aileana wedged her way through the crowd, who might have wished to help but created more of a hindrance by blockading the path.

"Pardon!" she called, nudging.

She collapsed to her knees beside the child upon Anag's lap, whose face was red and her hands at her throat, unable to gain a breath. Anag slapped her back.

"Maudie! Cough it out, sister!"

"Allow me," Aileana said.

"I'll no' allow a Grant to touch her—" Anag cut herself off.

Aileana ignored the knee-jerk admonishment and seized the girl out of Anag's arms. Grasping the child around her back, she wedged a fist in her belly and jerked it inward, pumping, pumping. Maudie's face was purpling. The bairn floundered desperately. Anag screamed and clenched Maudie's skirts amid the commotion of muttering and panic, pumping, pumping, sweat breaking out on her brow, until a wad came flying forth from Maudie's mouth as James, fresh from outdoors and still dusted in snow, shoved through the throng.

The wad bounced off his boot. Maudie inhaled with a gasp, crumpling against Aileana, coughing. Then came her tears, and she wrapped her arms around Aileana's neck.

"*Wheesht*, lassie," Aileana crooned, rocking her and smoothing her bonneted head. "*Wheesht*. All is well now. Breathe." She turned to the nearby kitchen maid, ignoring Anag, for her accusatory remark had hurt. "What happened?"

"We popped a piece of apple in her mouth as she went about her business," a kitchen maid admitted, dropping down before Anag and taking Anag's hand. "We was just tryin' to give the wee one a treat. I'm so sorry, Anag."

"It wasnae yer fault," Anag replied, wiping her eyes.

Aileana glanced up at James, whose chest still rose and fell from his obvious sprint indoors at the sound of distress.

"Ye saved the bairn, Aileana," he said gruffly.

And soon, other whispers of surprise circulated. "More benevolence from a Grant," another muttered, though the looks on the surrounding faces were surprised. And kind.

Still. She hadn't done it to be benevolent. She'd done it because it was what anyone would do for another, if they knew how to help, wasn't it? Tentative smiles met her gaze. She passed off Maudie into Anag's waiting arms and, having collapsed without care for her skirts, began to disentangle them to stand.

Anag snagged her hand. Aileana paused and took in the maid's distress. "My thanks. After losing my husband, I fear I'd never recover if Maudie were taken from me, too."

Aileana nodded once, the curt gesture all that she could muster. James extended his hand down to her, and while normally she would ignore a man's assistance, she felt compelled to take his offer now. His face was stricken, solemn. She placed her fingers in his, gazing up at him towering over her. From her vantage on the floor, she was eye-level with his knees, his great kilt draping over his thighs in thick folds. So close. So intimate, in front of so many people, for she was only a mere foot away from that which lay beneath the tartan.

He hoisted her upward, bracing her armpit with his other hand for leverage, and righted her. Then he bent to one knee and lifted Maudie's face to inspect her.

"Are ye well now?" he asked the child, who nodded and smiled up at Aileana.

Bless the lass. Aside from Brighde, Maudie had been the first and only other friendly face here.

"Bless yer wife, mi laird," Anag cried, still cupping Maudie's head and cradling her on her lap. "Bless the Lady Aileana for saving my sister's life. Mi lady, I'm sorry for what I said and for my anger toward ye."

Aileana shook her head, dropped her gaze, and worked her fingers together at her waist. "I'm sorry ye had cause for such anger toward my people."

"I'm indebted to ye, mi lady," the maid insisted.

James tousled the child's head, mussing her bonnet. "If ye wanted to shirk yer duties, lassie, ye had nay to go to such drastic measures." He chuckled, as did the others around them. "Put down yer chores and play tonight."

He winked at her, and Maudie grinned. Goodness, so James Moidartach, the Devil MacDonald, fed foxes, avenged his fated sister, Marjorie, by treating women with respect, enjoyed country gallivants, and doted on children. Not much of a warlord, as was her brother, Seamus, kind to those in his charge and good to animals. She'd been shocked at Anag's accusations, and it was becoming clear that neither man was a warlord, but rather a worried brother to his sisters, and that both clans had harbored misconceptions. It was easy to hate someone considered an "enemy." It was far harder to see them as human.

As James escorted her across the hall and up the steps to the hearth, he took up her hand and brought it to his mouth, then placed his lips upon her knuckles. "What did I say? Act like yerself, and they'd see who ye really are."

"I did nothing but what anyone would do had they learned the skill."

He shook his head, his lips still pressed to her hand, warming her. "How many noble ladies would have taken such action with no thought or even known what to do?"

Aileana, baffled, shrugged. "I do nay ken what ye're getting at."

"I'm saying that for all that yer tongue argues, even in the face of praise," he admonished with a smirk, "that ye have a deep love for yer people, and it shows." She looked up at him while they walked.

"These are *yer* people, Jamie. I merely did what I thought was right."

He swallowed hard, brought her hand down from his mouth, and gazed straight ahead of him. His jaw tightened, and he ground out his next words. "I suppose, then, that any man will be lucky to have ye as his wife and have ye claim his people as yer own, since I ken it willnae be me." He cleared his throat, his arm holding her hand stiff and his lips tight.

Hollowness ached in her stomach. Had she offended him? "Jamie, I'm sor—"

"No matter. Come. We light the Yule log."

Upon a flick of his finger to a cluster of men at the door, they pushed the door wide. Attached to chains was the Yule log, heaved home the day before by horse and cart. So that was what James had been doing outside before the commotion within had drawn his attention away.

"Gather 'round," the seneschal exclaimed, "as the laird hoists in the Yule log!"

Cheers rose loudly, and James installed her by the hearth, then dashed across the rushes to the door, taking up a chain alongside his men. The musician's music kicked up, and this time, as people passed Aileana by or clustered near to her, some regarded her with tentative smiles or uncertain glances.

"Thank ye, mi lady, for yer kindness," a serving man said, bowing to her as he went by.

She exhaled a shaky breath and nodded to him. The Yule log was supposed to be the spectacle, so why were so many of them still casting her surreptitious glances, making her forever feel like a novelty put on the spot? But the sting she'd seen on James's face at her remark still bothered her. What if these *were* her people? They already thought she was here to stay. If their acceptance should grow, would she ever gain their hearts? Would they ever gain hers? Could she abandon them so easily on Twelfth Night and reinforce their negative sentiments toward the Grants?

"This is my favorite part!" twittered Brighde, arriving

beside her and clasping her hand in sisterly affection. The lass was older than James, and yet still, girlish whimsy plagued her.

"What is to happen?" Aileana asked.

"'Twas our *faither*'s job before us and grand*faither*'s before him. My brother will crown the Abbot of Unreason for Christmastide, who will then order the Yule log lit, and such is always a surprise, for sometimes he picks a lad, sometimes he picks a guardsman. Last year, he picked the smithy, who ordered the laird bring him a tray each morn to break his fast."

Aileana laughed, caught off guard, as Brighde giggled beside her at the memory. "And he did it, I wager."

"Aye, and with good humor," his sister replied. "He lives for his people. He kens what it's like to nay be accepted and has always worked to be fair and honorable toward them. Little does the fool man ken that our people have never begrudged him for being born a bastard. Only my *mither* did. I was a wee bairn when he was born, but I remember much fanfare and feasting the night our *faither* presented his firstborn son and rightful heir to the great hall. A Yuletide gift, is how we always thought of him."

The sentiment lingered in Aileana's thoughts as Brighde prattled on, and the men hoisted the massive log through the hall, up to the hearth—parting the rushes in its wake like waves thrust outward by a boat. *What does she mean by Yuletide gift? Is James's day of birth during the winter season?*

The men unchained the log and tipped it beneath the chimney, and James dusted his hands and stood upright, unclasping his fur to reveal his tunic, coming unlaced at the top and exposing part of his pectoral. He didn't seem to notice, and passed the garment off to his seneschal, in turn, taking from him a crown of woven twigs and berries in hand.

He offered his hand to her now, in spite of the sweat

beading his forehead. She furrowed her brow. "Where do we go now?"

"Nowhere. Right here," he replied.

"Stand with him in ceremony, Aileana," Brighde encouraged, nudging her closer. "Ye're his wife. No matter how unexpected, 'tis yer duty to present these festivities alongside him. My *mither* always stood beside our *faither*."

A tick jumped to James's jaw at mention of his stepmother, but he nodded once in agreement. He leaned down to her ear. "Aye, lass. Until Epiphany, at least, ye're my wife. For ye to sit aside would nay be customary."

She took a deep breath and glanced around the expectant faces, so ready to make merry that they would forgive her her birth name for the moment. Aye, she and James had frolicked when they'd thought themselves alone, but to publicly display unity seemed to mean something. His palm was warm, rough. He turned over her palm, running a finger over her calluses. She'd helped her people reap what harvest they could, helped the healer time and again, helped her brother hunt, helped wherever was needed, and her skin wore the telltale signs of the underprivileged life thrust upon them.

"They're unsightly, are they no,'" she remarked, looking down.

"Sister," James said, ignoring her.

"Aye, James. What can I do for ye, *wee* brother?" Brighde replied.

His mouth quirked up at his sister's teasing. "See to it some of that cream yer maids make for yer hands is delivered to my wife's chamber tonight."

Brighde curtsied to her brother. "I'll see it done immediately."

Brighde scurried away, then James tucked Aileana's hand into the crook of his elbow as the folk teemed around them, ready for the season to officially commence.

"What sort of cream?" she asked him.

"Brighde uses it for her hands. To soften them. Ye're lady-born. Yer fingers should nay be so blemished."

She opened her mouth to argue that a lady's hands always looked best when serving her people, regardless of how soft—

"Nay argue, and accept the kindness. And by the way, I told the seamstress to make those gowns whether ye protest or nay," he admonished. "What sort of husband would I be if I nay provided my woman with the things she needed? Gather 'round!" he called, giving her no chance to reply as she gaped. "The time is nigh to light the Yule log, a blessing for ye all! Ye work hard all year long, and Tioram Castle would nay remain so prosperous without yer efforts to protect its walls and to protect each other from the MacLeods and the Gr—" He cut himself off.

From the Grants.

But knowing groans ensued, drowning out his blunder. James hushed them with an open palm.

"Lady Aileana tonight has reminded us of this very thing. To protect each other." She felt his eyes fall sidelong upon her, and she felt him squeeze her hand in his arm. "The maid Anag is nay doubt indebted to ye, for having the presence of mind to act, and so am I."

"I suppose that we can overlook the fact our lady is a Grant!" called a jest, which was met with good-natured laughter.

That familiar distaste nipped, but this time, Aileana quelled it. The faces looking upon her were expectant, as if they hoped she might return the ribbing.

"We feast tonight!" James boomed, and a boyish grin split his lips open, revealing a peek at his teeth and a divot in his cheek where a dimple had once dotted his face. The innocence of the smile, so unexpected, was wondrously beautiful, as copper light danced upon his skin from the hearth fire. "But first, it's my honor to announce the Abbot of Unreason! The laird to preside over the castle for the remainder of Christmastide!"

The people cheered, filling the hall with such vociferousness, Aileana had a mind to plug her ears. The tradition of selecting a layman to rule over the holiday festivities was an old one—a Lord of Misrule, as the Sassenachs south of the Scottish border called it. Nostalgia for times gone by afflicted her again. She gripped her stomach with her other hand to quell the unease it induced. That she should still stand here, enjoying the rich foods that her brother would be proud to provide for their clan, to rest in the security of these fortified walls each night, feeling safe and warm when her people did not...

James pulled her closer to his side amid the cheers, with the comfort and unconsciousness of a true husband accustomed to doing so, then slid his arm around her waist to secure his hold. She took a deep breath. What liberty he took! *Nay, ye're his wife. He handles ye as a husband would to convince his people.* But the reminder did nothing to calm her nerves. What a picture they must make, for his hand was grasping her hip as if he really did have ownership, and his smell, so intoxicating—riding leathers and wine and the faint scent of sweat. What would such skin taste like beneath her kisses—

She clapped a hand over her mouth at the thought.

"Are ye well?" James muttered discreetly, eyeing her.

Sunbursts flamed upon her cheeks. But just the thought, so close to his body heat, set free those butterflies in her stomach once more. Would she ever be rid of these girlish butterflies? Excitement skittered across her skin like flickering feathers. Still, she nodded—for words failed her at the revelation of how deep her attraction was growing—and rested against his chest.

Her hand, moments ago holding her stomach, migrated to sit upon his belly to brace herself. His breath hitched. She felt the intake of air beneath her palm, rather than heard it over the din. Felt his arm tighten in response to her touch. Warm. Secure. Security was something she hadn't experienced in so long. What harm was there in enjoying it? Her brother had sanctioned this arrangement in the span of an afternoon. Why feel guilty about finding a moment's pleasure? Goodness, such pleasure now was the same burning that had afflicted her in the woods as James had braced her playfully to the tree, as he'd pushed back her hair while they sat fireside on their trek to Tioram. It was the same pleasure she'd felt when he'd helped her dress and caressed her lips and kissed her knuckles. Feeling his eyes upon her again, she glanced up and held his gaze. He chewed the corner of his lower lip as if chewing upon words he wished to say, or perhaps uncertainty at how to say them.

"And as my bride is new here," he continued, finally looking up, though his voice was rough and husky, "I'll allow her to do the crowning!"

Aileana's eyes shot wide at the novelty as hushed gossip overtook the hall. "Pick the Abbot of Unreason?"

James nodded, that boyish smile teasing the edges of his mouth again.

She surveyed the expectant faces, then him again.

"It appears I've rendered my sweet-tongued wife speechless." He nodded with a satisfied smirk, looking down his arrogant nose at the jest only they understood. Damn the man. Sweet-tongued, indeed. She'd spent the whole of their first meeting slicing him with cutting words. "The honor is yers. Who would ye select? Some advice, though." He cupped his hand around his mouth. "Never select Smithy. He abuses his power!"

Rows of guffaws ensued—such a change from last night

and the tension surrounding the bean cakes. "Made the laird wait on him hand and foot, he did!" a maid exclaimed.

"Aye, and I might be sore about it, still!" James added with a grin.

Aileana giggled. "It might be nice, Jamie, to make ye run at my command for a fortnight. Mayhap I'd reconsider Twelfth Night if—"

Blast it. She jested. But a look of wanting so deep overtook James's face, his eyes glittering mysteriously, and she felt her stomach drop for having led him astray.

He wants me. Truly wants me. The revelation—that to him, this wasn't a farce—rocked her. *And I've gotten his hopes up.* Did she wish to stay? It was much too soon to tell. And besides, how could she abandon her people and take up residence as this man's legitimate wife?

He forced a strained smile that didn't meet his eyes, and she glanced over the expectant faces, the boys and men posturing to be seen, and the women…laughing and cheering their top choice on.

"Must I choose a man?" she whispered up to him.

James's brow knitted as he comprehended her meaning. "I suppose nay. I never laid out terms, now did I? I will say it must be a *person*."

"Nay a fox or a horse?" she added, her lips lifting in that smile of truce.

His eyes dipped down to her mouth, as if transfixed, and he brought his thumb up to caress across her lower lip. *Sakes.* Her smile fell at the sweep of his skin, the pad of his thumb roughened and snagging as he pushed the flesh out of shape. She'd burned for a kiss the last time he'd done this. And now he did it in front of all to see.

He cleared his throat. Dropped his hand.

"Who do ye choose?" he asked, relinquishing her waist, too. He took up her hand once more and tucked it in the crook of his arm, his throat bobbing hard. So formal a pose after their close hold a moment ago. Why was he putting distance between them when the closeness of their embrace had felt so good?

Knowing her choice, she leaned up to his ear and cupped her hand around her mouth. He leaned down to listen, furrowed his brow, then grinned. He nodded once, then looked around at the celebrants.

"I told my wife she may select anyone of her choosing! Mistress Maudie, come hither!" At first, no one came forth. "The wee lassie, Maudie!" he called again, and this time, the lass crept shyly from the shadows, circumventing the crowd, and padded across the rushes, shock paling her face.

"Did I do something wrong, mi laird?" the child asked, bobbing in a curtsy.

Sakes, Aileana hadn't intended to frighten her, but James scooped Maudie up onto his forearm.

"Nay, *lassie*," he said. "Quite the opposite. My bride is pleased with ye, which pleases me that ye would bring her joy. And we are all glad ye're well." He turned to the crowd again. "Lady Aileana has dubbed Maudie the Abbot of Unreason!" he boomed. "Or should I say, Abbess!"

Exclamations ran through the bailey and reverberated off the stone walls, as did clapping at the novelty of a girl wearing the title. Maudie's face split into a wide, surprised grin, and James lowered her back to the rushes as Aileana took the woven crown and placed it upon the child's bonnet.

"Per tradition, *Yer Grace*," James continued, teasing Maudie with a courtly bow as the people laughed, "ye must demand yer first ruling before ordering the Yule log lit. What be yer wish? A new dress? Sweets?"

Maudie beamed and clasped her hands in front of her, twisting from side to side as those gathered around her volleyed suggestions for her first command. She stared at the crowd, overwhelmed by the onslaught of demands, then glanced up at Aileana, a grin lighting her face.

"As the Abbot—Abbess of Unreason," she began with uncertainty, giggling, and everyone fell silent so as to hear, "my very first ruling is...that his lairdship..."

The silence, so deafening when the noise had moments ago been vociferous, gripped Aileana, too, as the girl covered her mouth to quell her giggles. What would the child request? Perhaps it would be enjoyable to see this warlord so humbled, toting trays of food to the child's bed pallet with a towel draped over his arm.

"That he kiss his new bride so that she kens he fancies her as much as Lady Brighde gossips he does!" Maudie called.

The cheeky lass! Aileana's stomach dropped. She'd thought wee Maudie was a sweet innocent, nay an urchin. James stiffened beside her, if only for a moment, then stood tall once more. A glance toward Brighde's smiling face, just returned to the hall, further defeated Aileana, for her sister-of-marriage seemed pleased.

"Kiss the lass, mi laird!" came the heckling.

Still, James did nothing. These folk knew nothing of the conditions of their handfast.

"Is the laird afraid?"

"We ken ye never flaunt yer women, cousin!" taunted Angus. "But is it because ye've never kissed one?"

Oh God. Attacking a man's prowess, especially one as purely masculine as Jamie, would never do. Aileana looked down as rows of laughter mixed with further heckling. Confusion churned with curiosity in her heart. Only Angus could get away with such a remark since he, too, was noble born and a close relation.

James turned toward her, dipping his head to her ear. "I promised yer brother I'd no' take liberties with ye." He squeezed her hands in his. "But hell if I havenae wanted to kiss ye since yer tongue first lashed me at Urquhart."

Her stare shot up to his.

He waited for her response, but her voice failed her. All she could muster was a nod.

"Are ye certain?" he whispered, his thumb rubbing nervous caresses across her clutched fingers.

Again, she nodded, a frantic gesture mirroring the excitement in her gut and the dryness that suddenly afflicted her mouth.

James relinquished her hand. A finger touched her chin, tipping up her face. His twinkling blue eyes held hers captive while his people laughed and goaded him to claim the prize. Such concentration.

He seemed intent and focused, then with a handsome smile that creased his cheeks and made nervous wings beat across her skin, said much louder now, "It's been so ordered. One cannae disregard the Abbess of Unreason's ruling, for it's akin to defying the king!"

And he dropped his lips to hers.

She stood frozen as the ruckus roared in her ears at the laird's audacity. How did one kiss? How did one breathe? How did one think? What was he thinking? The noise faded to the periphery of her thoughts. Her lips tingled where his touched hers, and—goodness, she needed to breathe. She sucked in a lungful, and God above, this enemy smelled so...*good*. Nay just like leather and wine and sweat, but like fire smoke and soap made of almond powder and marjoram mixed with the scent of his skin, a male musk all his own.

Her pulse raced away like Devil's galloping hooves. And then she felt his hands slide onto her waist, holding her hips, as if to anchor her. As if she needed an anchor! Her body felt rooted, leaden, her mind unable to communicate to her feet whether to stand, wobble, or dash away.

At some point, she became aware of his tongue, running

across the seam of her lips as if seeking for her to part for him. A hand snaked up her back to hold her at the nape, to fondle her hair netting tethering down her wild hair. His thumb raked up her other arm, across her collarbone to her jaw, where he rested it upon her chin. Fire lapped through her blood, pulsing hard in her ears, roaring at the sensation of such an intimate embrace. Was he finding amusement in fulfilling the bairn's order? Blast her for choosing the wee lass! She ought to have picked a nice old peasant man, perhaps a page or squire intent on personal gains instead.

Yet James's touch upon her chin and tongue upon her lips was persistent. And experienced. He'd kissed others, but as he'd admitted by accident, he used care and discretion—the only time he'd bragged being when he'd wanted to get under her skin at Urquhart, the infernal man. Her treacherous mouth opened without her permission, which was all he needed. His tongue pressed inside, bringing with it warmth, wetness, and the taste of wine. His hand now cradled her cheek, the other still bracing her neck, and a sigh escaped her throat of its own volition.

James pulled back at the sigh, his eyes furrowed in stern concentration and his lips damp, determined to understand what it meant. But she couldn't speak, couldn't move, his hold *still* strong upon her nape and his hand *still* cupping her cheek. Vaguely, the presence of others, cheering and laughing, filtered into her mind, foggy from his kiss. And then he leaned down to her ear, his breath a silky caress; his words, a balmy encouragement.

"I lied when I met ye at Urquhart." He cleared his throat, then whispered while his fingers caressed a path up and down her cheek, as if a mindless idle, "I'd say yer tongue is quite agreeable, as are these lips when they're no' slinging insults at me. With a bonny smile as my boon. My lady is without a doubt nay plain and every bit as beautiful as the wild Highlands."

Her breath hitched. She couldn't string a single thought together. In the face of her crippled tongue, he stood tall again, looking out into the crowd, and smiled, though it seemed forced, like an act, for it was too measured. Was he feeling as uncertain as she was?

"Let it be known, good folk, that the laird indeed fancies his bride, and let no one, most of all her"—he squeezed her hand, now back within the crook of his elbow—"question it!"

A new surge of shouts erupted. Sakes, but how could folk be so loud for so long? Her ears were ringing. Blush was burning her cheeks with its telltale stains of embarrassment, and she dropped her gaze to her feet. These strange new people were pleased with the spectacle, and she felt a tumult of the same confusion that had plagued her since she'd sat fireside with James. And a treacherous desire to be kissed in such a way again. Her knees, so weakened, wobbled. Her fingers dabbed mindlessly at the moisture upon her lips. He was nothing like the man he'd at first presented himself to be.

She needed breathing room and needed to make sense of what she felt, for how could she so easily enjoy such a carnal pleasure with James MacDonald when her own people were ushering in Christmastide with naught?

"Mi lady," Maudie now peeped, curtsied to her, with upset contorting her sweet face as she straightened the oversize crown. "Have I offended? I meant no' to embarrass ye."

"I'm quite well," Aileana said, patting her back reassuringly. "Though, aye, a bit embarrassed. Worry nay, and enjoy yerself this holiday. I believe yer next command as Abb*ess* is to order the lighting of the Yule log." She turned to James, breathing, "Please pardon me."

Aileana hastened across the hall, leaving James and the revelry behind her. Climbing the winding stairs, she clung to the rope railing until she reached the gallery above, where it was dark and shadowed.

"Sent her runnin', he did," she heard a couple of men jest below as she peered down upon the hall. "If the laird is wise, he'll make chase."

Breathing hard from her jaunt, she peered down at James to see if he had heard. He seemed to be clearing his throat, his face firm and his eyes fixed upon the stairway. He forced a strained smile, then took Maudie's hand, leaned down to her to listen while the child spoke in his ear, then announced, "The abbess rules that the Yule log be lit!"

Guardsmen cleared the benches, abandoning them alongside a wall and shifting aside the trestle tables while maids hastened to keep balance of the platters piled high with juicy meats. Folk took to dancing in the newly opened space. James straightened his belts, then stepped down from the fireplace as Sir Angus held a burning wick to the kindling wedged beneath the log. He glanced around as he walked through the throng, his eyes coming to settle on the gallery and, no doubt, the shadowed shape she created.

Aileana exhaled hard, resting a palm against the fluttering inside her belly that thoughts of intimacy with James had induced, and she backed up until she bumped the wall, losing herself in thought. *Is he coming to find me? Do I want him to?*

"Aileana?"

She turned at the deep brogue. James leaned around the dark archway, watching her. She gazed back over the gallery to examine the dancers' shadows lapping upward from ensconced torches around the great hall, feeling his presence as he stepped close. She could hear his soft breathing, smell his scent that had intoxicated her as his lips had pressed to hers—

A hand rested upon her shoulder.

"I meant no' to embarrass ye," he said softly.

Her nerves gnawed at her, and she chewed her lip.

"But I'm nay sorry I kissed ye," he added.

She gripped her middle now, unable to look up at him. He moved in front of her, blocking her view. Dim light glowed around him, casting him in a halo. A strange bout of laughter nearly gripped her. A halo? Just mere days ago, the thought of a halo upon the Devil MacDonald would have seemed preposterous. But now that she'd seen how he looked after his folk? Heard his clan's stories of terror brought on by her brother? She wasn't so sure the thought of a halo offended anymore.

He settled his other hand at her waist. Such a familiar touch for him to offer, and yet she sensed no attempt at liberties. "Aileana?"

His palm left her waist empty and slid up her side, over her shoulder, alongside her cheek to cradle her face, and like an animal in a snare, she withstood the eruption of desire and nerves it evoked, alone in the darkness while the revelers below intoxicated themselves on drink, dancing, and merriment.

"Are ye sorry ye kissed me?" His question was gruff.

Trembling, she shook her head, her sentiments betraying her and her tongue failing her *again*, rendering her unable to speak.

He exhaled with pent-up relief, nodding, and his fingers alongside her cheek fondled her coif as he studied it.

"And if I were to kiss ye again, in the privacy of this corridor, would ye reject me?"

Sakes above, was an entire spring faire turning flips in her stomach? She clenched her arms around herself and felt her blasted head shaking again, surrendering to the desire to know the tame side to this warlord. He leaned toward her, his fingers on her coif, sliding around her nape to cradle her head. He braced his other arm upon the wall, easing himself forward, encapsulating her in his body heat, and yet his approach was so careful, she wanted to smile in spite of her nerves.

Lips trembling, she closed her eyes and waited for the touch of his flesh upon hers.

She felt his breath first, heard his exhale close and smelled the familiar wine, waiting, waiting, until he finally, blessedly, ended the torture and pressed his lips to hers. She exhaled shakily against his mouth. Her hands, fidgeting, needed something solid to which to cling and hold herself steady. Her blood roared in her ears, pounding, pounding, and he relaxed himself against her, slipping his hips aside her thigh to better anchor himself. Sakes, the kiss downstairs by all accounts had been their first, and yet this alone, engulfed by his broadness, was far more special, and she released herself over to the sensation.

• • •

James sensed the moment Aileana capitulated. Her hands, twisting themselves, gripped him. Her mouth softened with welcome. And he was floating. Sakes, he loved this part of her mouth, the part that gave tentative flicks of her tongue against his. Her breath hitched so innocently. She trusted him, a *nàmhaid*—he grinned at the word, an insult now becoming a playful endearment—to have care.

He angled his head, unable to stop the passionate sweep of his tongue, and growled appreciation against her as she encircled his neck and held him close. He nipped her lip with his teeth, devouring the offering she made. Both hands now cupped her head and neck, so slight in his massive palms. His tongue laved hers—tasting hers, touching hers—and his control, barely held by a thread, threatened to snap.

His hand made daring roves up and down her side, caressing her hip, caressing dangerously close to the underside of her breast, causing a strangled whine to catch in her throat.

"Ye intoxicate me, lass," he muttered, delving in for another helping of her lips.

She squirmed and trembled in his grip, holding him tightly and arching by instinct against his touch. *Saints, take me now.* She liked this. It had been so long since last he'd slaked his lust with someone other than his fist, but this wasn't just lust. He was growing to know her, growing to understand how his clan's aggression against hers had tainted her. This lust was deeper. Because he wanted to do this again. And again. Not just with anyone. But with *her.*

And it's forbidden, man. Ye gave yer word to Lady Peigi that ye would return her untouched.

A groan worked its way up his throat to be absorbed in their tangling of tongues. This was wrong, but he didn't want to stop. How he would love to see her body, laid bare in the firelight, her limbs languid and sated from his rutting, his fingers swirling indolent patterns upon her skin as they basked in the glow of the hearth. Christ, she was slight, featherlight against him. Could his thoughts not keep course in one direction? For he felt as if his mind jumped from thought to thought like hens dodging a running mongrel.

"Aileana Grant, ye're a devil, ye are..." he breathed, deep and low, and nudged his hips, desperate to rut, against her, held her head tightly to his, anxious for the connection to gain more strength. "I want ye to be happy here with me. I nay want ye to leave. And I hope that my people and I can convince ye."

She froze.

He paused. *Why?*

Growing rigid in his arms, she dropped her grip upon him and palmed the wall behind her. He pulled back, cradling her face, examining her.

"What's wrong, lass?"

She looked askance and chewed her delectable lip, and slowly, the sounds from below filtered into his thoughts. What had he done? Then she wriggled for freedom. He stepped away, lest she feel ensnared.

"Speak to me, Allie." He swallowed hard at his throat, twisting in knots.

Instead, she scrambled away as if he were a leper, putting distance between them. Cool air enveloped him now, an unwelcome sensation considering the warmth he'd felt against her.

"Goodness, I'm shamed," she whispered, turning away from him.

The sharpness of her claim stabbed his pride, and he stood to full height, looming over her. No, Aileana was brash, and she threw her passion into whatever she wanted to do. How could she feel such maidenly shame? His hands hung awkwardly. He clenched and unclenched his fists to occupy them.

"We're man and wife," he said, tamping down the grumble to his words for fear they would sound angry. "Even if only for a fortnight. There's no shame in what we do."

She whirled around to face him, and *hell*, tears brimmed in her eyes, making them glisten.

"Aye, there is. *I'm* shamed. Because whilst *my* people suffer, I sit here in the lair of a man who they consider to be our gravest enemy, indulging in rich foods aplenty and kisses and basking in the desires of my flesh. Whilst my people go hungry from yer and yer men's attack on us. I ken now that there's more to it, that the Grants have wronged ye, too. I do nay blame ye in the same way I used to. But how can I ignore their suffering and indulge in such sweet desires? How will my people ever understand that this feud betwixt us all is more complicated than a game of pointing fingers? If I decided to stay, to let this union flourish instead of end it at Epiphany, how could they ever forgive me?"

Was she considering staying with him?

"*That* is why I'm shamed. For forgetting their suffering."

A tear succeeded in leaking down her cheek, clinging to her chin, and dripping onto her bosom.

"Allie—"

He tried to touch her again, but she was already hastening down the corridor, pushing into her chamber, closing the door. An unfamiliar ache lodged in his chest, and he took a deep breath to try and ease the tightness. Was this heartache? Whatever the wretched sentiment, it didn't dissipate. She had every reason to be angry at him. But was he supposed to let his ancestral lands surrounding Loch Ness go? All his life, he'd been tasked with the burden of reunifying the MacDonald birthright. Those lands had been wrongfully seized by a spiteful Crown. But Aileana had been right. It had been long ago, more than two hundred years, and the king who had stolen the land parcel was long since dead. Was it really MacDonald land anymore?

He thumped his chest with his fist, hoping to loosen the knot forming there, but the vision of pain on her face and the hurt in her voice wouldn't show him mercy; instead, it paraded across his thoughts. He'd done this to her. He'd put her and her people in such a desperate position that she'd thieved from him, nay to gain riches and wealth but to gain a night's meal—and a pathetic one, at that.

He strode down the corridor and shoved inside his solar, toeing shut the door to block out the sounds of celebratory music. His hearth was stacked with wood and ready for a fire. He pulled the flint and striker off the mantel and soon ignited a flame, then lumbered to his desk, where a fresh decanter of wine was laid out. He snagged it in his fingers and brought it to his lips. He inhaled deeply, taking another swig and letting the decanter dangle at his side.

He thought on Marjorie and his stepmother, and he realized that he'd gone a whole day without sparing them much thought at all when normally, they were always lurking in his mind like shadows that refused to be banished. Neither had he thought much about his inheritance—the impetus of this whole marriage. But Aileana's withdrawal now had been as powerful as a slap to the cheek.

He dropped into the chair and took another swallow of wine. The night wore on, and the wine in the decanter slowly emptied, leaving his thoughts blurred. He nodded off, slouching backward, staring at the dying fire and embers rolling in the hearth. If he didn't do his best to make things right with her and her clan, his marriage would end soon enough, and his inheritance would forever rest in donation to the church. If he didn't find a way to make her feel fully accepted here, then he might lose Aileana, after just beginning to realize how deeply he wanted her.

Chapter Nine

28th of December

Eejit.

James stretched and flexed his neck to rid it of the pinched muscles from sleeping in his chair when a perfectly good bed sat nearby in the next chamber. He shivered. His hearth was cold, and the chamber was as frigid as the edges of Loch Moidart. Feeble light rimmed his window shutters. What time was it? He shoved to standing, rubbing his arms through his tunic as gooseflesh prickled his skin, and unpinned his mantle to drape around his shoulders, shrouding himself in the wool. Contemplating taking a short nap before calling his soldiers for morning drills, he moved to the window to see how light it was. His head pounded. He'd drunk too much wine the night before as he wallowed in Aileana's rejection, considering what to do about his desire for her.

Ye have to go see her, man. He had to make sure that after their kiss that had rattled her and flooded him with the type of lust that turned a stoic warrior into a beggar for a lass's affection, that she was all right.

After pushing closed the shutter, he paused, then pulled it open again. A tiny woman upon the hill rising up from the loch moved among the headstones of the cemetery on her hands and knees, clearing each marker of snow and dormant weeds. Bright red-auburn hair hung loose, and a gentle breeze lifted the unruly tendrils. What was she doing?

"Sir Lewis!" James hailed a soldier below in the bailey, one of his skilled archers, who was striding to the well from the barrack, still disheveled from sleep.

"Good morn, my laird!" he called back up.

"Ask the sentry what the Lady Aileana is about so early this morning!"

Sir Lewis glanced to the open portcullis—though from his vantage, he likely couldn't see her—and shrugged. "She left nay long ago, telling the guards she wished for some fresh air and solitude!"

A walk among the headstones of MacDonalds for solitude? Sakes, if he wanted to find her, he had to go *there*? He would wait for her to return. Although, by the look of it, she'd only cleared a few headstones and had a row and a half to go. He might be waiting a while, and his apology needed to be swift, not belated.

Nay be a coward, man. Marjorie has been laid to rest for years.

He freshened his teeth with a pinch of mint, chewing on the leaves while he stripped and changed into a fresh tunic that didn't smell like yesterday's celebration. After strapping his calves and feet into sturdy boots for hiking, he fastened his leather doublet and drew his mantle down over his shoulder.

The morning meal was still being prepared—the fresh, savory smells permeating the hall from the kitchens—and though his stomach growled to ease the headache he'd brought on himself, he resigned himself to stop at the well on his way out of doors to drink from the bucket and ladle.

His thirst quenched, he strode through the bailey, beneath the portcullis, and across the promontory toward the mainland, rising the path to where he saw Aileana's tracks diverge into the snow. Sunlight broke in the east and cast shards of bright light through the crystalline trees above them. His heart pounded as the first headstone came into view, but he climbed onward until the stone cross protruding from the roof of the kirk rose above the horizon, too. He glimpsed Aileana's hair again—a beacon so bright and fiery, it gave her away—and noted her old gown, once more donned.

Slowing, he took in the sight of her working, as if the manual labor eased pain she might be feeling. Pain he'd caused by kissing her and daring to put into words his desire for more? He stopped in his tracks. Aileana faced Marjorie's headstone, and she'd brushed the snow away from it to read the carved inscription. After a moment, he resumed his climb again, and the crunching of snow beneath his boots caught her attention.

She glanced over her shoulder, her face brightening when she realized it was him, though she didn't smile; then she quickly turned away, shoving to her feet. But he'd spied the pink cresting her cheeks and nose, making it difficult to determine if she had blushed or if it was simply from the cold.

"Remembering our kiss, lass?" he jested as he came to stand beside her.

A mittened hand came up to cup her cheek. *Aye. Blush.*

"I'm sorry if I was untoward last night," he added, crunching up beside her.

She glanced at him at his apology, her face softening and a hint of a conciliatory smile lifting the corner of her mouth. "I'm sorry if I was skittish. I was just overwrought. I worry every day for my folk and felt selfish, indulging as I was."

"Ye needna' apologize. I asked ye for a kiss in front of my

people to placate them. I didna' expect ye to want it."

"Was that all it was, though?" she breathed. "A kiss for their benefit?"

He shook his head and drew a deep breath, running his glove through his hair tied back in an uncombed knot. "'Twas for my benefit, too. I wish it was also for yers, but ye've been clear from the beginning ye intend to return home."

"It was for mine, too," she whispered, like she were admitting something to herself instead of speaking for him to hear, her hand migrating to palm her belly as if butterflies fluttered within her.

It was what? It *was* to her benefit? She had enjoyed it? He'd felt that she had, up to the moment she'd stung him with her shame.

His pulse ticked up. He'd felt something in that kiss, and he'd worried all damned night that she'd not felt what he'd thought had passed between them like a river current.

"What are ye doing here?"

She shrugged. "In sooth, as strange as it may sound, I was homesick. Being close to my parents in our cemetery often makes me feel better. I have no family here, but the dead are always welcome listeners." She held out her skirts and knelt back down to push more pillows away from the remainder of the headstone so that the dormant grass beneath poked through. "I hope ye do nay mind. At Urquhart, I often tend my parents' graves, and felt compelled to do the same here. Yer cemetery is neglected, James."

He looked among the rows, from the oldest MacDonalds of Clanranald to the empty space beside Marjorie at the end of the second row meant for him someday. His legacy, denied him by a thread due to his bastardy. All that money would be gone in a matter of days, and it would never be bequeathed to a MacDonald again.

"I havenae come here in years," he admitted. "'Tis my

fault it's neglected."

"Why have ye left it so?"

He shook his head and shrugged, squinting into the morning light. "Memories I wish nay to dwell on, I suppose."

Still kneeling, Aileana brushed a fingertip over Marjorie's name, tracing the script. "I can tell how much ye looked up to her. Was she like a *mither* to ye, being so much older?"

James frowned but felt Aileana's gaze fall upon him. He nodded. "She never cared that I was bastard born. It meant something, to have both my sisters' acceptance when I'd never have my step*mither*'s. I wish I could have done more to protect her."

"Ye were still a lad, Jamie. How could ye have protected her?"

Jamie. The moniker was growing on him again. And as he stood here, before Marjorie's resting place, it felt oddly fitting. He turned and dropped down to his rear, too, the coldness of the snow biting through his kilt and nipping at the bare skin behind his knees, though he kicked his legs out and leaned back against his stepmother's headstone, to Marjorie's other side and next to his sire's.

"I was old enough to ken the sharp end of a blade from the hilt. Old enough to fight if needed. And fight I did. We tracked her husband down, attacked, and made sure the MacLeod whoreson knew it was us before we drove our dirks into his chest. I'll never forget the look upon his face, and I nay think I'll ever regret that moment of justice."

"Marjorie's death brought out the devil in ye."

James pondered her apt remark. He supposed it had. He'd never killed a man before that moment. He'd found his battle cry that day, and he'd used it ever since. Hell, the whole of the Highlands called him the Devil MacDonald.

"I imagine if anything happened to ye or Lady Peigi that Seamus would do the same."

He laced his fingers together to rest upon his belly.

"Aye, he would. And yet ye do nay seem much like a devil to me. Nay anymore." A gentle smiled creased Aileana's lips—a small favor he would tuck away with the other memories he was compiling of this woman. "What was she like?"

Memories of Marjorie's kind face; blue eyes; soft dark-blonde hair, which she'd always worn carefully plaited as a child and perfectly coiffed as an adult, swirled to life. The way she'd sung to him as a bairn, or cheered for him alongside Brighde at the occasional fair when he'd participated in a contest, had always warmed him and given him a sense of belonging among his siblings.

"She was much like Lady Peigi seems to be. Dutiful, never thoughtless. Somehow, she was always perfectly mannered, knew perfectly what to do or say in each moment. She was obedient, but she always defied her *mither* when it came to me. My sire's wife would have preferred her daughters shun me, but they never did."

"It must have been difficult, growing up as ye did."

But Aileana was prying deep down into the memories he wished not to speak of.

"Harder than some, easier than others." He shrugged. "What about ye? What was it like growing up a Grant?"

A wistful smile turned up Aileana's lips, and she huffed into her mittened hands to warm them further, staring into the distance as she thought. "Idyllic, I suppose, except for the occasional reave. Those were terrifying. But it seems everyone has wanted to get their hands upon Urquhart, and sadly, being prepared to hide during a reave became a routine. The first I remember, I was a wee one. Peigi and I were frolicking along the shore of the loch, collecting pebbles—well, *I* was collecting them and had my skirts tied up so I could touch the waters with my bare feet, though I could never submerge them for long. . . the waters are always freezing," she added with a smile.

He smiled, too, at the thought of a young Aileana, before freckles and beauty and dowries designed to capture a suitor had mattered and only a child's happiness had been the ambition. Her smile fell, and she began to swirl her mitten in the snow, making an idle spiral pattern.

"There was a commotion. My *faither*'s sentries upon the wall were shouting. Our crofters were running though the crops, screaming, trying to take shelter within the walls. Peigi and I didnae ken what to do and stood frozen. Should we thrust ourselves in the water rather than be taken prisoner, as we'd been told to do should we ever face an enemy's kidnapping?"

His heart clenched, and without much thought, he took her hand. This wasn't what he'd bargained for when he'd asked about her childhood. Hurt skittered through him for the frightened lassie she'd been, contemplating drowning in the icy depths of the loch instead of being taken prisoner, and yet after she'd endured listening to the hardships his people had suffered, he felt compelled to let her speak about this now.

"And then they *did* see us. And a massive horse galloped our way, a man in furs and with a claymore strapped to his back, bedecked in a metal breastplate, spotting us. He abandoned the crofters he was chasing and put us in his sights. Peigi screamed, nay knowing what to do. I tugged on her, panicking, and cried that we needed to jump in the waters, though I couldnae uproot her. And then Seamus was there, as valiant as a king. He was barely old enough to carry a sword, still gangly, nary a whisker growing upon his jaw and certainly had earned no titles yet. And yet he thrust himself in front of us, shouting at our assailant to nay lay a fingertip upon us. And so, ye see, I believe he *would* have defended us exactly the way ye sought justice for Marjorie."

James squeezed her hand, and she squeezed his in return.

"My *faither* arrived to defend us next, and distracted him whilst Seamus tossed Peigi and me upon his shoulders to run us to safety behind the castle and through the water gate, whilst my sire fought off the attacker, though the skirmish left him maimed. I remember Seamus telling us to stay hidden in a trunk, to nay make a sound, and told us to play a game, that we were mice trying nay to get caught by a lion, and the way he kissed each of our foreheads before closing the lid had Peigi and me terrified, for it felt like a goodbye—"

James dragged Aileana to him, wrapping his arm around her.

"Who attacked ye, Allie?" Gruffness laced his whisper as he pressed his lips to her crown.

She wrapped an arm about his waist, like a comfortable lover, nay the *nàmhaid* she'd once been. Yet he feared the answer, and for a moment, she fell silent.

"Jamie, it might be best nay to speak on those details," she muttered.

"'Twas my sire, was it nay?" He croaked. How dare Aileana have sympathy for him right now and try to shield him from the truth.

She said nothing, simply nodded, her hair brushing back and forth against his lips.

The air left his lungs. Gut punched.

Aileana looked up at him, but his jaw clenched, and he fixed his eyes upon Loch Moidart's wintery water.

"Are ye all right?" she asked.

He barked a preposterous laugh that she would be asking *him* that, after all she'd just revealed, then cinched her closer, burying his nose in her tresses and pinching his eyes. To imagine his father, of all the men—who'd once bounced him and his sisters upon his knee and allowed them to wrestle him playfully into submission in mock battles—terrorizing two wee bairns flooded him with fury. How dare the man? He'd never thought his sire would attack a child—and that one of those children had grown into this woman that he'd kissed thoroughly, held sweetly, and fantasized about a life together—ached. When Grant had attacked Tioram, his folk had felt this same fear. Had the children of Urquhart feared *him* in the same way, too, when he'd gutted Urquhart and claimed it for his own before the Earl of Huntly evicted him? He couldn't bear the thought. Couldn't shake the awful feeling making his body tremble and his stomach twist with regret.

Aileana squeezed him in return, nestling into his embrace as if she needed it.

"We sat in that darkness for what seemed like eternity, Peigi once in a while pushing up the lid to see if anyone was yet coming for us and to give us new air—"

"I need no' hear more, lass," he breathed gruffly, pecking her head, her cheek, her ear.

Distaste rolled up James's throat, envisioning a wee Aileana, probably no bigger than Maudie and with the same bright hair, shaking and crying in a trunk, hidden away from grown men striking fear in their hearts with every swing of their sword.

She glanced up at his show of affection, and in spite of the shame coursing through him, his gaze dipped down to hers.

"I worry, James. I fear that if the king's order for a recompense doesnae come soon, or if it's nay favorable in the way my brother needs, that my people willnae last the winter. I worry about Lady Elizabeth's babe, starving in her womb and killing Elizabeth in the process. My brother will never recover from the loss, he loves her so. 'Tis hard to think on fond memories to share amid so much suffering—"

His lips pressed to hers as they sat in a pile of skirts and tartan in the snow while the winter breeze stung their cheeks. Though this time, lust remained at bay. Desperation fueled him now. How did a man beg apology when he couldn't even make his voice work? How did he show how much he was sorry? He cupped her face, covering her reddened ear with his glove, and partook of a kiss he needed just as much as he needed to silence her with it so that the flood of guilt dragging him underwater would abate, so he could breathe again.

Slowly, he lay her down in the snow, leaning over her, his gloves still cupping her ear and head, as his kiss deepened. Her breath hitched as she received the stroke of his tongue between her lips and returned the gesture, holding him, her mittens kneading his hair and nape. Their torsos pressed together, he wanted to absorb her memories so they tormented her no more.

"I'm sorry," he murmured with his lips still smushed to hers, their noses cold and pressed against one another's, and she nodded, gazing up at him; then she resumed their kiss, held him close, and he relented to what she was silently asking of him.

He knew what to do now. The solution should have been obvious. It hit him like a wave crashing on the shore. Blast it, he'd sat up until late, drinking away his hurt, wishing he could somehow make this right. Aileana had saved wee Maudie's life. She'd given wishes to his people. She'd crowned the child the Abbess of Unreason and brought such joy to his folk in doing so. She was winning their hearts, slowly but surely. And here she'd been, clearing away the snow and reviving the fond memories of Marjorie that he should have tended to all these years. As he held Aileana here, the pain of Marjorie's demise was bearable for once but the realization of the depth of Aileana's scars wasn't. And he had to change that, for the sake of his conscience.

Whether or not he ever gained her true affection.

Chapter Ten

30th of December

Aileana awoke to a commotion in the yard. She lay upon her pillow, her brow contorting. It was too early for such activity. Morning fasts were likely barely being broken.

She pushed up from her bed as the portcullis chain ground out loud enough that even through her closed window, she could hear the faint disturbance. Abandoning the cozy covers, she pattered to her window and snagged a tartan shawl off her trunk to drape around her shoulders while dragging aside a tapestry. Cracking the window shutter behind it, the predawn light was still dull and the cool air sobering.

"But laird, that's half our winter stock," the seneschal was arguing as James strode beneath her window, dressed and prepared for an excursion in his furs and great kilt, his massive claymore strapped across his shoulder.

He moved from cart to cart, inspecting a procession lined up and ready to depart.

"Aye, and we still have more than plenty to make it through this winter and next," James replied.

"Oy, my laird, I cannae come to terms with this decision. Has she somehow addled yer mind?"

What were they talking about? *Who has addled who?* It had been two days since they'd sat together in the snow, sharing painful memories and finding the unlikeliest of support together. In spite of the bitter cold, that moment had been her first truly content moment here, and since then, he'd submerged himself in work, evaluating his winter stocks of grains and goods. And though she sat beside him at board, he'd spared her but a few strained smiles before departing back to his winter stores, as if he were avoiding her. Why had he been so occupied with work? In only a sennight, it would be Epiphany, and yet he wasted what little time they still had.

"They are still our enemy through and through." The seneschal wrung his hands. "Why do ye do this?"

James turned around abruptly, halting the seneschal in his tracks with a piercing glare. "I've so ordered it be done, and I'm the one ye ought listen to without complaint."

"But laird—"

"Yer concern is duly noted, man," James growled, and the steward heeded the warning and bowed.

"As it pleases ye, mi laird," he replied.

James seemed to soften, and he braced a hand upon his steward's shoulder. "I've always been fair to ye all. It's time I extend that fairness to others. Our conflicts were made by our fore*faithers*. I do nay have to perpetuate them."

A drover rode his horse beneath the barbican, draped in his red tartan mantle, which was pinned at his shoulder and around his head to stave off the cold. Upon his legs, he wore sturdy fleece-lined boots; upon his hands, thick gloves, as if prepared for a countryside trek. Did James have cows or sheep out to pasture during midwinter? Odd.

"What's yer report?" James asked as the drover pulled back the reins, the horse puffing steam on the air.

"Three hundred head in the outer pasture and ready to set out. Are ye joining the drive?"

"Aye." James nodded once. "I'll head the supply cart. We'll herd the beasts into their outer pasture where they can see 'em. Make sure yer MacDonald tartan blazes bright so it lures them out. I want them to ken it's us without having to talk to them."

The drover nodded and turned his mount, cantering from whence he'd come, while James returned his attention to the three carts stacked with crates and supplies. By the look of it, they planned to be gone quite a while.

Why make sure their plaids were visible? Aileana's brows knitted together. Was he...setting a trap for a raid? Was he going to use the cattle as bait to lure an enemy out into the open? During Christmastide of all times? Good God. He'd been gentle since her arrival, and she'd forgotten about this other side to him that swung a sword with expert precision. The side that raided without mercy. Worry twisted her gut. She whirled away from the window and dashed to the door to confront him.

Pattering along the gallery, she hurried down the spiraling stairs leading to the great hall. Distant clambering of soldiers settling into their morning meal as they prepared to take their posts clinked as she broke into the commons hall, though the dais sat mostly empty except for Brighde. A hush fell over them as she ran past toward the door.

"My lady?" questioned the guard manning the door. "Are ye well?"

"Quite, I thank thee. I have need to speak with my—" She still tripped on the word husband, for it was a lie. A temporary situation...wasn't it? "My husband."

The guard opened the door for her, and she stepped

outside. The sharp winter chill pierced her skin and froze her slipperless toes upon the stone step, and she tightened the tartan around her shoulders. Sakes, it was MacDonald plaid, and she'd barely noticed it as she'd flung it on. The carts were rolling, driven by two horses each. James, mounted on his massive destrier, was lumbering toward the portcullis, too far for her to catch up to him and too far for her to call without shouting like a harpy.

"Anxious to see yer husband off with a favor or a boon?" Brighde teased at her back, and she turned to see James's sister. Her cheeky smile dropped. "Whatever is wrong?"

"Oh, Lady Brighde. Why is James going reaving? At Christmas, no less? Pray I'm wrong and he's no.'"

Brighde's brow furrowed further, and she shook her head. "Who told ye he goes a-reaving?"

"The supply carts and the cattle, and he's armed to the teeth and demands they bait someone to the field with the sight of his tartan. I thought he—I thought..."

Aileana trailed off as confusion shown bright on Brighde's face. "Aileana, I ken nay of what ye speak. He goes to give aid to a clan in need."

He what?

Brighde smiled at Aileana's perplexity. "Did he nay tell ye?"

Embarrassment assailed her now. Nay, he hadn't even come to say goodbye to his wife.

"He'll be gone for two days, possibly three, depending on how long it takes to drive the cattle and wagons. Did he nay say farewell to ye when he woke?"

Blush infused Aileana's cheeks with such heat, she feared they looked wind-chapped. If only her shawl would swallow her within and make her disappear.

"I admit, he passes his nights elsewhere." Her voice sounded hoarse.

She cleared her throat, glancing James's way again to realize he'd stopped. He was looking over his shoulder, watching her, so much to say on his face and yet not returning to say it. To whom was he gifting all these things? Cattle and goods? What sort of goods? Blast him! To steal from her people and give to others. She'd thought he'd begun to care about her. He seemed to be looking her over from her toes to her head and back down again, taking in her state of undress, and instead of shrinking, this time she lifted her chin, unclenching her tartan to let it relax. As if to challenge him to keep looking. As if she wished him to return and sweep her back into his arms the way he had in the cemetery—

He sucked in a hard breath, his chest rising sharply, and quickly turned around to rejoin his contingent leading the procession of carts. Rejection nipped at her, and her shoulders slumped.

"What is all of this?" she asked.

"Grains for bread, seed stock, jerked meat and baskets of dried fruits, valuables, a household's worth of stock."

Everything a castle would need to survive until the spring. *Everything my people need, everything we've begged the Crown for.*

"Who—who does he give it to?" she croaked, gooseflesh rising on her arms, as if a premonition to the answer she wanted.

Brighde lay a gentle hand on her arm, squeezing it. "Why, yer brother, Laird Seamus Grant."

Aileana's stomach dropped and her tongue tied, unable to find the right thing to say. That rejection ebbed away as a chill of knowing prickled up her spine. Surely her brother's request for a recompense had finally come in. Surely James had been so ordered to give these things back. Perhaps a messenger had come, which was why James had practically ignored her these past days. Surely the man who fed foxes and tousled wee bairns' hair wasn't benevolent enough to bestow these things out of the goodness of his heart...was he?

"Did a messenger arrive from the Crown?" she whispered, for it was the only way her voice would work.

Brighde gave her a quizzical look. "I do nay ken what ye mean? We've nay had a visitor since the MacLeods attacked us from the sea this past summer."

Rooted to the spot, Aileana rubbed her arms, suddenly anxious to ask James why he'd done it. For if he hadn't been ordered, it meant he was doing it of his own volition. And if he was doing it of his own volition, then what did it mean about his intentions toward her?

"Come, Aileana. Let's go inside. Ye're in naught but yer chemise and will surely catch yer death. Ye'll see James soon enough."

Aileana let Brighde guide her away, back through the hall. Embarrassment pulsed through her, and she straightened her back to grasp at confidence she didn't feel. Everyone was staring at the display she'd made, flitting about the castle in such a state.

But the need to see James overpowered her, and she had to wait two, mayhap three, days for him to come home?

Home...

The declaration caught her off guard. *Home.* And yet she'd thought about what it would be like to call this beautiful wild place her home many a time, thought about how hard it would be to win the trust of his people only to vanish back to Urquhart at the end of Christmas. Her heart clenched at the thought of trading Urquhart for Tioram. But her heart also clenched at the thought of leaving Tioram for Urquhart. And if James was doing as Brighde said he was, then she wouldn't need to worry about her people overly much if she stayed.

Yet after James's silent treatment, the question now seemed, did he still want her to stay, as he'd professed more than once? Or had he given up on pursuing a marriage? Or worse yet, had he changed his mind?

• • •

31st of December

James blew into his hands as wind whipped through the glen. He watched the Grant guards scrambling across the outer walls, listened to the calls ringing down the line of men, and the portcullis chain lifting the massive gate. Smoke curled from the kitchen chimney, but no festive sounds or merrymaking met his ears. The cattle, huddled together as flurries swirled around them, were herded into the outer pastureland, and the carts—and horses—were parked upon what was normally a high road when the world wasn't covered in white.

"Retreat, men!" James called, and his drovers and guardsmen, farther up the glen, turned their horses.

He certainly had no wish to speak to a Grant and have it revealed in front of his men that his marriage would leave nothing but egg on his face come his birthday.

"We'll make camp for the night just south of Carn Eige and Loch Affric," he said, indicating the mountain and lake west of Urquhart.

As his party trotted off, James remained, waiting to see who would emerge from the gate. It was dusk, and already he had to squint to determine the details of the men he watched. Wind ruffled the fur across his shoulders and caused his braids to tap against his neck. A horseman finally trotted across the drawbridge. The Laird Grant, Aileana's older brother.

Good. There'd be no question that the laird saw him and knew who'd brought these things. Grant would know he'd returned what had been stolen. James pulled the reins around to join his men, urging his beast into a trot. The nerves that always pulsed through his blood when he readied for a skirmish skittered through him now. He hadn't come to make war or retaliate, and yet talks with the Grants always felt confrontational.

"Ho there, MacDonald!" called Seamus.

He ignored him and kept climbing through the glen.

"James! I ken ye can hear me!"

Be damned. James pulled back the reins, frowning, and dragged his horse back around.

"What are ye doing?" Grant demanded, a hand cupped around his mouth as he cantered through the snow to catch up.

"What does it look like?" snapped James.

"I've yet to receive word from the Crown about my recompense," Seamus replied as he rode closer, surveying the robust herd of shaggy cows, their brown-and-tan fur a splash of color on the landscape. "Unless the royal messenger came to ye instead and demanded ye return all that ye stole!"

"I've no' received a messenger," James replied, his jaw pumping, as he sensed he'd soon be admitting he was smitten with Seamus's sister and wished only to please her enough that she might give their handfast a chance.

"Then why?" Seamus gestured to the bounty around him. "Why give back when ye've never cared a whit about fairness before."

James clenched his teeth, and he quelled the ingrained reaction to lash out at Grant's challenging jibe. As if Seamus cared about fairness himself. Instead, he readjusted his reins.

"I'll see ye on Twelfth Night when I return yer sister."

Seamus held his peace a moment, sizing him up with a calculated squint. "How fares my sister? Unmolested by yer greedy hands, I pray?"

Again, James swallowed a biting reply, grinding his teeth and clutching the reins so hard, surely his knuckles beneath his gauntlets were white. Aileana had been kept in the finest care, and he was certain she and Brighde were becoming close, too.

"She's well. She keeps reminding me that this union will end soon, which should make ye proud."

He'd keep their kisses to himself. Seamus would surely draw his sword if he found out James's tongue had danced with Aileana's and that he hadn't wanted to stop.

Seamus scratched his head. "Then I admit, I'm baffled. Where has yer sudden burst of generosity come from? Unless…"

"Unless what?" James growled in Seamus's silence.

"Unless my sister has shamed ye enough to feel remorse or…" Surprise seemed to capture his brow. His eyes widened. "Or unless ye actually *like* her."

Christ. Was he so easy to read? Or had Aileana torn down his natural defenses? Liking Aileana was too benign a statement. *Besotted* was more a fitting term. Regardless, he said nothing to refute or validate the statement, and blast it, but Seamus's mouth was curling into a knowing smile.

"Aye, that's it, is it nay? Ye like her, and ye wish to make peace to impress her, in hopes that she might like ye in return."

Nay, on this account, Seamus was wrong. James didn't do this to impress her. He'd resolved himself to do this, to make his soul right with the maker again. He'd done it for Aileana, too, but nay in hopes it might score him points and make her love him. Whether she stayed or returned home, James had needed to do this for his conscience.

He pulled the reins around and nudged his horse into a trot, leaving Seamus behind, calling, "Ye'll have Aileana back as promised!"

"Unless she decides to remain with a bastard like ye!" Seamus shouted at his retreating back. "She's always loved a challenge!"

James stopped at Seamus's now-friendly taunt, Devil dancing at the bit for his master to make up his mind. Sakes, he'd always loved one, too. "I've conquered much in my life! But she's a conquest I fear I'll never claim!"

He rode off, certain he could hear Seamus chuckling at his expense. *And Seamus calls* me *a bastard.* But the truth hurt. Aileana had softened to him since he'd first packed her away from Urquhart. But she would never forgive him enough to stay with him and perhaps, someday, love him. *Would she?*

Chapter Eleven

2nd of January, 1546

Aileana frowned, walking along the frozen bank of Loch Moidart, gazing at the MacDonald horses rooting lazily through the snow for hidden grasses. James had been gone two nights, a third day had approached, and confusion had gnawed at her the entire time. What would she say to him when he returned? Surely he'd arrive home soon, wouldn't he?

Home. Such a strange way to think of Tioram, and yet the idea was growing strength in her heart. She meandered among the *currachs* and stacks of dormant fishing traps as her new burgundy damask gown swished around her. Such luxury. Such skilled tailoring. The seamstress had worked a piece of art in this beautiful dress. She was smoothing her mitten over the rich fabric when a disturbance along the walls caught her attention. She shielded her eyes against the sun to look at guardsmen blinking between the merlons.

"My lady!" Angus called down to her. "Come within!

Make haste!"

She furrowed her brow, pulling her cloak tight, and watched the soldiers gathering for orders.

"*Now*, lady! MacLeod balingers!" Angus shouted. "On the loch! 'Tis no longer safe to be outside!"

Aileana squinted onto the water. In the distance, several boats ran fast toward the castle, their sails filled with air. She dashed across the frozen ground as grooms hastened outside to round up the horses and herd them back around the castle through the portcullis.

"Run, lady! This isnae the place to be with MacLeods approaching!" a groom shouted to her. "They always assail us from these waters!"

She lifted her skirts, running, slipping upon the icy bank and collapsing to her knees. The boats were gaining on them. She shoved back to her feet, disentangling her legs from the infernal gown, when she saw movement in the copse that strung along the shore.

An arrow sailed past her.

Jesu! They were already among the trees. Had they feigned a water approach to distract the guards from spotting them taking position?

She hoisted up her skirts once more to run, screaming, "They're in the trees!"

Another arrow whirled near, and she dropped down again, shielding her head.

"Drop the portcullis! The horses are within!" a sentry announced.

"We have to retrieve the lady!" Angus shouted from above as the chains released and the portcullis jarred the earth with a bone-rattling pound.

"They'll use her as bait!" another cried.

More arrows followed. So many, she feared standing, for it seemed as if they missed her on purpose. Heart racing, she sucked in hard, trying to clear her mind, and scrambled on hands and knees behind the hull of a *currach*. If they weren't going to shoot her—on purpose—were they trying to lure MacDonald men outside the walls to aid her so they could strike them instead? Sakes, the Grants fought like gentlemen at a May faire compared to these MacLeods. She eased out from her hiding place, curling back upon herself as another volley of arrows sought to hold her in place.

"I'm coming, lady!"

Upon Angus's new plea from another direction, she looked up to see him outside the walls, withdrawn around the corner of the curtain wall. He inched out, making a dash with his targe shield guarding him, when the shooting kicked up once more, forcing him to retreat.

"Go back, Sir Angus!" she called. "They aim for ye!"

"James will have my bollocks if I do nay come for ye, lady!" he replied, peering back around the corner. "He charged me with yer safety in his absence!"

Again, Angus made a dash for her. Again, an arrow assault forced him back, and when a roar so piercing, so terrifying, lifted on the air, she froze. Her stomach dropped. Galloping thundered, and a string of warriors charged down the hill from inland, through the cemetery, a man in the lead with his claymore drawn, feral blond braids blazing upon the wind, red tartan a harbinger of retaliation. His drovers and guardsmen fanned out, metal gleaming high. This was not the gentle man who had confided about his sister's death but the warlord whom she'd feared ever since his attack on Urquhart.

She shivered at the sight of her husband, the famed, fearless Devil.

His fur lifted and settled with each bound. He expertly steered Devil with his knees, and as an arrow plummeted toward him, he thrust out his round targe to catch the projectile without a flinch. Moments later, MacLeod men jumped from the trees into the frigid water to swim toward the balingers. No way could they survive. Could they? Such relief poured like overturned casks through her. She sat stunned. Jamie was fierce, and with him arrived, surely they would be safe—

"Get ye inside, woman!" James shouted at her, snapping her back to reality.

She scrambled back to her feet, catching his gaze, as his chest rose and fell from exertion while he lifted his sword, his distant face shrouded in fury.

"Run, Allie! Run if ye can!" he bellowed.

Devil leaped into the trees and moments later, splashed onto the shore, into the water as the MacLeod archers swam hard. She ran as he demanded, this time unimpeded, for the assailants were now on the run. Angus dashed outside under his laird's cover, scooping her over his shoulder like a sack of grains, running her within. She gasped with each jar to her stomach.

"Lady!" Angus exclaimed as a sentry whinged opened the narrow gate for the two of them to squeeze through the gatehouse. He dropped her back to her feet, taking up her hand to kiss it. "God above! I thought they'd shoot ye!"

"I shall be fine—"

"I'll summon a maid to get ye abed," he interrupted.

"Sir Angus," she demanded, pulling free her hand. Now that the shock had subsided, how could she consider swooning abed whilst a maid pandered to her? "I'm unharmed. I've withstood a reave or two in my day and need no' a swig of whisky and a lady's maid to pat my hand. I would rather be useful. I must—"

"Christ, lady, ye nearly died. Ye'll do no such thing—"

"All hands can be useful," she snapped. "How can mine serve a purpose?"

An archer on the wall cried out, collapsing from sight. Angus eyed the wall walk with worry, then her.

"Go on, man," she chastised him. "As yer lady, I order it. Go to yer men and bring any injured down here to…" She looked about. "That shed. I shall round up medicinals and prepare a surgery. I can, and *will*, do more than whimper in a corner when there's work to be done."

Angus nodded stoutly, relenting to her order. "Account for the women and children as well, and hurry them to the buttery…"

Intent on getting to work, she dashed through the melee of servants securing sheds, stashing goods, and dousing the thatched outbuildings with water drawn vigorously from the well to prevent a blazing arrow from taking hold should it be lobbed.

"The boats arrive!" shouted a guard. "They turn the tables and push back the laird's line!"

Aileana froze in the doorway to the keep as more orders were shouted. *Is Jamie okay?*

"Is the gun powder on its way?" Angus demanded. "Be damned, we need it! Make haste!"

Gun powder? Tioram Castle has a cannon?

"Hurry, Aileana," she muttered to herself, tamping down the fear for James that gripped her. She had to help, and if she let worry cripple her, who would treat the injured?

Still, fear gnawed at her as she dashed indoors. Brighde stood at the hearth, quaking, as several serving wenches corralled the children within their huddle. She ran to Aileana, grasping her in a hug.

"Oh, Aileana! Is it true what they say?" she begged. "That ye were trapped outside and nearly perished?"

"Indeed it is," breathed Aileana, returning the embrace, then pulling back. "Where might I find bandages and salves?"

"In the pantry by the kitchen, mi lady," said one of her

maids with a curtsy. "We keep all manner of healing supplies there."

"My thanks. Now come, all of ye. I'm ordered to secure ye and the bairns in the buttery."

The women hurried the children with them, and Aileana snatched up wee Maudie's hand, who trembled, still wearing her lopsided crown of twigs. "Come, child. We cannae have our abbess left unsafe."

They wound through the corridor to the kitchens and detoured down the narrow stone stairs to the buttery, where the women huddled against the casks along the back wall, entombed within.

"Is anyone missing?" Aileana demanded, and after a moment, accepted the shakes of the head and turned to leave.

"Aileana, wait!" Brighde snagged her hand. "Ye must remain safe with us whilst the menfolk withstand the bombardment."

"Nay! Our men need a healer, and I've vowed to Angus to set up a surgery!" Aileana pried her hands free from her sister-of-marriage, but Brighde snatched her again.

"Ye cannae go outside! What if a stray arrow should clear the wall and strike ye down? Sakes, sister, are ye nay frightened? This enemy has been known to capture women and force them to wife. They nearly killed ye!"

Sister? Brighde accepted her as a sister through marriage? She summoned her resolve. Now was not the time to succumb to fear or sentiments.

"But they didnae," Aileana argued. "I've been in the fray more than once in my life, for yer own brother sacked Urquhart, or did ye forget?"

Shame darkened Brighde's fair visage.

Aileana took her hands, squeezing them. "I shall be fine, and will flee to safety should the enemy gain the bailey. Bar the door behind me, and open it for no one but our own."

She disengaged her hand once more from Brighde's delicate grip, ignoring the sting her remarks about James might have made upon the woman, pushing away what a claim to sisterhood might truly mean.

"But James will be furious that ye put yerself in harm's way. He would never forgive himself if anything happened to ye. The MacLeods killed Marjorie, and if they kill ye, he'll no' recover, for he's falling for ye."

The words hung in the air, suspended like icicles upon an eave. *No, nay dwell on emotions. Nay when lives are at stake.*

"James should ken well by now that I do what I must when I *deem* I must. 'Stand fast, stand sure.' That is the Grant way and is imbued in Grant men and women alike. Fear no' for me."

She pushed shut the door and was heartened to hear a bar slide across it. Hoisting up her skirts once more, she ran up the steps and emerged into the silent corridor, racing to the pantry. She scrambled for a basket and began dumping sun-bleached bandages, clay vessels of salves, needle and catgut, various bits of equipment, and soaps into the wide bottom.

With her arms laden down, she hurried through the abandoned hall to the door. The sound of weapons and shouting filled her ears. The bailey, mostly empty now except for the alarmed horses, was surrounded by MacDonald laymen and soldiers alike atop the walls, all able bodies ready to assist. Aileana waved to a pair of lads in homespun tunics, summoning them. They scrambled down the ladder and hurried to her.

"Bring me the pot of boiling water from the kitchens, and find me a flask of whiskybae."

The children ran off to do her bidding, and she carried her supplies to the shed in hopes that the thatching would protect her from stray arrows. The injured archer lay within, writhing in pain. Her pot of boiling water was brought outside soon after, each boy lifting it by a handle and walking it carefully so it didn't spill.

"They attack! They attack!" Angus shouted. "Gunners! Prepare a fire!"

Aileana closed her eyes, crossing herself, and offered up a Pater Noster as a shiver skittered over her skin. Not even Urquhart had a cannon, and the idea of one seeded terror in her gut.

The unified whirling of arrows sprang from MacDonald bows, and Aileana peered out from beneath the shed to see another archer fall backward with a cry, an arrow embedded in his arm. Aileana gasped, throwing her hand over her mouth. A fire arrow landed in the bailey, and servant boys tasked with extinguishing them dashed to douse it in water.

"Take him down to Lady Aileana!" a man at arms shouted, and the wounded archer was carried along the wall to the nearest ladder to be brought down, the arrow protruding from him.

"Over here!" Aileana called, and the men hauled him to her shelter.

She whirled away to treat the first man, an arrow in his shoulder, and rummaged for an arrow spoon among the supplies in her basket, finding one. Blast these sleeves! She ripped at the ties at her shoulder, slipping the folds from her arms and discarding them on the ground. So much for the beautiful dress. Rolling up her chemise, she held each arm out for the page boys to tie off with spare ribbons from her pockets and draped a sheet of bandage around her waist as a makeshift apron.

The arrow-shot man, groaning, was hustled in.

"Lay him over there; we'll start in the back and fill in to the front," Aileana directed, then knelt beside the first injury and called to the boys, "What are yer names, lads?"

"I'm Will, and this is Harris, mi lady."

"All right, Will, Harris. I'm going to need ye to assist. Can ye manage the sight of blood?"

They nodded earnestly, excited to help the lady of the castle. She turned to the two soldiers who had yet to leave. "I need ye to hold this one down, for I must get the arrow out and he is sure to thrash."

"Aye, mi lady," they replied, and Aileana washed the arrow spoon in boiling water.

"Master Will, run to the smithy and bring me a hot iron."

The child sprinted away, and Aileana readied to begin the grueling task of inserting the spoon into his wound to clamp around the arrow and drag it free.

She worked diligently, forming a routine with the two lads—

The cannon on the walls blasted. The report echoed.

Aileana closed her eyes and swallowed hard as the outbuildings tremored.

The second injured man, still waiting to be treated, groaned, sitting up. "I must rejoin the others."

"Sakes, nay. Lie down. Ye're in no condition to stand," she snapped, realizing he was the one they called Sir Lewis. "Harris, reheat the iron so I might burn shut his injury. Then, good sir," she said to the stubborn MacDonald archer, bracing his good shoulder to force him back down, "ye may rejoin the skirmish, if ye choose. But I warn ye, ye'll do Sir Angus no good by permanently crippling a wound that could heal easily with rest."

The archer grudgingly complied as he picked up her hand and swiftly kissed it.

"Mi lady, I owe ye my gratitude. I was among the laird's contingent that attacked Urquhart Castle two years ago. I nay deserve yer kindness."

She froze, felt her stomach plummet, then forced a smile, unable to spare the time such a declaration was owed.

The boy returned, the iron hot and ready.

Patting Lewis's arm gently, she said, "Rest, and I will help ye with haste."

He nodded, wincing at the pain, and settled backward.

Blood marred her apron. She cauterized the first man's wound, and as he screamed in pain, she smeared a salve upon it and wrapped it in bandaging. She moved on to Lewis, taking the same swift care, as her hair, styled fetchingly in her netting and beaded band, fell loose in wisps around her face, sticking to her sweaty skin, as another injured man was brought groaning into the shelter. Yet still, she worked. Never ceasing as the injuries mounted.

• • •

Fury, roaring through James's blood at the sight of Aileana under attack, had long since turned to distress. Had she been shot? Would Seamus ever forgive him if she had? How did a man focus on thwarting an enemy when all he could do was worry about his woman? How dare Laird Tormund MacLeod launch an attack while he was away and his bride was vulnerable out of doors? And for what purpose?

Affronted in a way he'd never felt before, he kicked up powder, his poor mount already weary from the three-day trek and now wet from the loch, oblivious to his men's victorious cheering, for the skirmish had been quelled and the enemy sent fleeing.

"Raise the gate! The laird approaches!" a sentry called as James thundered upon the causeway headed toward the portcullis.

He stampeded beneath the prongs, ducking, for the metal was still being lifted, and threw himself down from the saddle as his contingent straggled in behind him. One of his grooms raced out to take the stallion.

"He's been in the loch, lad. Make sure ye rub down his muscles good and hard and drape him in a coat."

"Aye, mi laird," the boy said, leading away the panting horse.

Angus hopped off a ladder to the wall walk, striding over to him.

"We've driven them back, cousin. A good day to celebrate—"

"Where are the bairns and womenfolk?" he demanded, undeterred, as he wiped a smear of blood oozing down his ear. He had to ensure that Aileana was well. He had to vanquish the images that had swirled to life and tormented him since the moment he'd seen her cowering behind the *currachs*, of Aileana hiding in a trunk, a wee child afraid for her life.

"In the buttery, safe and sound, thanks to Lady Aileana."

A wave of relief rolled over him. He dashed into the castle and across the great hall, jingling down the corridor, and descended the stairway to the buttery, testing the door. Barred.

"'Tis me! Yer laird returned!" he called, banging it with his fist, and the bar within slid away.

The door opened. "Oh, brother! Why do they continue to do this?" Brighde threw herself against him, and he wrapped her in an embrace.

He frowned. The MacLeods claimed to dominate all of these waters and vied to steal this land to secure their holdings of the Hebrides…just as he'd sought over the years to unify his own birthright from the Grants. Blast it all. That, and the MacLeods had never forgiven him for exacting revenge against Marjorie's husband.

His gaze darted over the women, alarm reigniting his blood. "Where's my wife?"

Brighde pulled back. "James, she wouldnae hear reason. I've no idea where she is, other than that she was setting up a surgery for the wounded."

James pulled back. *A surgery?* Of course, her family had made mention that she was a skilled healer. "But was she injured?"

Brighde shook her head and shrugged. "I do nay think so. Yet I ken no' if it would have deterred her if she was. She was determined."

A smile twitched his lips, if only for a moment. Aye, he could envision Aileana stanching her wound, then picking up tools to help another.

"The danger has passed, sister. 'Tis safe for ye to come out."

He jogged back up the steps, leaving the womenfolk, and dashed back into the hall. Where had she set up surgery? The hall was abandoned, save his pair of wolfhounds pacing and whining. He shoved back through the castle doors and scanned the yard. There, beneath a shed, he saw his reluctant bride, arms deep in tending an injury. Her hair was mussed from her labor, her sleeves removed, blood upon her fingers and wrists, yet she worked diligently and doled out instructions to two of his serving lads. Relief, once more, assailed him, and he exhaled hard to see that she seemed well. And nay hiding in terror, but strong and bonny. What a boon for him. A woman like her poured forth her passion in spades.

As if sensing his stare, she lifted her gaze to his, noticing him…and smiled. A big, broad smile of relief that lit her face with such natural beauty, the madness of the skirmish faded. And did he see her chest convulse? Was she shedding tears? He swallowed hard, to know she was pleased with his return. Aye, so she was well—in body, at least—but the skirmish had upset her. He nodded to her, smiling back, and was landing his stride to go to her when Angus jogged up, intercepting him.

"We took out two balingers," Angus finished. "Before

MacLeod found his sense and retreated."

"Good. Have the men secure our boats ashore so as to keep thieving MacLeod hands from sneaking back tonight and stealing what we sank." He clasped his cousin's shoulder. "I ken ye were nay keen on my wife when I first brought her home, but I thank ye for carrying her to safety."

"Of course, cousin." Angus dipped his head curtly. "I will say, I misjudged the lass based on her surname and saw yer handfast as a delightful political retaliation."

James shifted uncomfortably, glancing to his woman, who was consumed by work once more. "In a way, it was, but..." He let whatever sentiment he might utter go. Words couldn't express what her actions today meant, that she would help save the lives of men who had attacked Urquhart.

"Lady Aileana makes a fine chatelaine for our people. Five men were wounded. Thanks to her, they'll live to see another sunrise, for Sir Lewis took an arrow to a blood vessel and risked bleeding out."

James's chest puffed up proudly, a reaction he couldn't help. In fact, it looked like his man, Lewis, his trusted archer and guardsman that she stitched now, was gazing up at her, smiling in spite of the pain. "She makes me proud to call her my wife."

"And we're proud to call her our lady," Angus replied, solemn faced. "Truly. Grant or no."

Grant or no. Fok, but he'd been caught up in this illusion again, thinking of her as his own when he'd finally forced himself to accept the reality that she was going to leave. She wasn't his woman. He'd not even spoken more than a handful of words to her since they'd lain together in the snow, their emotions, hurt, and need to be close intertwining them in a long, unending kiss, wishing he could summon her to his chambers or visit hers, as a husband truly would, while trying hard to prime his mind for her inevitable departure.

She peered out of the shed with such anxiousness on her face, it compelled him toward her. And that fear he'd felt when he'd seen her cowering on the shore, knowing one stray arrow would be enough to kill her, hastened his step until he jogged. He needed to see and touch her with his own eyes and hands, to know that she was well and hadn't lied to their people about being injured to avoid sympathy.

Her skirts were dirty, a makeshift apron around her waist smeared with blood and grime. And on her face, she wore distress. For him? He arrived at the shed, his men lined up and bandaged, and snagged her around the waist, twirling her backward against a support, barely registering the tears brimming her eyes, and sank into a desperate kiss before he could think otherwise. His tongue pushed boldly into her mouth, his gauntlets gripping her head and waist possessively, and he shuddered with relief when she returned the desperate grip upon him. Carried upon the wave of initial panic, they allowed it to ease to simmering, and he pulled back to rest his forehead to hers.

"Angus reports that ye've made me proud, woman," he growled.

She swallowed hard, her brow marred with sweat. "Ye needed a healer, duties of which I can perform."

He kissed her nose, *her fairie kisses,* feeling such tenderness overwhelm him, feeling her sighs against his cheek, and he proceeded to kiss each one, gently, with painstaking care.

"Why did ye nay tell me ye'd be leaving and for the purpose that ye did?" she whispered, returning gentle pecks to his cheek.

He searched for an answer. Frowned.

"I remember a lass who ran from me with tears in her eyes after I kissed her, and when I heard yer grievance about my sire's attack on Urquhart..." He cleared his throat. "I knew I had no right to ever ask ye to stay again. And it stung me to be near ye and no' be able to kiss ye again for fear that my heart was on the line. I ken the terms of our handfast are real, lass, and it stabs my pride to be reminded of it, that ye'd choose to go home over me."

She opened her mouth to launch an argument, but he talked over her, quelling her, "Ye have good reason. I never should have forced yer hand to begin with. Regardless, I still wish to end this turmoil betwixt our people, and offering back what I stole was the first step toward establishing that."

Confusion marred her face. "Even if I go home?"

He nodded.

"Even though my brother raided ye, too?"

He swallowed hard, unable to answer honestly. He'd not done it for Seamus Grant. He'd done it because it was right.

"Why now, of all times?"

He closed his eyes, forehead still pressed to hers, and forced a response through tightened lips. "I've come to ken ye. I've come to understand that the origin of our clans' feud has no relevance today. I've come to understand, by hearing yer anger and hurt, that yer lands were never mine, and I was wrong to vie for them, as was my *faither*. And blast it, but seeing ye upon the shore, as the MacLeods attacked…"

Her lips pressed back to his instead. She strained on the tips of her toes to reach upward. He held still, feeling her grip on his neck and shoulders tighten, offering a piece of her affection, and he capitulated, sinking into the kiss. Gratitude and relief released like a coil needing to spring, to feel her desire acted upon.

"I'm glad ye're home," she whispered against his lips.

"I'm glad to come home to ye—"

He cut himself short. No more sentimental nonsense. After all that had passed and their passionate embrace now, as he whispered sweet nothings like a milksop to his mistress, she hadn't corrected him about her intent to leave. Yet she was smiling warmly at him. Sakes, she was in sore need of washing, as was he.

"Look at ye," he murmured playfully, "covered in blood like a hellion delivered from battle."

"Go on, man," she said with a giggle and pushed him away. "We make a scene, and ye no doubt have work to do in the aftermath of this reave. It always took my brother days to refortify…"

She looked away, catching herself, and he tried to swallow the distaste of her remark.

"I'm sorry," she whispered, unable to look back up at him. "I always speak before thinking, and forget how my words might be received."

She maneuvered around him, breaking contact, and began collecting her salves and supplies into her basket. Guardsmen were helping the injured stand and hobble to their barrack.

He forced a smile, following her, coming up from behind as she hoisted the basket onto her arm.

Guiding her face over her shoulder to his, he leaned down and placed a peck upon her lips, his other hand resting on her hip. "I've helped yer people. Ye've helped mine. I ken ye didnae mean to spike me with barbs and wish nay to dwell on it. The past is"—he looked away, too, then nodded—"painful. But the future doesnae need to be."

She nodded, squeezing his forearm, then strode across the bailey. He walked beside her, up the steps, and opened the door since his usual guardsmen were occupied elsewhere.

She stopped in the doorway, smiled, and fingered his bejeweled brooch clasping his tartan at his shoulder as if it needed intense inspection, then a droplet of blood onto his shoulder caused her brow to crease.

"Ye're bloodied as well." Her fingers splayed into his

hair, over his temple.

"I'm fine," he assured her, basking in the gentle inspection of a woman concerned for his well-being.

"Ye're nay injured elsewhere, are ye? Do ye need me to tend a wound?"

"Should I injure myself, then, so as to have yer hands upon me?" he teased, another smile shimmering across his lips.

She blushed. Sakes, this lass—bold one moment, blushing the next. He chuckled as she batted his arm.

"Ye promised my family ye'd take no liberties," she warned him, and yet a cheeky smile danced upon her lips as she glanced up from beneath her lashes.

"In sooth, ye seem to have a taste for such liberties, too, lass. Do nay blame it all on me," he jested.

She giggled. "True, aye. It's only taking liberties if a woman rejects yer advances…"

She sashayed away, a coy smile upon her lips as she glanced back at him.

He cupped his hand around his mouth. "And do ye reject them again?"

Disappearing into a corridor across the hall, she paused, flashed him another tantalizing smile, then left him rooted like an eejit, deciphering what it meant.

"Are ye all right, laird?" Anag curtsied to gain his attention.

"I…what?"

How long had he been blocking the door? She was waiting before him, clearly trying to exit, with an armload in hand.

"Aye." He stepped aside so she might pass, and the meaning of Aileana's smile finally struck like a kirk bell.

Did it mean she wanted him? At least, wanted more of him? Had his gesture of goodwill affected her that she would give this marriage consideration now? Fool that he was, he pivoted to return to his men and establish a tally of damages and depleted supplies with a merry skip to his heart. Mayhap this would all work out in the end, and he'd create the peace his father had seemed to want toward the end of his life. An alliance. Mayhap she would choose to stay.

Chapter Twelve

3rd of January

"It's good to see my wee brother so happy," Brighde said at Aileana's side, and Aileana hid her amusement at the thought of a *wee* James. "He cannae keep his eyes from ye for long, and when he does look at ye, he cannae seem to wipe that smitten look from his face."

Aileana waved her off as they sipped the potent mead, a cask tapped tonight to celebrate their victory yesterday that had taken well into the night to recover from. She inched closer to the smoldering Yule log to feel the heat warm her skirts and back while Jamie talked with Angus across the hall, idly stroking one of his wolfhound's heads. Her basket of ashen twigs lay unfinished beside her, but she and Brighde had long since abandoned the task.

"Nay, he's busy with his cousin—"

"Oh, posh," Brighde cut her off. "What ye did yesterday, Aileana, why, it's the talk of the castle, and he's proud of ye."

"Wouldna' anyone do as I did?" she argued.

"Nay, no' everyone, lady, and ye ken that well. And after the history betwixt our clans, it means much to us all, but especially to him." Brighde nodded toward her brother, who, blast it, was looking at her again.

She dipped her eyes downward, feeling warmth rise to her cheeks.

"All his life, he was trained to fight for our land, and that in order to be a worthy laird, he must keep up that fight until we achieved what our ancestors could nay—"

Aileana masterfully suppressed the retort on her lips, for Brighde spoke of conquering *Grant* land, and this drink had a tongue-loosening effect.

"But James is a, well, an introspective sort at heart, nay so much a fighter, believe it or nay. Our sister Marjorie's death affected him deeply and turned him into the warlord he's reputed to be. He turned into a brooding soul after losing her, for Marjorie was much older than him and was more of a *mither* to him than ours ever was," she lamented.

"I was sorry to learn of yer sister's passing," Aileana said, taking her hand. "Jamie—*James*," she corrected herself, although Brighde smirked knowingly, "told me about her our first night together and has confided more since."

"Then ye should consider that special. He'll nay even speak of Marjorie to me. He must trust ye, to open that wound to ye."

Brighde smiled wistfully and looped her arm through Aileana's, gazing at the castle folk drinking heartily and eager to celebrate. Aileana tightened the sisterly embrace. Peigi had a habit of looping arms, too, and it made Aileana both long for Peigi's affection and take comfort in Brighde's sisterhood.

She swallowed.

This sisterhood didn't have to be severed at Twelfth Night. She hadn't accounted for the possibility that she would grow to like these people and that they might like her when Seamus had tied those cuts of tartan around her hand and declared her married. Not once had she anticipated finding friendship here, or kindness. Certainly, she'd never anticipated finding acceptance.

"Our *mither* never forgave our *faither* for taking a leman and took out her anger on James. It's made my brother self-conscious of his bastardy his whole life. I always felt badly for him, for he was birthed into this world through no fault of his own, and although our *faither* broke his marriage vows, James was the son and heir he needed.

"But because he was a bastard, his claim to Tioram and the Earldom of Ross has been nothing but contested. His chief competitor, our second cousin Mathus MacRuaidhri, claimed his lairdship is illegitimate and that the line of succession should flow to them. 'Tis why they employed the Frasers and the Grants—" Brighde caught herself. "I'm sorry, Aileana, to speak so accusingly of yer people."

Aileana forced a smile. Sakes, but would this rivalry never be put to rest? "Worry nay, lady. Ye are one of my people, too. Please continue."

Brighde restarted upon a deep breath, squeezing her arm. "'Tis why our cousin MacRuaidhri employed the Frasers to oust him four years ago."

"How did James regain this stronghold?" Aileana asked, eying her *nàmhaid* husband, whose demanding and desperate kiss yesterday had left her flustered ever since.

"We're loyal to James. He's always protected his folk and handled their disputes with care. We didnae make it difficult for him to creep in under the cover of night with his men. He ousted the puppet laird easily and sent him packing back to whence he'd come. But I fear he didnae forgive yer brother, Laird Grant, so easily."

"Nay, I remember that day too well," Aileana said.

"Granted, I knew no' how my brother had joined forces with the Frasers and have spent much time hating James for the reaving."

"I fear many of a woman's troubles are brought on by men and their disputes," Brighde remarked, sipping her mead.

"I suspect my brother involved himself with the Frasers to retaliate against James for a past reave, but true, we often bear the brunt of their decisions, no?"

Brighde nodded. "I'll drink to the sentiment." They both imbibed another sip. "But it's nay just his stronghold he had to win back. As ye ken by now, my *mither* burdened him with conditions placed upon his inheritance because of his bastardy. He's had nothing but a rough go of it, and yet he still finds a way to overcome."

Aileana frowned. "What conditions?"

Brighde opened her mouth, then shut it, then looked down. "Surely he told ye. By now, I mean. Ye do nay ken?"

"What are ye talking about?"

"Ach, 'tis nothing." Brighde took a nervous sip. "I swear, this drink makes me heady. I'm just glad James found happiness with ye. He positively glows when ye're near to him, and I never thought he'd find such contentment. He deserves it. So do ye."

"What does that mean? Ye confuse me."

Brighde sighed, as if caught in a folly, and Aileana's skin prickled. "I shouldnae have said anything. His inheritance is his business to tell ye about."

"Whatever do ye speak of?"

"Well, surely he told ye about his inheritance, aye? Held in trust at Fearn Abbey?"

Of what on God's green earth did Brighde mean? And yet Brighde continued spilling.

"It was my *mither* who put the condition on his inheritance, for even she contested our sire's line of descent going to James—"

Brighde cut herself off, a guilty look marring her brow.

"Did he nay receive his monies and title upon yer *faither's* death? As his heir?"

"Oh, his title, aye, and the castle's coffers and these lands, but in order to claim his personal money, he needs to complete a couple tasks to the satisfaction of the abbot with writ of proof—goodness, it's nothing." Brighde waved her off, readjusting her hold on Aileana's arm.

Yet Aileana pondered. What secret was being withheld from her? She'd suspected Jamie had initially intended to make an example of Clan Grant when he'd married her, a notion further bolstered by his soldiers' gossiping about subduing her abed. But she'd chosen not to believe it. After all, Jamie had given back her earrings, ordered her gowns made, kissed her passionately, and made reparations to her people of his own accord—that, and he had yet to take her to bed, thus honoring his promises. But now, with Brighde's alcohol-loosened tongue, suspicion niggled once more. What had James's true reasons been for demanding this marriage? He'd still not told her, and she, overwhelmed by all that had happened, hadn't thought to press him.

And yet the way he was looking at her now...

Their gazes connected once again, and he offered her a playful grin, lifting his tankard in salutation, as Angus chattered on about something and James stroked the massive hound's head. Nothing in his gaze felt false. It felt right. So why did something feel so wrong about Brighde's admission?

"I just thought ye should ken the truth," Brighde added, "because, well, ye make it all possible now, giving yerself to him, and I ken it means much to him, considering our clans' contentious past." She shook her head to herself. "My, what a birthday gift this makes."

"Birthday gift? My handfast?" Was Brighde speaking in

tongues?

"Why, James's day of birth falls on Epiphany. He hates to acknowledge it, but did he nay tell ye?"

Aileana frowned. She had thought to leave Jamie on his *birthday*?

"I fear I've somehow confused ye—oh, the bard is going to sing!" With a nervous sigh, Brighde peeled herself away to gather around the bard and musicians tuning their instruments, decorated in Yuletide splendor of rich evergreen velvets.

Odd. What did she make possible for James now? Losing herself in thought, she stared at nothing, feeling the fire heat at her back, feeling numb. It was as if Brighde was avoiding telling her more—

"My lady," a deep voice thrummed beside her, and she looked up. James stood beside her, his brow soft and content, holding out his arm to her. "May I join ye? We burn the *Cailleach* tonight, though mayhap, considering our poor luck yesterday, we should have burned it sooner." He chuckled, for all knew that burning the *Cailleach*—the wooden carving of an old hag—was supposed to bring good luck.

She nodded and slid her arm into James's bent elbow, forcing a smile, as wee Maudie entered the hall, still donning her crown and carrying a small log in her arms with the carving upon the bark. The hall hushed, and the lassie, struggling to carry it, made her way into the room, resisting young Harris at her side, who tried to help her with her load.

Shuffling across the floor, she eventually made it up the steps to the hearth, and this time, as she fumbled it onto the grate, spraying sparks, James scooped the child out of the way and picked up the log, repositioning it in the flame.

"Easy there, Yer Grace," he teased. "We cannae have yer tunic going up in flame."

Aileana giggled, then clapped her hand over her mouth.

Had such a girlish sound just escaped from her? Aye, this drink was potent, for she was feeling light-headed. And, sakes, James was looking down at her, his elbow tightening around her fingers. His eyes dipped to her lips. Her tongue flicked out to wet them nervously, and blast it, but his gaze remained fixed there, unabashed yearning on his face, Aileana's cheeks stained pink beneath his assessment. Had she really suggested that she might consent to more with him?

He dipped his head to her ear. "Pray the lassie orders her laird to kiss his lady once again. I should like every chance I can get before Epiphany to taste such a treat."

She sucked in hard, held her breath, unsure what it would sound like coming out. How bold! And how she wished he would kiss her again, feel him encapsulate her in his arms once again. Feel his arousal, and know it was his attraction to her that compelled such a reaction of his body. Did he burn inside as she did when they kissed? Did it feel as if his blood was on fire, thumping hard and fast like galloping stallions? As he'd said before, there was no shame in sharing sweetnesses, for they'd handfasted.

And should their handfast dissolve, there would be far less shame in having shed her maidenhead should she choose to explore her attraction to him more deeply—*God above, what am I thinking?*

Yet there was sadness in his words, too. Acceptance that he only had a fixed amount of time, or perhaps he was offering her a chance to correct him and announce she would like to stay. Sakes, Twelfth Night was fast approaching, and now that she knew it was his birthday, guilt settled in her gut. There were only a few more sleeps until Epiphany. She needed more time! How did one make such a life-altering decision so quickly?

"Ye're fretting. Are ye well?" he asked, his brogue rolling low and soft at her side and a concerned furrow creasing his brows.

She nodded, swallowing in a futile attempt to wet the chalk in her throat. "Just shaken from the attack. 'Tis all."

He pulled back, determined to look at her more deeply. "A lie, I'd wager," he said. "Ye're thinking about something far more serious."

As if the MacLeod attack hadn't been serious. And yet she didn't sense malice in his statement. He'd always been good at reading her thoughts.

"Would ye like to retire for the eve?" he asked.

"Goodness, no. I wish to celebrate the victory." This time, her smile softened genuinely.

He lifted her hand from his elbow and placed a long, hard kiss upon her knuckles, then enveloped her in that warmth she'd been fantasizing about, which only added to the turmoil she felt about leaving. She rested her head against his chest. He'd clearly bathed, as had she. The smell of soap was strong upon him. His tunic, too, was sun bleached and freshly scented with dried herbs, and she buried her nose against it to inhale his musk. Did she want to give up this feeling and return to Urquhart? Nay. But after Brighde's remarks, ought she ask him what his sister had been talking about?

He looked down at her, as if he had more he wished to say. But didn't.

"What's yer first command of the night, lassie?" shouted a guardsman at Maudie.

Goodness, she'd forgotten about all the people watching! She pulled back, knowing her cheeks burned pink once again. And yet no one seemed to notice. It was as if they accepted her with their laird and paid their affection no mind.

Maudie looked up at them both, an impish smile curving her lips and lighting her eyes with mischief.

"I might just get my wish," James murmured.

Aileana chuckled, raising her eyes heavenward.

"I command that the laird and lady share the first dance of the night!"

A cheer rose up. Even the arrow-wounded soldiers who sat along the wall on benches shouted approval, and the troupe struck an initial cord and launched into a reel.

"Oh, goodness, I—"

"Come, my lady, it's been so ordered," James taunted, cutting Aileana off and grinning so big, he revived the boyish divot in his cheek.

The song was spritely, and James dragged her into the center of the hall where the rushes had been swept away as their people gathered around, laughing, clapping; she fell into step, twirling, such a joyous release. How long had it been since she'd been so carefree? James spun her. The gathering stomped and clapped the rhythm. Her hair, secured in netting, loosened with each jump and twirl until a pin fell loose.

"My hair!" she fussed, grappling for it, but James pulled her hands away and dragged out the remaining pins, discarding them carelessly over his shoulder.

Her auburn curls tumbled loose.

"I could get lost in yer tresses, Allie," James declared, fondness causing his blue eyes to warm.

"Bonny lass!" she heard an old man shout. "If the lady wasnae already taken, I'd dub her the winter maiden!"

Aileana tipped her head back and closed her eyes, twirling around, giving herself over to the mead and basking in the warm gaze of her enemy husband, basking in the happy crowd, content to know her people were warm and well fed and likely feasting, thanks to James's change of heart. For the first time since arriving here, these people's innuendos about her and James didn't upset her. They emboldened her.

The song concluding, James caught her in his arms so they could catch their breath as the troupe launched into another reel and the people around them flooded in to dance.

Brighde had once mentioned James was light of foot, and such wasn't a lie. James hoisted her up in his arms.

"Jamie!" she gasped, gripping him around his corded neck, but he only chuckled and carried her through the crowd amid whoops and whistles, until they reached the main door. A guard dragged it open, and he stepped through into the crisp night air, where he finally set her down.

"Ah, such fun." Aileana sighed. "I havenae danced since before the…"

Since before the MacDonald attack two years before. James's glittering eyes went dark, and his brooding furrow returned. He looked away, letting go of her and raking his fingers through his hair. "Aileana, I—"

"I forgive ye. As I hope ye'll forgive me for what my brother has done to ye. Brighde told me about yer cousin MacRuaidhri's attack. And how my brother involved himself."

The statement left her lips so swiftly, she scarcely realized she'd uttered it, and a breath later, she was pushing up on her toes to press her lips to his. He held still. Rigid.

"Kiss me, James. I nay want to lose the happiness I'm feeling tonight," she whispered.

He relented, sinking so heavily into the kiss, he gripped her tightly, growling as his tongue thrust boldly against her. He exhaled hard, inhaled hard, and, *sakes*, was she floating? Nay, he swiveled her toward the outer wall and braced her there, his body blanketing hers against the chill as the stone against her back pierced her with cold. Yet she only felt heat. And hands. And his mouth crushed to hers. And his thighs straddling hers, and his… God above, the stiff column of his arousal pressed mercilessly against her hip, infusing her with wanton heat. Or perhaps it was the mead warming her, for she'd consumed a fair amount of that…

She clung to his neck, kissing him fervently back, anxious

to feel more, to be more to him. Her fingers splayed into his hair, over the healing scab above his ear, gripping his nape and braids, while her other hand smoothed over his shoulder and around his back to clench his tunic.

"Ah, lass, ye make me mad for ye. Ye make me mad for the things I cannae have from ye, what I want from ye."

His declaration, a low rumble as their lips clashed, caused her to arch instinctively against him and tighten her arms. He sucked in hard at the reaction, ground himself more tightly against her waist and hip. His fingers kneaded her hair and back, wrapping into her tresses and gripping her there. With a tug on her hair, he tipped her head, improving his angle and control, and yet she sensed if she balked even slightly, he'd step back.

"Jamie," she whined, unclear what else to say.

"Christ, but if I carry ye above stairs, I dare say we'll have a flock of revelers taunting us through the keyhole," he murmured before partaking in another helping of her lips.

"But where can we go?" she whispered.

He dusted kisses along her cheek, her crown, then as his lips reconnected with hers, he paused.

"I've a thought."

Scooping her back up, he strode across the bailey, beneath the silent but vigilant eyes of his night watch upon the walls. Snowflakes, kicked up in a breeze, sprinkled upon them, and beneath the bright moonlight, the tops of the hay carts and thatched roofs of the outbuildings looked frosted in iridescent white.

"Naybody will want to venture out in the cold when they can dance and feast," he said.

"Yet we're in the cold," she teased, unable to suppress her shiver.

He winked at her. "Nay for long."

They came to a small byre along the far wall, and the

sheep within rifled around at their arrival through the gate. James set her down, latching the pen behind them.

"A sheep byre? Are we to sit in the muck with them?" Aileana quirked her brow with amusement, but James only grinned. "Why do I feel like a lass sneaking off for my first kiss again?"

He paused. His grin fell, and his eyes widened upon her with genuine surprise. "Ye mean my kiss was nay yer first?"

"Was my kiss yers?" she returned, lifting her eyebrows and giggling.

He cleared his throat, then cleared it again while looking askance, and did it appear that his pride had been stabbed? Or mayhap that in the light he might be red in the cheeks? "Nay. But it has indeed been my favorite and all I can think about," he muttered. "Does yer brother ken about it?"

Aileana laughed. "All of Urquhart knew, for it happened when I was a mere lass of twelve and before I'd even begun my courses."

The strained look on his brow seemed to ease. "Before yer courses? Then ye're..."

She rested her hand upon his arm, teasing softer. "My first kiss with ye was my second. And I would like it very much, man, if ye'd kiss me once more so I might decide which one is my favorite. Even if we must hide in a byre so our parents willnae discover us—oh!"

He scooped her back up, grinning. "Cheeky wench," he teased, nipping her lips, and carrying her to the back of the byre where a stall sat unused, piled with fresh straw.

The body heat of the sheep did much to insulate them from the chill, but still, James lay her down upon the straw and proceeded to unwind his mantle from his shoulder and waist to drape around them.

"Suppose I banish from yer mind yer first kiss for good," he teased, stretching out beside her and leaning over her to entrap her beneath his torso. Her skin buzzed at such unchecked intimacy.

She nodded breathily. "Of course ye'll have to throw yer effort into it, man—"

His lips landed upon hers with a growl, and she couldn't help but grin as he cupped her face and pushed his body against hers. Whether it was the drink that had relaxed her defenses or the underlying desire for him finally brimming to the top, she opened her lips for him to pillage with sheer desire.

"Aye, I'll steal what kisses I can," he murmured.

"Typical reaver," she admonished.

He grinned arrogantly. "Aye, Devil, I believe ye've dubbed me. But my wife has always had an unruly tongue," he added. "I dare say I should silence it with mine."

But her grin had already fallen as heat surged through her, as her belly warmed in the way it was coming to do when he showed her affection.

She sucked in air, exhaled raggedly, and he pulled back to look into her eyes in the darkness. She studied him, muted by shadow, barely an outline, but she could tell he was studying her shift in demeanor. She threaded her fingers into his feral hair and pulled him back down to her, and this time, he sank with quiet determination into the kiss. Against her leg, she felt his hardened manhood press against her, easing off gently, pressing again, as his tongue courted hers and his grip upon her softened to an exploratory caress.

The heat upon her skin turned to gooseflesh. The nerves in her belly turned to fire, as his hand slid over her stomach, around her waist, up her side, while his lips plied hers, his skilled seduction serious and wanting. She arched into his roving caress and heard him hiss an inhale.

"Ye like that?" he murmured gruffly by her ear, nipping at her lobe and pecking his way across her cheeks back to her lips.

She nodded, more frantically than she'd intended, though she was losing herself in his touch. He undulated against her more ardently. She gripped him tighter, arching and exhaling and suckling upon his lips as he was with hers, and he groaned long, low.

"Sakes, lass, ever since I met ye, I havenae been able to get ye from my mind," he said, so gruffly, she knew he was spiraling out of control.

She nodded again, agreeing that she'd felt the same way, for her mouth refused to produce words. He shifted atop her, pinning her beneath him. His kiss deepened, his head tilted, his hand gripped her crown while his other roved more haphazardly down her arm, around her waist, then up her stomach to cup her... Goodness, his hand was upon her breast! Again, she arched into his touch, her body knowing what it wanted, and she had no control over it. Again, he groaned long and low as his fingers began to gently knead her through her bodice ribbed with stays, frustrating him in the most delightful way.

He tore his lips away from hers and kissed down her neck, across her chest, and fought with her garment to pluck her breast from the low-cut neckline. She ought to be scandalized! Instead, she felt herself wriggling to be freed from the restrictive garment, reaching behind her back to pull the lacing her maids had worked hard to tighten.

The bodice slackened. He inhaled gratefully and dragged his nose over her skin to kiss his way to the rises of flesh below her neckline. He eased the fabric down, nudging a pert peak from its hiding place, and pulled back, a reverent softness on his brow.

• • •

James gazed at the dusky tip of Aileana's breast, uncertain how to proceed. Her chest rose and fell in fragmented breaths, her bonny lips, plump from his devouring, parted so gently as she gazed up at him; he knew he'd never tire of seeing such trust in her eyes. To see this lass, so defiant against his might, so giving in her love and labor for others, was enough to give him pause. And consider. He dipped his lips to her breast, pecking it, then gently suckled it into his mouth, laving his tongue over the delicious flesh.

She inhaled hard, a whimper on her lips, and gripped his hair as if to anchor herself to him. It anchored him, too, for he was damn near to floating away. Outside, snow swirled, yet within the byre's primitive privacy, he had Aileana Grant—nay, *MacDonald*, if only for a couple more days—beneath him, wanting him as he wanted her.

His hand skimmed down her arm, over her waist, over her hip, down her thigh, where he slipped his palm beneath her hemline, slowly, slowly, inching up the fabric. She squirmed. A soft whine seemed to catch in her throat.

"James, I'm...I'm burning," she whispered.

Sakes above, she was going to drive him wild with words like those. His eager manhood begged him to move fast. He resisted, sliding his palm over her stockinged calf, over her knee to where the ribbon held it in place, over her thigh. Christ, it was smooth, like freshly churned cream. Surely his calluses scratched it. Up he ventured still, until his knuckle grazed across her privy hair, and she jumped, clinging to him so tightly, he was certain she would tug his braids from their roots.

He grinned, dragging a finger over her seam, damp and warm for him. Was she as anxious to join with him as he was with her? For once they started, he might not be able to stop. He would want to do this again and again with her until he had to give her up.

I'll have to give her up. The day is fast approaching. She's nay staying; she's made that clear. Can I really do this?

Damn that voice of conscience, like ice dumped upon a fiery ember. There was no harm in what they did right now as man and wife, but could he deflower her *knowing* she would return home? Knowing she would forever be stripped of her maidenhood because of him? He'd stolen much from her—he saw that now. They might tease about stolen kisses, but could he steal her virginity, too, perhaps sow a child upon her, then leave her on her brother's threshold?

Christ. He could never sire a bastard. The urge to plow headlong into this new frontier with Aileana ground to a halt. His cock pulsed with frustration, demanding to rut. But he just…couldn't. Not when he knew they had no future.

Moments lapsed, when he realized he'd ceased kissing her breast, his palm frozen upon her thigh. Her fingers slackened their grip, and he felt her shift beneath him. He looked up to see her gazing down at him, concern marring her bonny face.

He withdrew his hand, then pulled up. Then sat up. Then raked his hand through his hair and shifted from her to face away, feeling the straw shift and her skirts rustle. When he finally glanced back, she, too, was sitting up, clutching her bodice upward and casting her face downward.

"Did I do something wrong?" she whispered on a thread. "I, I ken no' how to…how to act…"

"Wrong?" he gripped her hand, dragging it free of her garment, though it was stiff and her posture wary. "Aileana, ye're like fine wine I want to guzzle—"

"Am I nay to yer liking? Oh God."

She gripped her stomach, then pushed to standing, dragging his mantle with her to wrap around the laces hanging loose down her back, a telltale sign of what she'd been doing, and smoothed her hair to rid it of stray strands of straw.

Speak, man! For her vulnerability was unbearable, and

she was about to leave. He, too, shoved to standing.

"Aileana, if ye think ye're nay to my liking, then ye havenae been paying attention. I want ye. More than I can describe," he growled and took her shoulders, turning her back to him. "Ye drive me mad with want of ye."

"But?" she asked, looking up at him and piercing him with her hurt stare.

He sighed, then slid his hands down her arms to take her fingers in his.

"But I ken ye wish to return to Urquhart. And I'll no' steal yer innocence as mine, and sow a bastard upon ye in the process, then give ye back. There's been enough stealing betwixt our people. And I ken all too well what it's like to be born out of wedlock, having to fight hard for what yer peers are given for free. Any man ye marry willnae want to raise another man's progeny—"

He turned away once more, severing his touch, frowning at the sour taste thoughts of Aileana abed with another left in his mouth. Yet he couldn't leave her alone like this, with her clothing mussed in a sheep's byre.

"I'm sorry, but I've grown to care for ye." He swallowed hard.

Her hand took his, and he turned to gaze at her, her messy hair framing her face endearingly.

"Actually, James, I'd thought to discuss that matter with ye. I...cannae say living here has been so bad as I thought it would be. Yer sister has welcomed me, and yer people are growing on me. Wee Maudie is indeed a sweeting."

"She's a cheeky imp," James admitted with a weary huff of laughter.

Aileana smiled, too. "I admit, when ye demanded a bride, I imagined myself enslaved, made to fulfill orders and humiliated at every turn. I feared Peigi would never withstand it, but I knew that I could."

He shook his head, but she continued, causing him to stop.

"Ye've made great peace with my people and taken care with me. I'm nay averse to, eh, reconsidering my original plan."

What was she saying? That she might stay? Or more importantly, she *wanted* to? His heart leaped at the thought. He searched her eyes for some sort of clue.

"Be clear with me, lass, so I'm nay led astray. Do ye want to remain with me?" he asked, the words raking over his unusually gruff throat. "Do ye wish to make this marriage permanent?"

She gazed shyly up at him, nodding. "Could it be that I've grown to care for my *nàmhaid*, too?" she whispered.

He grinned and took her upper arms in hand, wanting to hold on tightly, and dropped his lips to hers.

"And does that mean ye want to lie with me?" he murmured, his mouth renewing its dance with hers, his nose nuzzling hers.

Again, she nodded. And this time she ducked her head in embarrassment. "Will it hurt?"

Sakes, but the last thing he wanted to do was hurt her. His dipped to her ear, nipping the lobe, felt her sharp intakes of breath as her grip upon him regained strength, felt his frustrated loins surge with renewed desire.

"I'll have care, Allie. And I promise, I'll do my best to please ye."

She lifted her chin in that defiant way that she always did, as if prepared for any challenge.

"Then, Jamie Moidartach MacDonald. I'm willing to lie with ye and give myself to ye as yer wife, if ye promise to always treat me with the goodness ye've used so far."

He nodded, dragging his finger down her cheek to linger on her lip. "Aye, *nàmhaid*," he murmured so fondly this time, it was a wonder the word had ever been an insult.

He felt her lips curl up in a smile, and God, but it felt good, and new, and profound to know he'd be a husband honestly, as if they'd only playacted to this point. "And we'll call upon a priest so that we can make this right with the church. I'll give ye a proper ceremony, and together, we'll align our clans, and lands, instead of remaining divided."

She turned her face into his to capture his lips, and he gave them willingly. Ought he to take her to his chamber? Bed her like a proper husband would bed his new bride instead of rutting in a sheep shed like a lad and lass evading their laird's scrutiny, as she'd jested? Except she was pulling him in. She was holding him and drawing him close to her.

He shed his mantle from her shoulders once more, letting it slip through his fingers to drop to the straw, easing her back down upon it. She lay beneath him, and he sank to his knees, straddling her, wanting her, and eased her bodice back down over her bosom.

"So beautiful," he murmured with appreciation, caressing a callused finger over the mounds and down the valley between them. "Curse the souls whoever told ye ye were plain."

She shivered but arched toward his touch. So bold. So confident. So Aileana, to seize the moment instead of shying from it.

He lifted her hands and placed them upon his knees, skin to skin, sliding them upward. "Have yer way, lass. As I would with ye."

At this, she turned her head away with embarrassment. He held still, waiting for her curiosity to get the better of her. He guided her face back with his finger, and she swallowed, then trailed her hands over the hair upon his thighs, the sensation both tickling and agitating in the most delightful way, inching closer, closer, to the mark. His breath caught.

His bollocks tightened. It had been so long since he'd been touched so, and to feel Aileana now, to have won her stubborn heart, made this moment so delectable, he couldn't imagine thinking of another—

"Jesu," he hissed as she grazed over his bollocks, and he looked down to see sheer fascination on her face as she explored this unknown, the veil of his kilt obstructing her view, turning this into a game of touch and exploration.

He tightened at the base of his spine, within his bollocks, and blast it! He was about to finish like a green lad! He ripped her hands away, dropping down atop her, and fought to drag up her mass of skirts.

"I want a union with ye, before ye make me so pleasured, I end this before I can even start it," he growled, nipping at her ear, her cheek, her chin, returning his lips to hers.

He found her core with an urgent finger, felt along her seam, swallowed the hitch in her breath such a touch induced, and positioned his helm at her entrance. Plunging with barely harnessed control, she cried out, arching, and tensed beneath him, and God above, he fought to remain still, fought to regain his patience so that her untouched flesh might soften to him.

He kissed her idly, plied her breasts gently, as he held the union, sheathed to the hilt, waiting, as she relaxed, as her tight warmth gripped him and caused him to tremble with need.

"There," he whispered against her ear, clenching her tightly, feeling his heart open farther in ways he never knew it could. "Ye're mine, as I'm yers. I want it no other way."

She nodded against him, clinging hard to him, her nails biting through his tunic to clench his back, her legs cinched tightly around his rear. "Aye, Jamie, my...I—"

He froze, then his pride, like a strong wind, soared away with his heart. Was she about to say what he thought she was? Surely it was much too soon, as she'd concluded by silencing herself. But as he tried hard not to grin a lopsided grin, he sank into slow, gliding thrusts, easing himself upon his woman and basking in this Yuletide miracle binding their people, and their hearts, together.

Yet her ankles came around his legs, clinging to him, as soft cries welled from her throat at the new sensation of loving, encouraging him to give more. Try as he might to be gentle, her encouragement teased him. He felt her fingers glide up his abdomen, around his rear, clenching him, pulling him more forcefully to her as if she needed him, and as his thighs and arms trembled from holding himself steady, he relented to the wildness he felt.

He pulled back on his haunches, gripped each of her creamy thighs, and dropped back his head as his cock thrust harder and faster, galloping his way home. She cried out, a seductive, pleasured sound that rolled over his ears and infused him with energy. A groan, low and rumbling, vibrated in his throat, the primal pride a man felt when he pleased the woman who seized his heart, bubbling over his lips, where it had been brimming. With a thread of control, he gazed down at her, his eyes hooded with hot lust. Her face was tossed to one side, eyes pinched closed, sweet moans of pleasure encouraging him from her delicious lips as her fingers moved frantically upon him to grasp hold.

"Jamie, Jamie," she murmured, though there was no direction to the utterance, and he dropped down upon her to capture her lips in his as the tingling of release throbbed low in his spine, tightened his bollocks, hastened his pace…

"Lass, I…"

He pinched her lips in his teeth, staving off his release as her moans grew into a whine, gripping him, as his pace increased and his skin smarted hers. She tossed her head and tipped it back and gripped him tightly around the waist and rear as her whole body shook. Her legs tightened upon him.

She froze, clinging to him, and a delightful moan welled from her throat, her nails biting through his tunic.

Warmth coated him. Her thighs trembled. Ah, there it was: his woman's pleasure, sweeter than fine sugar. He was the lucky bastard to claim this cherished prize, and he drove himself once more, a swift, hard, desperate thrust.

A roar tore up his throat, and he kissed her hard, forcing the guttural exclamation into her mouth, spilling his seed within her in pulsing surges as he released and flexed helplessly, at her mercy. Panting, his body tingling as if he'd just sprinted an entire league, he finally opened his eyes—which had at some point, fallen shut—and noticed Aileana gazing into his face, such softness and wonder on her brow as she idly twisted his braid in her fingertips, a languid smile shimmering over her lips.

Their lips met—soft pecks, no words spoken—as he pulled free his tartan and shook it out to lay atop them. Cocooned together, he held their union while he softened. Lazily, his lips roved over her nose, her cheeks, as she continued to toy with his braids.

There would be time for their affection to grow and blossom into that love that James felt in his heart and knew that Aileana felt, too. Now, as he basked in the warmth of her flesh tangled with his, there was all the time in the world. He couldn't be happier.

Chapter Thirteen

4th of January

Aileana had floated through the night and all through another day. Who knew such an act as the scullery maids oft tittered about was really as amazing as they'd said? She smiled idly as she glided down the corridor toward Jamie's chambers, for he'd asked her to join him tonight, and every night hereafter. His *Allie*. Goodness, she could scarcely keep her feet anchored to the ground, as if her heart had grown wings and was carrying her away. Would her brother ever approve? It was too late now. Her body shivered with happy afterthoughts, memories of how her husband's body had felt upon hers, within hers, how reverent his hands had been, how sweet his tongue had been, whispering encouragement to her all through the night and into the wee hours of morn, together entwined in warm bliss beneath his tartan in that byre.

She approached his door, wrapped in her robe, and was lifting her fist to knock when she noticed his solar door beside it ajar, flickering light coming from within. Soft talking could be heard through the crevice. Was he conducting business so late?

"But, brother, why have ye no' written the abbot yet?"

Brighde? The festivities in the hall had long since died down, and yet the lady wasnae abed?

Jamie sounded as if he'd sighed. "I will, in time. The festivities and the MacLeods have taken much of my attention. I'll send an emissary to Laird Grant on the morrow, informing him of..." His voice murmured inaudibly, and compelled by curiosity, Aileana moved closer. "And I'll ask him to put his mark upon the formal agreements of the marriage date, which I'll need as proof for the abbot to approve."

"But why did ye nay sign the formal agreement when ye married?" Brighde pressed. "Ye knew ye would need it."

More silence. Another inaudible utterance from Jamie.

"This is all such good news. I'm so fond of Aileana. She's strong, like Marjorie couldnae be. She gives me a sister again. I trust in time she'll truly accept me as one."

Aileana smiled. Brighde had been nothing short of kind. What a blessing it was to find such companionship at Tioram.

"But I cannae understand why ye didnae write to Fearn Abbey the moment ye brought her home as yer bride."

"As I said, I've been busy," James replied, an air of annoyance accompanying it.

"Too busy to claim yer money? Sakes, brother, but it's near four hundred pound."

Aileana's smile fell. What did Brighde mean?

"Is that nay what ye intended when ye took a Grant to wife?"

He sighed with exasperation. "Aye, in the beginning, but... *Shite*."

The latter sentiment was nearly spat from his mouth, like the taste of rancid meat. Aileana could picture him, raking his hand through his hair in frustration.

"Who would have thought marriage to a Grant would work so well? It was a brilliant plan," Brighde said.

"I sense *Faither* tried to achieve a similar union with Marjorie's marriage," James replied, and Aileana peered through the crevice in the door to see James swig a dram of whiskybae in nothing but his sleeping braies slouched around his hips, as if he'd been prepared for bed and Brighde had interrupted him.

The long, toned planes of his muscles, bronzed in the firelight, sent reminders skittering through Aileana's belly as she remembered the strength and stability they'd exuded as he'd held her and enveloped her in his warmth while his body made love to hers. But wariness prickled now as she took in his agitated state, as he paced and took uncomfortable swigs from his dram.

"Aye, but our *mither* never put such conditions upon Marjorie, that she must gain the submission of an enemy's lands and be married to them by a certain age," his sister replied. "She did that to *ye* out of spite at *Faither*. And it's done nothing but delegitimize ye and cause incessant competition for yer earldom and inheritance."

"Brighde, nay now." He pinched the bridge of his nose the way Seamus often did when he was burdened. "I need no reminders of the past."

What on earth are they talking of?

"True, the past was oft dismal, but that ends now." His sister took his hand affectionately. "Ye've achieved the conditions placed upon ye and get to claim that money. Aren't ye pleased, James? Who knew ye would succeed at it?"

"I'd given up thinking much on it," he said dismissively, tossing back another swallow.

"How could ye nay think on it every day?"

James shrugged, sipped, and said nothing.

"However did ye manage to twist Laird Grant's arm

into giving her to ye, anyway? Ye've never told us. Ye merely showed up with her and have refused to give anyone yer reasons."

A fist of dread tightened upon Aileana's throat. Whatever they spoke of, it wasn't good, at least, not for her. Straining to hear, she felt her fingers migrate up to her throat to clutch her robe shut. Vulnerability infiltrated the happiness that had soared since the night before, when they'd both finally been spent and she'd lain in the warmth of his embrace, tracing idle circles upon the hair sprinkled upon the ridges of his stomach muscles littered with olden scars.

"I admit, I forced his hand. 'Twas before I knew Aileana—"

Aileana pushed the door open, unable to continue eavesdropping.

"What are ye talking about? Yer inheritance?"

Was this what Brighde had gossiped about before the Yule log? James froze like a deer sensing danger.

Brighde's face dropped in surprise. "Lady, I had no idea ye were here."

"Allie, I'm nay sure what ye heard, but—"

"Was this all a design?" Aileana asked, illness roiling in the pit of her stomach. "Subduing the Grants? Through marriage? Just as yer men once jested?"

"It's nay like that," James replied, coming to her to take her hands. She clutched her robe harder, refusing to accept the gesture.

"Then what is it like? What are yer reasons for forcing my brother to give ye one of his sisters? Why did ye have to marry *me* to gain yer inheritance?"

"Let us retire, wife," James replied, his lips flattening into a firm line and worry in his voice. "So I might explain."

"I would have ye tell me now. I ken ye wished to humiliate me when ye first demanded a wife. I just thought..." Her tongue failed her, as did her intellect, for no more words came out.

She turned away, trying to make sense of her jumbled thoughts. The remarks of the man as they'd hunted for the Yule log swirled with Brighde's slips of the tongue during the celebration the night before. James took hold of her shoulders, attempting to ease her distress.

In sooth, attempting to placate me so that I nay learn the truth.

She turned around, refusing to fall victim to the panic in his blue depths. "Was I a wager?"

"Nay," he growled. "I was petty when I forced Seamus to give ye to me. And I regretted it almost instantly."

"Then why did ye nay sever the handfast right then? Why be kind and good to me and try to win my trust? Ye gain something from marriage to me. I can sense it."

He looked down and stepped away, and his face went ashen. "In sooth, I'd forgotten much about my original purpose..." He glanced back up, a furrow to his brow. "As I fell for ye."

"About *what*, James?"

At her quiet but unyielding enunciation, Brighde slipped through the door, clutching her stomach. "I'm so sorry, Aileana," she whispered, disappearing.

Aileana clenched her trembling hands. Sakes, but could she not master the nerves chewing through her stomach?

He rested his hands at his waist wearily and took a deep breath.

"When my *faither* died, I learned that he'd ordered my personal inheritance be kept in trust at Fearn Abbey until the end of my twenty-fourth year. He did this because my step*mither* was furious at him for taking a lover and getting a bairn on her—*me*. She wanted me to get nothing and instead see my money donated to the church, as his penance for straying from her. After years of arguing, he finally agreed to her terms, with a condition of his own."

James sighed. Swallowed. Took a deep breath as if giving his last apology before an executioner dropped the hatch to send him swinging.

"He wrote that if I could unite our ancestral lands once more or negotiate a marriage with the Grants, I would be able to inherit, as it would prove my ability to fulfill the role of laird and solidify our holdings in spite of my bastardy." His eyes dropped. "My twenty-fourth year ends on Epiphany. This year."

"That's in two days," Aileana croaked, shaking her head. "So my thieving gave ye opportunity to... All of this was, in sooth, an effort to gain my brother's lands and put a Grant in yer marriage bed. For a purse of coin?"

"Aye—*nay*." Nearly pleading, he came to her and pried her hand free to hold in his broad ones, though there was no mistaking his shaking fingers and tremoring lips. "At first, I was irritated that ye got the better of me, stealing from me, but I saw how scared ye were at Urquhart. I knew I couldnae trick ye the moment the demand left my lips. When yer brother requested that ye have the right to leave me, I knew my claim on the money would be foiled. But I agreed anyway."

"And proceeded to sweeten me to ye this whole time so as to convince me to make it permanent? Make me like ye? Mayhap grow to l—" She cut herself short as a lump rose to her throat and thickened painfully. "Ye buttered me to ye so I'd agree to stay. So ye could get yer money." She nodded. "'Tis grand ye'd get everything ye wanted, James. But that's the MacDonald way, no? Reave what ye will, claim whatever and whoever ye want."

"A lie," he practically snarled, but she gave him no mercy.

"I'm sure ye saw giving up some paltry cows and home

goods to my brother as a small price to pay for the coffer awaiting ye. Four hundred pound gained if ye give up three hundred pound of cattle? Why, that's a one-hundred-pound profit—"

"It's no' like that, Allie—"

"My name is Aileana. Aileana *Grant*." Her rising voice couldn't be calmed. "'Tis a proud name, and one that isnae owned or used. My people got what they finally deserved from ye, and—" Blast it all, but tears were spilling down her cheeks as her words lodged in her throat. She brought her kerchief— dammit! The white kerchief of truce he'd gifted her upon a jest—to hold at her mouth. "I suppose my maidenhead was a small price to pay for that."

He exhaled as if she'd gutted him. As if she'd accused him of high crimes and gouged him with a sword.

"Ye promised to return me home on Twelfth Night," she whispered, catching the ridiculous cry with the back of her trembling hand before it could become a sob, turning away.

James loomed at her back, and she took a deep breath, pinching her cheeks and drying her eyes.

"I never anticipated wanting ye, but it's the honest truth, lass. I *need* ye to believe me. I came to dread the thought of Twelfth Night, when ye'd leave."

"How much was I worth?" she lifted her chin, turning back to him. "Is there more at stake than just yer four hundred pounds? How much more do ye gain from subduing a Grant abed?"

"*Stop,*" he growled, distaste so thick in his voice, it was nearly chewable.

"We had an accord, and I want to go home."

"Lass, hear reason," he croaked so gruffly, she almost believed his convincing charade.

"Ye've played me like a lute. I feel so foolish." The tears flowed again, with no cork to stem them.

"God, lass—"

"Surely ye'll complain to the king now over, what was it? A bundle of vegetables?"

She shook her head. He grabbed her hand, his voice so gruff. *Aye, gruff, because he kens ye're ruining his scheme.*

"I beg ye, woman. I want this, with ye."

"And I'll believe that when the Loch Ness monster dances jigs at the faire."

He stood up straight, his broad chest widening farther as he inhaled a deep, trembling breath. He dropped her icy fingers. The anguish on his face was soon schooled to impassivity. He backed up a step. Swallowed hard. Turned away to face his fire, which was leaping merrily, as if pleased that Aileana's world was crumbling. Silence stretched, filled only with the sounds of crackling wood.

"I'll see ye to Urquhart at first light," he muttered, his voice gravelly, his chest once more rising and falling on a shaky breath as if he summoned strength, and his jaw muscles twitched. "Consider our handfast void. As promised." He chewed his cheek, his brow drawn tight, his profile hard, stewing on thoughts he struggled to articulate. "Just say that ye'll…" He shook his head, fighting for words.

Instead of finishing his sentiment, he strode across the floorboards, through the private door to his bedchamber. He shoved it shut with a hard thud, and as the moments stretched on—turning to minutes—and as the fire crackled, enhancing the deafening silence, she realized he wasn't coming back.

· · ·

5th of January; day before Twelfth Night

The sky was heavy with clouds prepared to dust the earth with more snow, matching James's mood. They plodded along silently, and blast it, but each time he felt Aileana move behind him, shift against him, adjust her hold upon him, he bit back a desperate plea that she reconsider this severance. Losing her touch after barely acquainting himself with it ached so deeply, it was like a fist to the gut. Her unwillingness to hear him had left an acrid aftertaste in his mouth. But why *would* she believe him when their clans had never afforded each other a shred of trust before?

He took a deep breath and pounded his chest, recalling wee Maudie running to Aileana as she left amid the hall, stunned to silence, as if a funeral procession passed by. He recalled the child's cry, begging to know if she'd done something wrong and given Aileana cause for displeasure. Bless the lass. And damn Aileana, winning the fledgling's heart only to discard it so easily.

"We've arrived," he finally muttered, stating the obvious as dusk darkened the sky further.

They rode toward Urquhart's main gates, where Sir Donegal was upon the gatehouse, calling for the portcullis to be raised.

"Lady Aileana is returned!" he called, and a general echoing of cheers arose from within the walls.

Devil lumbered across the drawbridge, but as he reached the portcullis, he couldn't bear to go farther, stopping just short of the thick stone wall and grate. His lungs burned as he heaved in air, and he was certain his hands hadn't stopped trembling since the night before and his ruse had been exposed in all its crude glory. The urge to pound his chest again and clear his throat was overpowering, yet he managed by a thread to remain stoic.

Looking within, he could see the castle folk had paused their tasks, their happier faces not so gaunt from hunger as before. Evergreen sprigs decorated the doors. Smoke rose from the castle chimneys. His repayment of goods had done this, given Aileana's people back their sense of worth and their smiles. The door to the keep opened, and blast it! He couldn't face Seamus Grant, now striding into the bailey, followed by a fretting Lady Peigi. He reached behind him, grasped Aileana beneath her arms and hoisted her down. She gasped, caught her footing, and gaped up at his unceremonious severance.

"Allie," he managed to croak. "It stopped being about the money the moment I woke up to ye in my arms by the fireside. It stopped being about the lands as soon as I caught ye when ye fell ill. And ever since then, this handfast... It started becoming something much more, when I realized I was falling—" He caught his pathetic admission. What man of worth spouted such poetics? And yet the gruff edge to his voice turned thick, and he could feel his blasted eyes rimming red. "I'd rather give ye up to make ye happy than make ye miserable with me. I just beg one thing. I thought ye were mine when I bedded with ye, and if a bairn comes of our union—" His voice cracked, and he cleared it angrily. "I beg ye have sympathy for its bastardy. The stigma of such is a shame I'd no' wish on anyone, least of all my seed." Damnation, were his eyes now misting? "My inheritance will be past the point of claiming by then, but I'll gladly take ye back."

He dragged the reins around and tapped Devil into a canter, then as hard a gallop as his weary horse could muster. Relief and hopelessness twined themselves together in a tangled bundle of regret. At least it was over and he could get on with life. He never thought this severance would be so painful. Surely it was only his pride wounded. Surely he hadn't been about to declare that he'd fallen in love. But it was too damn late. He knew he had. And his heart had just bled out like a sword thrust through it.

• • •

"What did that bastard do to ye?" Seamus demanded,

racing to Aileana's side as tears flowed unchecked down her cheeks. "Christ, wee sister. He didnae even provide ye with a wardrobe. Look at ye—ye return to us in the same rags ye left in."

He wrapped her in his arms, and the strange need to defend James overcame her.

"He *did* provide for me, but I refused to keep anything—"

"I fed ye to a wolf who would dump ye back at home like a rejected sack of grain," Seamus continued, too consumed to hear her.

Bless him, she thought, resisting the urge to look heavenward. He knew exactly the *wrong* thing to say as he squeezed her in his protective embrace.

"My thanks, brother, for likening me to such a commodity; it makes me feel much better about my situation."

"I'm sorry, I'm forever guilt-stricken about the decision I had to make. But I thought that he might fancy ye. I began to think he was taken with ye."

She looked up at him, dabbing futilely at her puffy eyes. "Why would ye think that?"

Seamus tightened his hold. "When he delivered the cattle and the home goods, he could barely answer my questions about why he'd done it, and when I guessed that it was because he liked ye, he turned beet red, like some lovesick lad."

A tingling of wariness lodged in her stomach. Had James been telling her the truth about his feelings? Nay, preposterous. He'd already admitted his motives for forcing the handfast.

"And when Seamus suggested to him that ye might actually be happy in that brute's house with him," Peigi chimed in, petting her hair back, "our brother said the MacDonald felt certain ye would never be happy there, and the sound of James's voice was…"

"Forlorn," Seamus clarified. "I could tell he was smitten.

Or at least I thought he was."

Aileana pulled back, suddenly aware of all the eyes peering onto the drawbridge, watching her. She was never so weak as to break down crying, but now their people, who were used to her strength, were watching her whimper like a pup. Peigi turned her around, taking her hands.

"But these tears, sister, can only mean a few things. Was he cruel to ye?"

She shook her head. "On the contrary. He was kind and protective."

Peigi's voice went soft so no one else would hear the personal question. "Did he force ye to his bed?" She eyed Seamus stiffening at her side, his knuckles whitened on the hilt of his dirk perched in his belt, as if prepared to chase down James and administer justice if she even hinted at impropriety.

Again, she shook her head. James hadn't forced her to do anything. She'd chosen to lie with him, encouraged him to do so when he'd shown restraint. "Nay. He was honorable, nay the devil we all ken him to be..."

Peigi smiled fondly and squeezed her hands. "Then is it possible, sister, that ye've become smitten, too, and these tears are from heartbreak?"

Aileana froze. Indeed, she had grown fond of him. She'd taken a risk and opened her heart. She'd let down her defenses, begun to care for his people, especially Maudie. When he'd given back her earrings, shame sagging his brow, she'd known there was good at his core, even if conflict had shaped him into the warrior he was. When he'd fed foxes, held wee lassies on his arm with such comfort, and sat beside a feverish woman's bedside through the night, she'd known he was gentle at heart—someone she could love. When she'd learned of his tragic upbringing, she'd sympathized with a lad who'd had to fight for his legitimate title in ways no other heir would have been required. How would she have survived if she'd been born of her father's indiscretions and raised by a stepmother who'd sabotaged her at every opportunity?

"He only married me to gain his inheritance, for the conditions upon him were such that he needed to marry a Grant before Twelfth Night of this year in order to be given the coin," she said begrudgingly. "I thought he meant it when he said he wanted to give this marriage an honest try, but in sooth, I was nothing more than the key to his wealth."

She looked askance, explaining the conditions to her siblings' shocked faces, and continued to dab her splotchy eyes. Sakes, the truce kerchief. She suddenly sobbed at the sight of it, burying her eyes within it.

"And yet he brought ye home," Peigi finally said. "He's given up his money for ye. Did he reject ye?"

Oh, her foolish, foolish pride! He'd done the opposite—he'd begged her to stay.

"I insisted on being returned. He's simply honoring my wishes."

Peigi smiled, then shook her head with the closest thing to incredulity Aileana could remember gracing her sister's porcelain face. "Then are ye so blind as to nay see what I see? He cared enough to let ye go. To let all of it go. Because he couldnae have yer honest heart."

"Damnation, I hate to give that *nàmhaid* any berth for sympathy, but such actions only speak of"—Seamus cleared his throat to force something distasteful from his lips—"love. And if all of this is true, then I'd say ye took the best revenge a Grant could ever take on a MacDonald. Ye stole his heart, then ye broke it. And for some reason I'll never comprehend, I feel sorry for the bastard."

The statement spiraled through her mind again and again as Peigi led her inside, where Aileana glanced around the great hall and took in the festive evergreens, the rich smells coming from the kitchens. These people's lives had been made full again, thanks to James making amends, regardless of how the feud had once started. And yet while the castle folk sang and laid out food for the evening board, Aileana swallowed at the hollowness in her stomach, like an empty cavern, envisioning the redness that had rimmed his eyelids as he'd departed. Had she made a mistake?

I have. Oh, I have! And just as suddenly as she'd demanded to be brought home, she bolted to her feet and abandoned the dais, dashing to her chamber to change. She had to go to James, and her clothing was still damp and cold from the snowy journey home. He would stop for the night somewhere soon, and if she were quick, she'd be able to follow his tracks.

· · ·

Of course, the only place to stop for the night was the rocks under which James had first slept with Aileana. But if James pressed on, there would be no other shelter for leagues, and blast this winter, but it was already dumping more snow upon him. Continuing in such a downfall could prove folly for poor Devil.

He dismounted with a reluctant sigh and blotted out the images of Aileana sleeping so soundly upon his chest by this very firepit. He unsaddled Devil and rubbed him down. Blessedly, the remains of their first fire and stack of unused wood still lay untouched.

He heaved his packs within and rummaged through a pouch for his flint, cracking it upon the striker to make sparks. At last, one spark took hold on a dried leaf still clinging to a twig. He nurtured the flame until an ember took hold and eventually, a blaze.

Drawing his mantle over himself, he sat back against

a rock and stared at the dancing fire, recalling Marjorie's humiliating deliverance home, recalling the years of his youth when his stepmother had snubbed her nose at him. He hadn't mourned his stepmother's passing—it was because of her he'd lured Aileana into the handfast. But if Aileana carried his seed, would his bairn be raised by a stepfather someday who detested his child as much as his stepmother had detested him? Could he claim paternity and usurp her custody? The thoughts did nothing but cause his stomach to roil, for such a legal course would only stoke the fires of rivalry betwixt their clans and make her hate him more.

As he closed his eyes and swigged his flagon of whiskybae, trying desperately to doze so he wouldn't have to think anymore, he heard Devil grunt. His eyes popped open. Devil was hard to see in the darkness and downfall of snow, but from the firelight's weak reach, he could determine the horse's ears pricked forward.

He stood, slipping his claymore from its sheath beside him, and rose, stepping out of the rocks. Two shadows on horseback approached, cantering out of the darkness. He patted his waist, ensuring his daggers were secure, felt his *sgian dubh* in his boot, *sgian achlais* in his armpit. If these travelers meant trouble, he would need every blade to fight himself free.

Except one shape was much smaller than the other, and long fabric flowed from...*her.*

Aileana. His heart leaped into his throat with hope at the same time that it seemed to drop to his feet in wariness. Did she want to come back to him? Or had she come to add further insult to injury? Had she brought her brother to accuse him of forcing her to his will or taking liberties?

His body, charged for a confrontation while his heart squeezed, sent an ill feeling swirling in his gut. But as they neared the firelight, his confusion mounted, for Seamus wore a humored, patronizing smirk, as if the bastard were about to make a jab, and James couldn't help but think it would be at his expense.

Aileana fanned her skirts over the saddle and dismounted before James could consider assisting her, and when she turned toward him, her eyes looked sore. He wanted to brush his thumb across them to push away the moisture but refrained, for she was no longer his to touch.

"Jamie, I…"

Jamie. How he loved the moniker. How it brought back fond memories of both his childhood and the affection he craved from this woman before him.

"Were ye really going to walk away from all that money?" she asked.

He twisted away from them, tossing down his sword with a clatter and heaving a sigh, perching his hands at his waist.

"Lass…" He turned and eyed her over his shoulder. "When I chased a lad back to Urquhart, I had anger in my heart. I intended to make ye pay for stealing and saw an opportunity to fulfill the conditions put upon me." He turned away again. "But the moment the demand for a bride left my lips, I knew I was embarking on something bigger. I knew, when I saw the fear on yer face, that I didnae want to hurt ye." He shrugged. "I need the money, aye, but I want *ye.* And if I cannae have my Allie"—he shook his head—"well, what's a purse of coin in this short life we lead?" He shrugged again. "I never had it to begin with."

A hand settled on his arm. His heart skipped a beat to feel her touch.

He glanced down at the gloved fingers, so slender and delicate, it was a wonder that they'd helped her people push ploughs and heal injuries. "Jamie? When I overheard ye and Brighde talking, I thought the worst. It seemed like something the Devil MacDonald, who'd raided us, would do, and I didnae honor our truce and give ye a chance to explain, nor did I account for all the fine things ye've done for me since the moment we handfasted but saw them as ploys to win me into staying. And when ye left me this afternoon, I couldnae make sense of why I felt so sick until my brother and sister..."

"She loves yer ugly face, man, is what that stew of words means," Seamus said with brotherly ribbing, to which Aileana scowled back at him.

James glanced to Seamus. Odd, he was never off his guard, but for a moment, he'd forgotten about the enemy laird nearby.

"We told her she belonged with ye," Seamus continued, "for it's clear as day ye're smitten with her like a wee milksop for a mistress, and obviously she's gone and turned traitor on us all."

The anger that would normally spike at such insults didn't this time. Aileana was in love with him? Sakes, but aye, he was smitten like a wee milksop, and he didn't care who saw it. He turned to face her, his eyes searching hers as his hands unconsciously migrated to hers to interlock with her fingers. His brow furrowed questioningly, awaiting her elaboration.

She took a deep breath. "I want ye to give me another chance, if ye'll have me. Ye proved to me today that I matter more—"

Somehow, she was in his arms, and he was bent over her, his lips crushed to hers. Relief loosened the noose that had been suffocating his heart. Her fingers snaked around his nape, her body snug against his as he encompassed her in his arms. He lifted her up, uncaring of Seamus watching him maul his wee sister, and was carrying her toward his fire when Seamus cleared his throat like a church warden.

"I handfasted the lass," James retorted over his shoulder.

"Aye, and ye severed that agreement. If ye want my sister,

then new terms and agreements are in order."

Aileana giggled, looking up at him with softness in her eyes; James wanted to bask in such a glow forever and never again see the angry scorn that she'd once bestowed upon him.

"No going back this time," he whispered.

She shook her head. "No going back."

He reached into his sporran, withdrawing two folds of fabric—cuts of MacDonald and Grant tartan.

Her eyes widened, and she touched them, too. "Ye kept them?

He nodded, then felt a smile etch into his solemn face. "Do the honors, *brother-of-marriage*." He held them forth to Seamus.

Seamus, groaning at the title, took the fabric, joined their hands together in an intertwined fist, and knotted the tartan around it.

"James Moidartach MacDonald of Clanranald. I give ye my wee sister, Aileana Grant, *again*. What are yer terms this time?"

James looked down at Aileana, who returned his gaze. She smiled. Sakes, what was she about to demand?

"To live a long, happy life together, with fidelity betwixt our hearts and peace betwixt our people. For the reaves and retaliations to cease, for the cause of such feuds be put to rest. And for any child born of us to never be a bastard."

James's heart clenched. He squeezed her hand in response, nodding once.

"Then let it be so that yer marriage remain until death parts ye," her brother said. "The deed is done—*wait*."

James grinned as he swung Aileana up in his other arm, their hands still knotted, carrying her fireside.

"Wait one bloody second," Seamus continued, snarling, grabbing his shoulder. "How could yer child be born a bastard unless..." His brow grew stormy. "Ye dishonored my sister?

Ye *whoreson*—"

"'Twas no dishonor," came Aileana's soft voice—so solemn, considering only moments ago, she'd been giggling.

Seamus stopped and looked at her, his face softening in the doting way only an older brother could look at his sister. "Aileana, he promised he'd respect ye."

"And he did," she said pointedly. "Peace, brother. From today onward, and always. Is such an oath so quickly discarded?"

Seamus backed up a step, his temper causing his lips to quiver, but nodded. "Aye, peace. Such a thing would be quite the accomplishment with this lot."

And as snow drifted down, as the fire crackled and filled the enclosure with woody scents and Seamus Grant departed to leave them alone, James settled his furs over them, as they'd lain their first night together. Quite the Yuletide boon indeed.

Author's Note

In 2018, I traveled through the unparalleled mountains of the Scottish Highlands. After touring the Isle of Skye, the guide returned us to Inverness, on the northern tip of Loch Ness, while entertaining us with trivia and folklore about olden clan feuds that prompted me to go in search of more information. Urquhart Castle overlooking the loch was one of our last stops along the way. Clan Grant had once controlled Urquhart, and the MacDonalds in particular had been hostile toward them. At one point in 1513, shortly after the Grants had been instated by the Earl of Huntly, the MacDonalds raided Urquhart. They temporarily commandeered the castle and made off with about three hundred head of cattle and several hundred head of sheep. Just a few decades later, another raid, specifically by the MacDonalds of Clanranald, depleted countless household goods, furnishings, and livestock. Certainly living in such a time would have been frightening, but what a delicious backstory for a romance! My curiosity was piqued. But it wasn't just the Grants and MacDonalds who once argued. The MacDonalds and the

MacLeods had a particularly nasty feud around the turn of the seventeenth century, brought on by a MacDonald chief rejecting his wife, who was sister to a MacLeod chief. As lore suggests, the wife was blind in one eye and was sent home on a partially blind horse and accompanied by a partially blind dog. This contemptible dishonor did not go unchallenged and led to a series of bloody retaliations. No longer merely curious, my writer brain was thrust into overdrive. Before leaving the Highlands to fly home, I had already conceived this book, and I immersed myself in the tumultuous histories of these three clans. The astute reader will note that I've taken quite a bit of creative license with my dates, in part due to the fact that at the onset of the Reformation, attitudes toward Yule shifted, and eventually Christmas was banned in Scotland. Additionally, Lady Marjorie's plight in this book, based loosely on the aforementioned marriage feud, is a MacDonald, when historically, the insulted wife was a MacLeod. I hope that you enjoyed *Twelfth Knight's Bride* and that the tidbits of history that birthed the concept of my story give you intriguing things to ponder!

Acknowledgments

First and foremost, I need to thank my family: my husband who believes in my writing, my kids who tolerate the long hours writing requires, my mother-in-law, and my extended family who take the time to read my work and cheer me on my way. I couldn't do this job that I adore if it weren't for their love and support. There are many others, too, who've helped me during the course of writing this book. My morning writer group fondly called the "Morning Writer Chicks" has helped keep me focused on multiple goals, despite the ups and downs the year 2020 has produced. Shout-out to author Christi Barth, too, for being such a supportive writer and for critiquing my blurb and synopsis for this story. It's thanks to her that my confidence as a writer continues to grow. And where would my story be without a fabulous editor? Erin Molta is a joy to work with, and I'm ever grateful for her expertise and belief in this book. Lastly, I'd like to thank the entire team at Entangled, for the opportunity to see this book born into the world, for all the expertise that goes into producing a book from start to finish. My deepest thanks.

About the Author

Elizabeth is convinced life is better with good coffee, chocolate, and a pair of hiking boots. Ever since her elementary school librarian "published" her epic childhood tales—complete with handmade covers—she's enjoyed writing. She loves exploring history through literature, and the world through hiking. While studying prehistoric Britain at Newcastle University and roaming castle ruins and Hadrian's Wall with her kids, Elizabeth found story inspiration in the tumultuous history of the British Isles and the folklore of Scotland.

A recovering archaeologist and biomed research coordinator, Elizabeth is known for her Ladies of Scotland series, as well as her HEA at *USA TODAY*–recommended *Christmas Wore Plaid*. She spends her days penning rugged heroes draped in tartan and chain mail, and the willful heroines who ensnare their hearts. She currently lives on a mountainside in West Virginia with her husband, sons, and various pets. Because she's always honored to hear from readers, make sure to follow her on Facebook, Bookbub, Twitter, Goodreads, and Instagram.

Get Scandalous with these historical reads...

The Highlander's Unexpected Proposal
a *Brothers of Wolf Isle* novel by Heather McCollum

A lass begging to marry him tops the list of "oddest things to happen," but Chief Adam Macquarie is desperate. And he's not above lying to get what he needs. Lark Montgomerie is thrilled the brawny chief agrees to save her from her father's machinations of wedding her off to the first fool that agrees. Nothing will dampen her spirits. That is, until she arrives and realizes things are amiss...

HER ACCIDENTAL HIGHLANDER HUSBAND
a *Clan MacKinlay* novel by Allison B. Hanson

Marian, Duchess of Endsmere, is on the run from the English Crown after killing her abusive husband in self-defense. She has only one safe place to go—her sister's clan in Scotland. When one day a disheveled lass runs from the forest with an English bounty hunter right behind, War Chief Cameron MacKinlay feels compelled to protect her by claiming she is his wife. But he certainly didn't intend to marry her for real!

HIGHLAND RENEGADE
a *Children of the Mist* novel by Cynthia Breeding

Lady Emily has received title to MacGregor lands and she's
determined to make a new start. She just has to win over the
handsome Laird MacGregor whose family has lived there for
centuries. Ian MacGregor aims to scare her away. But despite
his best efforts to freeze her out, things between them heat up.
Highlanders hate the Sassenach, so Ian must choose—his clan
or the irresistible English aristocrat who's taken not only his
lands, but also his heart.

HIGHLAND OBLIGATION
a *Highland Pride* novel by by Lori Ann Bailey

Due to a violent attack, Isobel MacLean will do anything to keep her family safe—except marry infuriating Grant MacDonald. She wants justice, not a damn husband. Unfortunately, we don't always get what we want... Grant MacDonald is determined to tame the hellion wife he was forced to wed. And he'll need to use every tool in his arsenal to distract his alluring wife from her quest for vengeance...before it's too late for them both.

Made in the USA
Middletown, DE
31 October 2023